NORTH HAVEN

SARAH MORIARTY

NORTH HAVEN

A NOVEL

Published by Little A, New York
www.apub.com

Amazon, the Amazon logo, and Little A are trademarks of Amazon.com, Inc., or its affiliates.

ISBN-13: 9781503941519 (hardcover)
ISBN-10: 1503941515 (hardcover)

ISBN-13: 9781503941526 (paperback)
ISBN-10: 1503941523 (paperback)

Cover design by PEPE *nymi*

Printed in the United States of America

First edition

To my sister, Cally, and my brother, Brad,
and
to my second mom, Priscilla

PROLOGUE

The mud came early this year and has stayed late. It pools in the ruts of the drive; it eddies under the open mouth of the drainpipe by the side door. A truck comes jumping down the lane, heralded by the scratch of overgrown brambles. The caretaker is coming to wake his charge, which has been waiting here hunched and quiet through winter, covered in snow. The gray shingles have flayed out as they thawed. They curl at the edges, snaggled and striated like teeth. Parked under the oak sits a pollen-caked jeep; the truck stops behind it. The caretaker is a local, employed by the family. They call him Remy, he calls them Willoughby.

He goes to the pump house first, unlocks the padlock with a tiny key, the smallest on his key ring. He kicks over a bucket and sends robins up from their nest under the small eave. Then the whir of the pump brings water up from the well. This is the third house he has opened this week. He walks across the sodden meadow toward the back of the main house. The toes of his boots turn black. The three steps of the back porch sag beneath his feet. *They should fix that.* The bolt in the door is reluctant to turn, a rusty joint. Once he is in and the foundation settles a bit, the shingles bloat out further. When the mud goes the lichen will grow, moist fissures will dry and crack, then the frost will come again, go deeper into those spaces, work them wider with the leverage of winter.

The wet comes inside too, through loose seams, under eaves. It sends rivulets down the chimney, leaching into the plaster. Even their mother and the children, no matter how grown, don't realize that there is more to fend off than fog. They have never seen snow here. To them weather is cause for a fire in the rug room, an excuse to turn the dock light on early. Their father was better, mending loose porch boards each summer, caulking window casements. He taught the children to watch the wind, to move the boats. But even he let the big things go too long. Now he is gone too long.

And she has followed him.

Down the back hall, the caretaker flips in loud clicks the circuits in the fuse box, and the windows seem wider, the sun brighter. He opens the side door, stands on the little sunny landing just outside. He steps onto the soft earth and faces the wall, stoops to turn the valve and let the water back into the pipes. Now the blood is flowing. Now the dry mouths of faucets are quenched as he goes around first to the downstairs bathroom sink and then the kitchen to open spouts. He runs the air through, makes sure the water is running clear. It is. It is a flood of gratitude. Awake, awake. The dust in the basins is washed down the drains; spattered drops will stay on the porcelain rims for hours after he has left. He opens and closes the empty refrigerator, twists some cans on the pantry shelves. He walks slowly through the first floor, looks at the ceiling, shakes his head at the water stains. He would do more if he could; if they asked; if it were his place. But he doesn't like to think that way.

The vultures are starting to circle, he thinks. Just the other day some mainlander asked about it. The guy stood on the ferry landing, his foul-weather gear stiff and shiny as a taxicab.

"How much you think that place is worth?" asked the taxicab, all casual.

"About as much as you're willing to spend, I'd guess," said the caretaker.

"Could you introduce me to the owners?"

"They ain't here 'til summer."

"Maybe you could give them something for me," he said, holding out a note.

"Post office's right over there." *Vultures.*

The Willoughbys will be back soon. But not their parents. Now the kids are in charge; *God help us,* he thinks. He doesn't know that something is better than nothing.

They will throw up sashes and put in screens; they will sweep out the poison from under the kitchen sink, and the bodies of a few desiccated mice. They will leave windows open when it rains. They will tire the plumbing. They will wear holes in the elbows of this place. But they will light the stove, and steam will rise from kettles, from baths, from bowls of soup. They will hang wet towels on porch rails. They will light candles and pick wax off the dining room table. They will chatter the silver in its velvet-lined drawer. They will build fires and warm the very spine of these old bones. But not until the mud dries. Not until the lobsters return, and the ferry changes its schedule. Soon.

PART I

ONE

LIBBY

July 1

Libby had woken up early, knowing they'd be on the first boat. When she tied up the *Misdemeanor* at the town dock and climbed the gangway, the ferry was still a ways off. She headed up the road to the post office.

"They're coming in today," Libby shouted to Bev, the stationmaster.

"'Bout time. Gwen owes me money."

"She still thinks she won," Libby called across the parking lot.

Bev rolled her eyes.

Libby tossed a wave to Smitty at Bigalow's Boatyard. He pointed at the incoming ferry. She gave a thumbs-up.

After a quick stop at their PO box, Libby stood in the middle of Main Street between Anne's Gift Shop & Gallery and the post office, sorting through her mail. Addressed mostly to "occupant" or either of her dead parents, the mail wasn't, strictly speaking, hers. But it was hers to open and answer: a bill from Remy for an unspecified boating issue ("Misdemeanor $72," handwritten on an invoice form, which looked remarkably like a restaurant check from Schooner's), a large envelope that declared she might already be a winner, and a note with no envelope. She stared at the small piece of paper creased at the center. Had Patricia sent her a love letter? Libby looked over her shoulder, wondering if Patricia could be staying at The Casino. But she wouldn't be. Patricia had made that abundantly clear.

The note was small, written in an unfamiliar, tight cursive. As she read, Libby held the small piece of paper tighter and tighter. Libby had the urge to eat the note, chew it apart like a beast, like the mother of beasts. To keep this secret in her belly. *Thank God* I *found it,* she thought. She had no intention of showing it to anyone. As long as she kept it to herself, it was her decision to make. And it was made.

"You send Gwen my way when she's got time."

"What?" Libby looked up to see Anne standing in the doorway of her store.

"We need to talk about her next show," said Anne.

"They're on the early boat." Libby shoved the paper in her breast pocket. "I can send her up."

"No, no. Let the poor girl settle in."

"Alright." Libby waved the mail over her head and walked down the small hill to the ferry landing.

The ferry bumped and jockeyed its way into the landing. Libby watched the passengers head below for their bags and heard the whoosh of car ignitions. The ramp was lowered, and as the cars clunked their way ashore the ferry bobbed ever lighter. Once the cars were off, the passengers came next in small, red-cheeked groups. The hour at sea had done them good.

Gwen stepped off the ferry first. Libby felt her chest contract for a moment. At thirty-six, Gwen looked just like their mother had when Danny was a baby. Beauty swelled over her. Her hair had grown darker; what was once sandy had become chestnut and then deeper, like wet earth, the same color as their father's. Gwen had grown it long and kept it tucked behind her ears, as their mother had. This summer there was a different flavor to her. Libby noticed it right away. Like a song she couldn't place. There was something slippery and new about her sister.

"What have you been drinking?" said Libby as she hugged her. "You look great."

"I'm on a frappé diet at the moment, calcium."

"And I've been wasting my time on soft serve, bummer. Where are the Y chromosomes?" The two of them turned to look back at the ferry. Danny and Tom were each pulling a small handcart stacked with coolers and duffel bags. Libby walked down the ramp and took the cart from Danny and hugged him. He sort of leaned against her, his arms by his sides. Still acting like a sullen teenager even when he was almost done with college. Still her baby brother.

"How was the drive?" Libby noticed the three of them exchanged a look.

"Long," said Tom. He took the cart from Libby.

Libby looked at Gwen, who opened her eyes wide, which meant, *I'll tell you later.*

On the town dock Tom and Libby made a small luggage brigade, passing coolers and duffels from the dock into the boat. Gwen sat in the stern. Danny hadn't even gotten into the boat. He still wobbled around on the planks of the float as if he were surfing.

"That's everything," said Tom. Libby started the engine. Danny stepped into the boat and pushed them away from the float. The smell of diesel came up strong as the water bubbled behind them. Tom pulled in the bumpers.

Libby steered them across the wakes of other boats, weaving between buoys. She loved this part, picking them up, the ride to the house, the first expectant moments of their visit. Later, she would miss being alone, sitting on the porch in quiet, listening for the soft purr of motors on the water.

From out in the thoroughfare that ran between the two islands, the house seemed disguised at first, like a gray boulder alone on a point standing guard over the busy waterway. But as she drew the boat closer, the house, as always, revealed itself. Its two halves, each with their covered porches and peaked roofs, were connected by a column of bay windows. A long, low side wing wended its way through the pines, windows and chimneys peeking out from behind treetops. As with all the old houses here, the front of the house faced the water, reminding her always that it was meant to be approached by boat, like an undiscovered continent.

Libby pulled up to their mooring and let the boat idle in place. Danny sidled passed the cabin roof to the bow. Down on all fours, Danny slapped the water repeatedly with the boat hook, trying to fish out the mooring line. His brown hair flapped long in his face with his effort.

"Dan, stop smacking," shouted Tom, leaning over the side. "Slice at it. Pick it out of the water."

It begins, Libby thought, *before we even set foot on the island.* Tom, always acting like the authority on any given subject. True, the line was nearly impossible to see, obscured by the mooring and the bow, but did being two years shy of forty give him some specialized degree? They were all old now, all of them over thirty, except Danny. Danny, still with youth in his cheeks, still savoring the legality of drinking, still red-eyed over their mother. He didn't need this.

Tom braced his thighs tight against the rail and leaned further, pantomiming with both hands, one as a rigid hook, the other as a limp line.

"He can handle it, Tom," Libby chided. "Don't backseat drive." Her eyes on the water, she watched for a shift in wind. She had to keep them from being blown back toward the float, while keeping the bow steady for Danny's slippery hands.

Gwen sat with her feet propped up on a pile of life jackets, her arms resting open and wide along the back of the seat. *Like she's sitting in the back of a water taxi,* thought Libby. Libby saw Gwen as all Riviera and Grand Canal, and herself as rocky coastlines, channels marked with rusting nuns. Now, with the glinting sun, the water shone like the Adriatic, the scrubbed evergreens like the parasol pines of the Italian coast, but stronger, taller, more timeless, almost prehistoric. It was a place where a divine hand touched earth, where gods could mingle with mortals. Libby would not have been surprised to see a swan stand at the edge of the woods or drift past their float with an eye on her older sister. She was sure that Gwen had the power to draw gods down from their mountains.

Libby, who had never missed a summer here, was not the object of any swan's gaze. She was just a mortal living at the edge of something, which seemed about right to her. Someone needed to tend the track, to keep this world from disappearing into so much mist.

"You could've just dropped me with the bags on the float," Gwen said to Libby. "I don't think we all ought to squeeze into the dinghy." Libby ignored her.

"G, just pull *Little Devil* in. Dan's got it now." Libby turned off the engine and locked the cabin door.

Gwen took off her sunglasses, folded them, and hooked them on her shirt, lenses on the inside. Over her lifetime Gwen had dropped a dozen pairs overboard. As a little girl, Libby had wondered how things like glasses became more important than toys. Watching her sister stand teary at the edges of boats and floats, staring into the green water as each pair drifted out of sight, had taught Libby to avoid sunglasses altogether.

With the boat moored, each of them stepped or slid from the stern into the *Little Devil.* Shaped like a large bathtub, the dinghy was named for its notorious tendency to dump its passengers into the sea. Gwen sat in the bow, a hand trailing in the water, while Libby did the rowing, and Tom and Danny sat side by side in the stern. Danny stared back toward town as if he'd forgotten something. Tom looked over Libby's head, hands pressed together, fingers pointing toward the house. If Libby drifted off course, Tom's hands shifted. He was the compass needle, and the house was north.

"I can navigate the forty feet between the mooring and the float, Tom," said Libby.

"You want to strain your neck turning around every other stroke? Fine." Tom let his hands hang between his knees.

"When are Melissa and the kids coming?" said Libby.

"Tomorrow. Kerry and Buster couldn't tear themselves away from their busy social lives before then." Tom rolled his eyes, a good impression of his teenage children. Libby began to mentally revise that day's menu. Tom's hands were pointing at the house again.

"Tom, did you see those dolphins swimming with the ferry?" said Gwen.

"They're porpoises," said Danny.

"Those ferry windows are so scratched you can barely see out. They should really be replaced," said Tom. He always spent the majority of the ferry ride in the cabin working. Libby was surprised he wasn't on his phone right now.

"I don't know how you can sit below without getting sick," said Libby.

"Porpoises or porpoi?" said Gwen absently.

Libby's knuckles kept knocking against Danny's knees. "You got to put those somewhere."

"Maybe I should just get out and kick," said Danny, paddling the water with one hand. "We might get there faster."

"Oh, I'm sorry, would you like to row the five-hundred-plus pounds of Willoughby around the thoroughfare?" said Libby. "Actually, I'd love some help; why don't you just dive right in and give us a tow? The water's so refreshing." Refreshing. That was their word for freezing.

"Forget it, you're doing great. I like the scenic route," said Danny.

On her next stroke she gave his knees a particularly powerful knock.

"It's porpoises," said Tom.

"Porpoi, sounds like pork pie." Gwen.

"Pork pie." Danny sighed. "When's lunch?" Up here eating was a sport, and Danny was a champion, his teenage appetite yet to abate. Though Gwen was capable of giving him some stiff competition, at least when lobster was involved. The dinghy squawked against the rubber bumper of the float.

"Pork pie is a hat," said Gwen. "You're thinking of pork buns." She hopped out of the boat and knelt on the float, holding the boat close so the others could get out.

Libby couldn't remember the last time they had been up there just the four of them, no friends, no spouses. Just the kids. That's what their parents would've said. But now there wasn't even one parent left to say that, to remind them of the intimacy that they all came from that bound them together in ways that went beyond ferry schedules and Christmas cards.

Three summers ago, their father died. Only their mother had been there. She had watched him walk through that screen door, as he had every summer since 1972, and collapse on the porch. He had seemed never to age to Libby, still able to pick her up in a hug, still sailing the sloop by himself, still climbing on the roof with a hammer in hand. "I can smell a leak," he'd say. She had watched him push her dead car down her long, narrow driveway so that he could jump it. He had waved away her help, as if she might hurt herself. When she was little she had thought someone that tall could never die. But since the summer she turned ten, Libby had watched for it. Once she knew what to look for. She tried to stay close, to be sure he didn't slip away from her. And then he did, on a Tuesday, when she wasn't even there. She hadn't been able to stop it at all.

Bob Willoughby was just sixty-one when he died. They scattered his ashes in the thoroughfare. That summer their mother, Scarlet, had stayed in the house much later than usual, well into October, until

Remy told her that the water had to be turned off or she ran the risk of bursting a pipe. The float was pulled up the day she left. Now she was gone too.

On the float, they picked up items from a pile of duffel bags, totes with stitched initials, two small coolers, and a case of wine. It was only ten. Loaded down, they teetered up the ramp. The skids of their shoes scratched against the asphalt paper. Through the fabric of her thin shirt Libby could feel the note stiff against her skin, trying to push its way from her pocket, trying to be seen.

"God, it smells so fucking good here," said Gwen.

"You say that every time," said Danny as he came up the ramp behind her carrying a case of wine.

All Libby could smell was Gwen's suntan lotion and Danny's sleeping bag, the warm, earthy smell of a dog bed. She was too accustomed to the dry smell of pine needles and lichen, the salt of seaweed and wet rope. She wanted to read the note again; she wanted to tear it up. But she couldn't do that with them here, ready to take it from her, to wrestle the reins from her hands.

It was low tide, making it a steep climb up to the pier. Libby, a bag in one hand, a sleeping bag in the other, headed up the twisting path hemmed by rocks and beach roses. On the porch she held out the duffel and sleeping bag to Danny. "Your bedroll and valise, sir." He typically responded to her Victorian bit with, "I'll take a snifter of brandy in my chambers at the usual hour," or something similar. The hours of watching BBC dramas with Scarlet had rubbed off on him. Today, though, he just stared at the water, biting his nails, before he realized she was talking to him.

"Dan, your crap."

He turned to her and shook his head. "Sorry, the view, it sucks me in." He shrugged, took his things, and headed upstairs.

Now Libby stood alone on the porch, among the coolers and the case of wine. Her siblings apparently thought the food would just magically float onto the shelves in the pantry. They never thought about logistics, about the number of beds divided by the number of invited guests, the cubic space of a side-by-side refrigerator, the amount of wine that people consume while on vacation. They bought and brought what they were told. They were good about sticking to the menu she drafted. But she was the one charging any dry goods they couldn't carry from the mainland over at Fairholm's. Her siblings seemed to forget that their mother was gone. There was no one who diligently carried and stowed. No one who cataloged and restocked. Well, there was, of course: Libby. Really, in the three years since their father died, Scarlet had been receding, leaving Libby to pick up the various tasks left behind. She wasn't sure what was worse, to replace her mother or to be ignored as the replacement.

She didn't want to be her mother. Scarlet had been the fire of her hair, of her name. And Libby had been burned. All of them had. Except Danny. To her face, she was called Mom, but between them, she was always Scarlet. Because she was bigger than the diminutive; because, like a hurricane, she needed her own name. And now she was just a swirl of sand in an urn, a ship in a bottle.

After dragging two coolers into the kitchen, Libby knelt on the floor of the pantry in front of the open refrigerator and attempted to put things away. Soon every shelf and drawer was full, and she sat on the floor with a jumbo jar of mayonnaise and a pitcher of iced tea. No matter the configuration, she was inevitably left with two extra things, jam and a block of cheese, a head of lettuce and a family-size tub of hummus, a net bag of lemons and two pounds of sliced ham. Finally, she shuffled and stuffed and finagled the lemons and the tea as the remainders, and she left them both on the kitchen table, its oilcloth shining in the sun.

A glass of iced tea in hand, Libby walked through the dining room toward the door to the porch. She stopped in the entrance to the great room, and glanced up at the door to her parents' room at the end of a long balcony. It was separate with its own porch and bathroom. When she had first opened the house she had left her parents' bathroom empty of soap or the bucket often needed to assist the plumbing. But she had made their bed. The sight of the bare-buttoned mattress had made her cry. That was three weeks ago. Now she was settled; she hadn't cried since. Libby hated missing her mother and hated hating her, so she didn't want to think of her at all. Libby looked over the great room; through the bay windows the sunlight stretched beneath the Ping-Pong table and wicker chairs showing the dull spots on the floor fringed with white water stains. She added "refinish floors" to a growing list in her mind.

The house was sinking, growing old, and that list was getting longer and longer. The chimney was cracked above the fireplace in Libby's room, and her Toile de Jouy wallpaper had faded so much she could barely read the months that were spelled out beneath each bucolic scene. The great room's white cathedral ceiling, girded with beams, was veined with brown water stains. Sailing pennants and animal heads—moose, deer, a boar, even an angry-looking fox—that hung from the interior balconies that looked out over the room were shaggy with dust. The house had come to them as it was: furniture, animals, pennants that marked races beginning in 1914, the 1938 ferry schedule still pinned to the kitchen wall. This was what happened when you bought from the wife of a disgraced politician who had fled in the middle of the night with his starlet girlfriend, leaving all the furniture behind, leaving dishes in the sink. To this they gradually added their own permanent features: a toddler's shoe resting on the stovepipe, a feather tucked in a cracked tile on the dining room mantel, a sketch of the fireplace pinned beside the same fireplace. The kitchen doorframe was repeatedly marked in pencil with the same names, different years, different heights, each of them growing steadily past the latch.

Libby returned to the porch steps with her iced tea and sat down looking out toward town. Tom sidestepped Libby and thumped down the steps.

"Taking the Whaler for a quick ride," he said. He scrubbed her head as he went by.

"Have fun." *Thanks for asking.*

Six months ago, three years after their father had died, their mother Scarlet became sick. Her thyroid. Normally the easiest type of cancer to fight, but they had found it too late. They agreed that Tom would pull the plug. Tom said it should be him. Gwen tried to talk him out of it, tried to say she was the one to do it so he wouldn't have to. Libby didn't volunteer. She had spent the last seven years wishing her mother was dead. Some irrational part of herself worried that she had somehow caused the cancer. Her rage had grown a tumor in her mother. She couldn't bear to kill her again. And Danny was practically catatonic already. So it had to be Tom or Gwen. Tom just made up his mind and closed the discussion, like he was finishing some giant leather-bound book.

Afterward, they wanted to be at the house, they wanted the comfort of it, of their childhood, a place where their mother could still be, a place that could never be robbed of her presence. But it was winter, and so they had settled in Tom's living room with its brown velvet upholstery and Tiffany-blue walls, and each took turns holding Danny. He couldn't stop crying, not to eat or drink. He even cried in his sleep, struggling with the sheet on Libby's foldout couch.

Danny had held Tom's beagle-terrier mix, much to the dog's dismay, until Melissa replaced the dog with a large glass of wine. When she wasn't holding Danny, Libby washed dishes, dried them, and then washed and dried the dish rack. When she started in on the oven, Melissa put her to work making pasta for dinner. From her place at the kitchen counter, through the darkness of their front hall, Libby had seen Tom go to his wife. Then he kissed Melissa, pulling open her shirt and grabbing at her breasts, her neck, pulling her hair, as if he wanted to devour her, as if she was the one who was dying, and he could save her by eating her alive. He crumpled against her, and Libby heard him say, "Now we can finally sell that fucking house." She had never heard him swear before. Libby had looked away, back to her pasta.

From the porch she watched Tom glide out into the thoroughfare. Libby finished her tea, picked up the case of pinot noir, and headed into the house. She could hear running water from the upstairs bathroom. After depositing the bottles in the sideboard, Libby readjusted a straw hat with fake lilacs and a yellow slicker on their hooks in the small hallway off the dining room. She held the brim of the hat for a moment. The last time she'd seen her mother wear it, Scarlet had been standing in the kitchen, shirtsleeves rolled up, arms mud smeared, audibly glugging a glass of water. Sometimes she had seemed almost human, wearing hats and everything, not some great scaly beast. Libby could hear Gwen and Danny upstairs.

"These mattresses are gross," said Danny. "We're going to be asphyxiated in our sleep by all the camphor. What's with the fucking mothballs anyway? Is it 1953?"

"Let me just take some quinine for my rheumatism," said Gwen, "and a DEET rubdown to soften my skin."

"You're both going to burn in hell," Libby called up the stairs. "I should've just let the mice nest in your beds. Then it could be toxoplasmosis for everyone."

"We'd have to eat the mice for that to happen," shouted Danny.

Gwen broke into a chorus of "Burning Down the House."

"Do you think David Byrne and Jeff Goldblum were separated at birth?" said Danny.

"Or they're soul mates," said Gwen.

Libby climbed the stairs as Gwen walked from Danny's room with a pillow under each arm. Libby followed Gwen into her room. There was no better view in the house than the one from this bed. When she was alone in the house, Libby liked to read here when it was raining and watch the storm move through the thoroughfare. They called Gwen's room the Pilot House because of all the windows. But it felt like the room at the top of a lighthouse, and Gwen was the light, a beacon shining out to sea, out at the thoroughfare, toward town. That light was a signal to all the local boys who had wanted to conquer a summer girl.

"What's wrong with your pillows?"

"We're swapping. I need something with more heft." Gwen tossed the pillows at the head of the bed and then unzipped her duffel. Libby sat down on the bed and edged the door shut with her foot. Gwen glanced at the door, then sat on the floor facing Libby.

"He freaking wiped down the dashboard when we stopped for lunch. Who does that?" said Gwen.

"He's in rare form. I thought he was going to make Dan cry on the boat." Libby imitated Tom's hook-and-line pantomime.

"This is why I won't go sailing with him anymore," said Gwen. She unzipped her duffel and pulled out her kit.

"Were there rooms left at The Navigator?" said Libby.

Gwen nodded. "We stayed up way too late heckling Lifetime movies."

"With Tom?"

"Yeah right. Tom wanted us to all stay in one room. He said something about a slumber party. But I was not about to put up with him for the night. Dan slept on a cot in my room. How's it been here?"

Libby looked out toward town for a minute, as if her eyes could travel into the post office through their little brass box and back in time to see a man carefully writing the note on the counter. She wasn't able to keep secrets from Gwen. Libby took the note from her breast pocket. She stretched her arm out over the bed and passed it to Gwen. Gwen put down the pile of underwear she was shoving into a drawer and read the note:

To the Willoughby Family,

If you ever consider selling, please contact me. Your property is truly unique, and I would, contingent on inspection and confirmation of acreage, be prepared to offer approximately 3.1 million. This offer stands as long as I do.

Sincerely,

Rafe Phillips

Attached was a business card bearing his name and beneath it, "Vice President, Kallman Enterprises."

To Libby hearing the words aloud was like being hit on in the worst way: "I'd like to give you a *real* pearl necklace." As if just by virtue of having a beautiful house, she was some kind of property slut. She wouldn't have wanted to sell even when her parents were alive, but now that they were gone, now that it was hers, well, all of theirs, certainly not.

"Holy—When did you get this?" Gwen fanned herself with the note.

"This morning."

"So you haven't shown it to Tom?" Gwen examined the note again as if she were a graphology expert trying to suss out some hidden message.

"As far as I'm concerned, this isn't worth a second thought. He'd want to analyze it. He'd be all over it. He'd be a shark," said Libby.

"And this is one big bucket of chum." Gwen dangled the note, pinched at one corner like it was a dead fish.

"It's probably not even for real. I mean, why would anyone offer that much sight unseen?" said Libby. She lay down on her side, her head propped up on her hand.

"Maybe 'cause our pal Rafe"—Gwen waved the note—"doesn't give a shit what it looks like."

"But it needs so much work, to get this place back to what it was . . . I can't even imagine."

"Oh, Bibs, Money Bags isn't looking to restore. He's looking to demolish. That price is for the land. He'd just build some giant McMansion or condos. He's probably a developer."

Libby sat up and took the note back from Gwen, stared at it as if she had missed some key sentence. Up here, there was no computer to look up this viper, to see how many Levittowns he had probably perpetrated over wetlands and burial grounds.

"Throw that shit away," said Gwen. She took a stack of moth-eaten sweaters from her duffel. "Or actually just give it to me. I could use three million."

Libby stood up, crunched the note into a ball, and shoved it into her pocket.

"Over my freaking dead body."

"Language! There are ladies present!" Gwen put a hand to her chest and widened her eyes. Libby threw a pillow at her.

"I have to save it up all year; now that I'm on summer vacation I'm going to let loose on you guys for the next week. I'm going to work blue blue blue." Libby swung open the door. "Now I have to put the freaking laundry in the freaking dryer."

"It's cool. Start slow. You have to build up your tolerance. We can work on 'crap' tomorrow," said Gwen.

Libby gave her the finger as she walked out the door.

"Progress already!" said Gwen.

Back downstairs in the dining room, Libby could see Danny in the rug room, a book in hand, settling into one chair before moving to another, and then another. She found her wallet resting on the sideboard. Libby took the note from her pocket, smoothed it out, and slipped it into the worn leather. It was like a foreign bill, some piece of currency valuable here only for its novelty.

TWO

GWEN

July 2

Gwen made Danny pick blueberries with her. She had to keep busy or she would be tempted to talk. They stepped into tall rubber boots by the back door and headed outside. Libby was bringing in a batch of sun tea as the last bit of morning sun swung around the house.

"Leaving the house already?" said Libby. "It's only your second day. Tom, yes. He made coffee for everyone and is already out on the boat. But you guys? This is really more fourth-day behavior."

"I'm on dessert tonight," said Danny.

Gwen looked at Libby and mouthed, *I'm on dessert.*

"I saw that, smart-ass," said Danny. "I'm happy with Hydrox and ice cream. I'm not the fancy one here."

"Forage away," said Libby. "Just watch out for the poison ivy; it's looking a little aggressive up there."

The ground tipped slightly under Gwen's feet, and she did a small cha-cha step, hoping to cover up her stumble. Lately, nothing felt solid.

She actually preferred to be on the boat; dry land had been making her nauseous; the dip and swell of the water seemed to equalize things. She had even started to wear wristbands that activated pressure points, which so far had only succeeded in making her wrists hurt.

She knew there was a better solution, and she had an appointment for the third week in July. It wouldn't be the first time. There was once in college, and then again, six months into her eighteen-month marriage. Being with the man had seemed like a great idea, the baby not so much, and then she realized maybe she could cut herself out of the marriage too.

The backyard wasn't a yard so much as a meadow between the house and the woods. A large oak tree dominated the meadow at one end, and the other end swept past the south porch and down through poison ivy thickets, raspberries, and dead pines to the rocks of the shore. Gwen and Danny walked up the peak of the small hill behind the meadow. The water, busy with boats going in all directions, rolled away from them toward the neighboring island. *Like a bustling intersection.* Danny swung his bucket while he walked and hummed a tune in time with his steps. He walked ahead of her, up toward the tree line, where the blueberries grew thick and low.

Gwen believed in choice, in control, in self-sufficiency. She believed in any pagan ritual that brought women dancing naked around a fire. She did not believe in the sacrifice of the self. But there was the lowest whisper inside, something dim that pushed her to delay the appointment. Those other times, there had been no hesitation. It was just part of life, like getting strep or breaking a bone. No sexually active collegiate woman with an ounce of self-preservation could avoid it, at least no one like her with the impulsive nature of a blotto frat guy. But now she was uncertain, and that uncertainty felt weak. It embarrassed her.

Indecision was for people who didn't really know themselves. Gwen did not linger over menus, in dressing rooms, or in relationships. She believed in first instincts and gut feelings. Only now her gut had been hijacked and, therefore, her instincts potentially skewed. Her hormones were pounding out some genetic rhythm, beating incessantly through her veins. Not telling Libby was a way of guarding against that feeling. Libby would say those words that held to the shadows inside her: "What if it's your last chance?" And yet she hated that Libby didn't know. She had never kept a secret from her sister.

The grass had grown knee high, and she pulled her boots through it instead of stepping over it.

"This always seems like such a good idea until we actually get out here," Danny said as he began putting the first few tiny berries into his bucket. He took his phone out of his pocket, swiped a few times, and put it back.

"We're doing as the original rusticators did. Just keep thinking: blueberry crumble, blueberry crumble." It was Danny's favorite, and the only thing Gwen felt like eating right now. That and lobster. Everything else made her feel tired and gray.

"Please, they had their servants do this shit," said Danny. "They just sat on the porch under parasols drinking Chartreuse or something."

That sounded like heaven to Gwen.

"Been keeping up with your *Masterpiece Theater*, I see."

"There's more to me than High Life and ramen, thank you very much." He threw a berry at her.

Gwen tried to catch it in her mouth, missing, by a lot.

She worked quietly for a while, smelling the warmth of the grass and salt, the richness of pine tar. Nothing about a baby seemed practical to Gwen, even this simple act of plucking blueberries from their brittle stems. *How does one even do this with a child? How do you keep them out of the poison ivy, out of the frigid sea that wants desperately to devour them? Their warm flesh must hold something more vital, more enticing, than the porous husks of adults. The gentle lapping waves always seeking to pull them from docks, from the sterns of boats, even from the pebbled shores of quiet coves. How could a life jacket hold back all that hungry ocean?* She had seen the sea's appetite all those years ago, when Libby lay blue-lipped and soft on the hard stones of a beach.

Gwen stood and stretched, looking out at the harbor. The boats on their moorings and the birds perched on the rocks all faced into the wind. The cormorants held their wings wide open to dry. Gulls jabbered over a slow-moving lobster boat. *With crawling and crying, how do parents ever enjoy silence again?*

"So, are we going to talk about it?" said Danny.

"Hmmm?" she said, mouth full of blueberries.

"Who's the daddy? You're gonna have it, right? 'Cause don't get me all excited about this uncle crap if you're just gonna flush it."

Gwen sat down with a clunk of her pail and stared at Danny for a moment.

"Well, fuck." She pushed his shoulder, trying to knock him over. "What gave it away?"

"You've been turning down booze. And you're a fat cow, obviously."

"So tough. You're the kind of guy who'd run out and buy miniature high-tops before the thing's even firmed up."

"Everyone needs a pair of high-tops. Besides, the little bastard is going to need one sensitive man in his life. Wait, you did do this with a guy, right?"

"I realize it's surprisingly traditional of me. We'll leave the turkey baster to Bibs."

"Have you told her? She's going to be pissed you told me first. You told me first, right?"

"Dan, I really don't see motherhood as the next step in my artistic development, okay? So can you just dial it back a little. Plus, you guessed, so I haven't technically told anyone."

"Guessed or saw the pregnancy test box in your recycling. Whateves. Either way, don't go that route with her. She'll kick your ass when it comes to technicalities. What about a name? The Executioner?

Bonecrusher, maybe El Diablo?" he said, kneeling with his arms held high like Godzilla over Tokyo.

"No wrestlers, no hair bands, no serial killers. If I were to have a baby, in the distant future"—she pinched her thumb and forefinger together and pointed at him, as if to pull any sense of excitement from him—"I would not let you chose the name. If it were a boy? Maybe Robert." Their father's name.

Danny sat back on his heels, his bucket dangling from one hand, and began to cry. Gwen took his bucket and set it on the ground. She scootched toward him until they were hip to hip, and she rubbed his back for a second.

"For now you can drink for two, okay?" she said. He nodded, gave a short chuckle between sniffs. She hugged him and passed him his bucket. He sighed. She hated to take this from him so quickly.

"How you feeling?" Danny asked. "Seeing your breakfast in reverse?"

Danny smiled at her and put three blueberries in his pail—plink, plank, plunk. She was only eight weeks pregnant, but she could feel his smile was not just for her. She felt both his love for her and his love for what she carried. It felt good and sad. In a few weeks, he would love her less.

"You gonna tell them?" Danny asked, checking the ground for a clear spot and moving to a different bush.

"Soon there will be nothing to tell, and I don't want to hear it from Tom." Gwen moved next to him, and they both looked down the slope toward the water. "Why tell them? So they can tell me I'm not getting any younger?"

"You might push Tom over the edge anyway. He seems like he's hanging by a thread. That shit with the Windex in the car?"

"Everyone puts their feet on the dash. I don't know how that is news to him," said Gwen.

"I thought he was going to leave you by the side of the road. His ears turned purple."

"It was a spectacular freak-out." Gwen swept one hand wide in front of her as if gesturing to the word "freak-out" spelled in glittering lights.

"Dude, he was about to turn green and burst out of his clothes. Unless he's now selling plutonium instead of media strategies, something's up."

"Maybe he's selling plutonium strategies."

"See, you are totally ready to be a parent. You're thinking outside the box." Danny patted her shoulder.

Not getting any younger. *My youth is closing,* she thought, *and that great expanse of middle age is opening its door.* She saw an illustrious theater with gilded chairs and red plush curtains, filled with the quiet rustling of programs and the adjusting of jackets and purses. The wink of opera glasses being opened and lights that seem perpetually dimming, something always about to start, but never does. This was what Gwen saw through those doors, this stuffy world, this interminable waiting.

"I'm not going to spend *my* life sitting in a carpool line." *Always waiting, always keeping up appearances.* "No fucking way."

"I'm pretty sure there's more to it than that," said Danny.

"You're right. It's a fabulous parade of bodily fluids and sleep deprivation."

"You know, if you spew this much negativity the kid is going to grow a tail or hooves. All I'm saying is keeping secrets is a bad idea; that's how people get tumors. You'll end up with a Minotaur baby."

"I thought about telling her, it's just . . ."

Four weeks ago, three days before Libby left for the house, Gwen and Libby had had dinner at Gwen's place in Cambridge. Gwen had wanted to tell her then.

"Your doorbell isn't working," Libby had said as she peeked around the corner of Gwen's house to find Gwen watering the garden dressed in a half-slip, bra, and wellies. "Christ, you're gonna give Mr. Ciccone a heart attack."

Gwen's outfit was partly for practical purposes and partly because this was what summer looked like to her. For the last eight years she had lived in the same first-floor apartment of a triple-decker. She usually paid Mr. Ciccone her rent on time, though she had bounced two checks, only because he cashed the checks too soon, too enamored of her to suppose she might not have the funds to cover it. He made those checks their private joke, happy to have something to share with her, since he couldn't rib her in any other capacity. He didn't care about the shavings of paper glued to the herringbone floors, or the charcoal fingerprints all over the front door. He spontaneously upgraded her appliances and fixed dripping faucets. The last time she came to Maine she returned to find he'd retiled her bathroom.

"If you aren't careful, he's going to break in and mosaic your name into the kitchen floor, or maybe he'll just slip between the sheets and wait for you," said Libby. "Betcha he's a rose man." She pantomimed clenching a flower between her teeth. Here was Gwen's chance: "I'm pregnant with his baby, ha-ha, just kidding, about Mr. Ciccone, not the baby." But she just overwatered the peonies instead.

"Men are pathetically dependent on flowers," said Libby, "and women, on letters."

Gwen thought of a letter she had sent nine years earlier; she had drawn doors all over the envelope, all shut with dark, gaping keyholes. But one small door, in the lower right corner on the back, was open just a crack. There had been no reply. *Maybe I would've had more luck with flowers. Maybe I shouldn't have left in the first place.*

Gwen pointed a dirt-rimmed finger at a bottle of white wine and an empty glass on the porch.

"Where's yours?" Libby asked.

"I'm working," said Gwen.

Libby was quickly distracted, and they moved inside, dishing out dinner in the kitchen.

The two of them ate on the porch, plates balanced on their knees. Gwen complained about the ivy creeping over the neighbor's fence, about the morning glories that looked so sad and deflated in the shade of the cedar tree. All spring she had wanted to attack the garden, restore and revitalize it as a way to thank Mr. Ciccone, as a way to show him he would never get anything else from her.

"We could move the morning glories to the south side, over there past the fall of the shadow." Libby pointed with her fork to the far corner of the garden. "Or you could chuck them completely and put herbs there, and maybe ferns under the cedar here."

Gwen put down her plate and went and stood in the bramble of flowers and weeds, demonstrating the sun's daily path with a sweep of her arms. Between the main course and dessert they managed to rip out half the garden. They stood in the turned soil, detached roots worming sadly toward the sky, discussing the risks of moving peonies and the life span of the skeletal rhododendron. Back on the porch they worked up hasty, dirt-smeared sketches while they ate cold, store-bought pie. They envisioned the woolly yard as a garden of wildflowers and herbs, with cascades and falls and sprays and mountains of hairy blossoms, of petalled eyes, of spiny-leafed monsters. It would have the look of an abandoned English garden, the yard of some doddering vicar. They had done the same thing to Libby's dining room eight years before (her drop ceiling dismantled during dinner), when Gwen couldn't manage to tell Libby she was getting a divorce.

Even though this house was full of projects to use as diversions, it would be hard to hide from Libby for a week.

"Libby is going to kill you if you keep it from her much longer. Better tell her before *el bebe* starts to show," said Danny, poking her belly. She knew Danny was confused as to the pace of things.

Just then in Danny's face she saw their father, whose smirk she knew was in all of them. Would her child smirk? Was this her only chance of having a child who would see this house, who would run barefoot down the steps, hold sparklers on the dock, eat lobster and emphatically state that, when pouring the liquid off, "Ewww gross, it's throwing up," as Libby had? What did you do with jars of murky watercolor rinse? With palette knives and tubs of glue? How were you supposed to wear a papoose when on your hands and knees uprooting ivy leaping over your neighbor's fence? Her house was a beautiful poisonous garden, something from the illustrated conservatory of Charles Addams, flowers made of razor blades and giant insecticide pumps full of aerosol glue, beautifully illustrated seed packages full of toxic pigments. Contents under pressure. Combustible. Maybe she could raise a dismembered hand, but that was it, nothing whole.

"If Tom knew, he'd try to change my mind. He'd give me a combo it-takes-a-village and life-begins-at-conception speech. He'd try to get me on his side about the house. He'd want me to be reasonable, whatever that means. Maybe we could keep the house without him. You and me and Libby."

"Is that really what he's thinking? He'd seriously want to get rid of this?" Danny waved at the house, the sea, and her eyes followed.

"He doesn't have the power to obliterate a landscape, don't worry. He just might be intrigued by the cash money involved. His ears would perk up for three million."

"That's awfully specific there, G." He turned to face her and stroked his chin like a villain.

"There is no secret. I mean, besides the one you already guessed— snooped. The point is moot. So you don't need to stress." She patted his knee. Danny gave her a sidelong, yeah-right look.

"Fine. It can just be you, me, and Bibs. And baby makes four. I can drop out of school and help you," said Danny. He patted her belly. Gwen shoved him over. She was sure he believed in that math, that the addition of a baby would make everything better. There had existed some sort of magic between their mother and father and Danny. The three of them. But Gwen was not three. She was only two. And soon she would be one.

"Sorry, D, you're stuck in your ivy-covered prison for another year. You'll have to run away and join the circus on your own time."

"Don't tempt me," said Danny. Propped up on his elbow, he had his phone out again. "All I'm saying is Little Junior Mint needs to see this place." He cocked his head toward the house. "Maybe they should be called Embryo Mints; they sort of have that curled up, fetal look. Stupid reception."

"Gross. You just ruined my favorite movie snack." Gwen pointed at his phone. "You gotta go to the float if you want that to work." He rolled his eyes and put the phone back in his pocket.

"Sure you're not just getting fat? Maybe it's a beer baby? Just name him Stella. I know, Frito." Danny pulled a few more berries off a bush.

"Please, he would be a genius. Fig Newton is way more appropriate." Gwen was using both hands to separate branches, to search out the hidden berries.

"As in Wayne?" said Danny.

"As in Isaac. Aren't you in school?"

"Now I'm craving beer and Fritos. Sympathy pregnancy." Danny stood up and brushed off the seat of his pants. He walked up the ridge a bit to get a better look at the view. Suddenly, he started waving one hand around his head and jumping up and down.

"Bees!" he shouted. Gwen ran down the ridge twenty feet and turned to see Danny running in circles. "Bees!" he cried again. Now he was swinging his bucket wildly and whacking his back with it, blueberries flying. She tried to say something, but she couldn't stop laughing.

"Run toward the house," shouted Gwen, "not in circles, you fool." She wasn't sure he could hear her over the thunks of the bucket and the snapping of brush. She started waving her arms toward the house.

Danny, bucket helicoptering overhead, jelly-legged on the uneven ground, veered toward the house. He bore down on Gwen, who stood directly in his path.

"Move!" he shouted. Now she was running too. The two of them sprinted across the meadow as if a cloud of killer bees pursued, as opposed to a trail of squashed blueberries. They ran through the house, buckets still in hand, and out onto the front porch.

On the porch Danny lay down on the warm planks. "I think we lost them." Gwen headed into the house, the screen door slamming, then she was back out, ordering him to sit up. She had a bottle of ammonia and some cotton balls.

"Let's see," she said. He lowered his head and showed a sting on the back of his neck and two on his arm. She swabbed down the bites, blew on each one.

"I lost all my berries." He held his empty bucket, slightly dented, between his knees. "I told you this wasn't a good idea. You really need to start listening to me."

Poor Danny. He just wanted a little more life and a little less death.

THREE

Danny

July 2

Danny woke up from an unintentional nap in a chair on the porch, his book was closed in his lap. He'd lost his place. Maybe that was for the best. He'd been reading the same page for weeks. Thirsty, he looked over his shoulder at the house. He could hear someone in the dining room opening and closing drawers in the sideboard. Libby. He decided he'd have to go in through the great room door if he was going to avoid her.

Libby was fairly good about letting everyone read or laze around on the porch, but if she caught one of them walking around, on their way to the bathroom, getting a glass of sun tea, she inevitably had a job for them. Danny was an expert at avoiding her. To get to the kitchen for a drink he would have to go up the main stairs and down the back to avoid her as she probably sat at the dining room table sighing over the week's menu. This was a habit she had picked up from their mother. The preoccupation with food: purchasing, storing, preparing. He recognized it, and knew, as with Scarlet, the best defense was a good offense. If he could have, he would have walked the ridgepole to get out of doing work.

Danny walked softly across the porch and opened the screened door to the great room, slowly, to keep the hinges quiet. But once inside, he nipped fast to the base of the main stairs to stay out of sight, and pressed himself against the wall directly under the taxidermied moose head. Then began the painstaking process of getting up the old stairs silently. This was an exercise in hope and memory. *Which side of the third step creaked?* He always got it right. At the top he walked quickly down the hallway. He descended the back stairs mostly using his hands on the banisters to support his weight. He emerged into the bright kitchen, to find Libby holding the compost bucket. *Damn it.*

"Oh, good. I could use a hand." She held the bucket out to him. And then she went back to, he wasn't sure, checking the levels of the various cooking oils?

"Mother!" he said under his breath. He put the bucket down in front of the sink and took a drink from the tap.

"When you're done can you dig a trench?" Libby had a pencil behind her ear and a list in her hand. This was a bad sign. She said it like she often asked people to dig trenches.

"A trench. You mean like a long pit, that kind of trench?" Danny knew there was a reason he should've stayed in bed this morning.

"Is there another kind of trench?" Libby wasn't even looking at him but at her list. "It needs to run from the side door around the back to the pump house. We've got to lay some new PVC."

"Sure . . . That sounds relaxing."

Now she looked at him. "You big baby. Dump the food and get a shovel. I'll help for a bit, then I have to go get Melissa. She's on the late boat."

"I'll be right back." He took the plastic bag out of the bin and headed out the back door. There was no way he was coming back.

Danny stood at the lip of the old empty swimming pool, upending the plastic bag of fruit rinds, rotini, and coffee grounds. The pool was a small oval of concrete, ten feet deep, lined with cracks and moss. On buying the house, their father had decided to try to fill it with brush and compost to eventually create a small garden. But over the last forty-four years, they had managed to only fill it halfway. While Danny didn't appreciate Libby's constant assignments, he did love coming out here. He liked to empty the compost bucket. To duck low branches and step over roots, to come out to this slight rise between the house and the boathouse beach, all hidden in woods.

He liked to imagine how this must have once looked. The mild elevation would have given a perfect view of the water, if some trees were cleared. He wondered if, beneath the fallen logs and ferns, there was a mosaic floor, some Gilded Age extravagance depicting seals and porpoises, where tanned feet once slapped out a spray of water before them as they walked around to the deep end for another dive. The sunset would have been beautiful then. The waters of the sea and the pool would've reflected back all those long waves of light, the reds and oranges. He could see the long dresses, the seersucker blazers, the rolling trolley with spirits and ice. He imagined his parents, lean and tall, like Grant and Hepburn, dressed in white, drinking cocktails in low glasses.

He had often begged his father to restore the pool. But the B.O.B. reared its head. This was the nickname they had given Bob Willoughby anytime he acted particularly lawyerly—stating the case, reviewing the facts, explaining the obvious and clear course of action. His father argued against Danny's plea—the costs, the broken pumps used to bring the salt water up from the sea to the pool, the decadence of a pool with the ocean right in front of them.

Danny thought his father was calling him greedy. It was one of the few times Danny had ever felt belittled by him. Danny only wanted a place to actually swim, not just jumping in and out again because the water was so cold it burned. He wanted to do strokes. Sometimes

Danny thought his father had been right. He was greedy. Greedy for time. Standing on the mosaic terrace that existed only in a world buried under a hundred years of pine needles and moss, he felt the vastness of time stretching out beneath him, and at the same time how quickly it got eaten up. He thought of his father, napping on the porch. No more. Now under the water, sleeping with seaweed. He thought of his mother, but then he didn't. He wouldn't.

After his father died, he could think of nothing else. Of all the moments that Danny had tried to catch his father's attention, fixed always on his mother, like the sea always tending to the rocks, whispering, comforting, sometimes pleading, sometimes pounding. And she, like the rocks, seemed both to resist and absorb it. She would bathe in it, bask in it. There were moments of storm, too, of eruption of water, and the groan of rock shifting. Losing his father was almost worse, never having lost something before. It was losing something he'd never had, and again time felt both quick and slow. But it wasn't worse. This was.

Danny shook the plastic bag, let long threads of carrot peels slide forth, falling on corncobs and watermelon rinds. *Must be Libby's from the week before.*

"Hurry it up, Dan," Libby called from the house. He ignored her.

He'd had Scarlet those last three years, when she was no longer submerged in her love for her husband, or in his love for her. Really he had her before too. She was never so lost as his father. She could look up from beneath waves of devotion and see Danny, make some joke about deep-sea diving or mermaids, about how sweet and silly it all was.

One night when Danny was twelve, she'd been standing at their kitchen table chopping tomatoes, pulverizing them, actually. His father stood behind her, one hand searching for the weather station on the radio, the other rubbing the back of her neck.

"If you're not careful, I'm going to chop my fingers off," she said to him.

"A delicacy I will devour with my supper," he said, kissing her behind the ear. She looked at Danny sitting across the table from her, bugged out her eyes, and stuck out her tongue, as if to say, *Oh my God, I married a cannibal.*

But now, he couldn't think of her. He couldn't eat tomatoes or listen to the weather. He could think of his father, but not his mother; he could not let himself. He had to be vigilant, or he began to see her hands; thin with long fingers, the age spots beginning just below the knuckles; the rings, wedding, anniversary, something amethyst for the day he was born. He pressed a cut on his hand until it stung. It cleared his mind, and he stopped seeing her. He wanted his mind blank. He wanted to shut out all stimuli until his mind was just white noise.

Danny walked around the pool, stopping at one end. The edge of the pool curved in, rounded by moss. The toes of his sneakers stuck out over that edge as if he were about to dive in. He wondered how much it would hurt to dive into branches and leaves. Would there be enough of a cushion or would he hit the bottom? His mother was an excellent diver. She used to dive off the bow of the sloop when they went sailing. Just the three of them. He stepped back from the edge, picked up a pinecone.

In the woods toward the house he heard the crunching and cracking of footsteps. Libby. Man, she was really invested in this trench business.

"Seriously, we need to get started," she called again, much closer this time, but still out of sight. Danny looked around, trying to figure out where to hide. There was only one place. He sat down on the edge. At this end, the pool held mostly dead leaves and brambles. A vine grew into, or out of, the tangle, crawling up over the side. He lowered himself down onto the pile of detritus, and squatted, his back pressed against the side of the pool, the pinecone still in his hand.

"Dan, where are you?" Now she was close enough that her footsteps sent an acorn skittering into the pool three feet from him.

"It's just one little trench," she shouted in her sweetest voice. "We could have a digging race. You start at one end, and I'll start at the other, and we'll see who gets to the middle first." *She can't get out of the nursery school teacher zone sometimes.* To be fair, those tricks used to work on him really well. He heard her footsteps retreating. She must have thought he'd gone back to the house, snuck by her through the woods instead of sticking to the path. The pockmarked cement of the wall made his back itch.

Danny couldn't believe what Gwen had said, that some bloodsucker was after their house. *What's wrong with people? Should we have draped the place in black, like a giant covered mirror? Black sails on the sloop. Oh, but the sloop is gone. Maybe just hung a sign on the pier: "Do Not Disturb, In Mourning."* He turned his attention back to the pinecone. Seeds and symmetry were better things for him to focus on.

Avoiding thoughts of his mother had gotten harder and harder. At first, being at school felt helpful, the space, the sympathy. You are forgiven for falling asleep in class, or talking incessantly about the importance of wetlands in the midst of your Gothic literature seminar, or telling your TA that she has perfect thighs, or staying in your dorm room for days, for weeks. When you are twenty-one and your mother dies, there is a pause that exists. Like when you stay home sick from school and you have run out of things to watch on TV and there is nothing left to do but take a nap.

It was good to have permission to be sad, to have a nameable reason. But that pause, that grace period, was coming to an end. He could feel it happening, a hardening of things, of people. So he had to leave campus, because it wasn't over for him, and he couldn't stand to do what was expected of him.

Extensions turned to deadlines, phone calls turned to e-mails, a double room turned to a single. Finally, he decided to go and find time, to give it to himself. On any given day he could decide how much time he needed. He could tell people his mother had died the week before or ten years before. He had wanted a journey to real emptiness. The Grand Canyon.

In the four days it took to drive from Bard to Arizona, Danny had imagined standing right at the lip of the canyon, but, once there, a post-and-rail fence had kept him back from the edge. Someone had dropped a magnet in the dirt, an image of a red convertible parked at the rim of the canyon. Danny wondered why it looked better in the picture. It wasn't what he had been expecting, at least not in a strict sense. It was beautiful and big. But some things are just too vast to be understood. It was easier to feel just a part of it through the TV screen than all of it through your skin. So the fifteen minutes he stood at the lip of the Grand Canyon felt too long. But he knew it was just long enough that he could say, without lying, that he'd been there. He had watched tourists moving along a path, black specks on a trail, ants in their farm. He couldn't understand those people who wanted to hike down to its vascular center. Why would they want to feel the chill crawl over their bodies as they distanced themselves from the sun, to follow a path, past the striated sediment of millions of years in a few hours, on a mule led by a guy named Paco John who was from Michigan and wore a Baja? He wanted to feel time flow at its natural pace, not sped up. He did not want a millennia-lapsing hike.

But life away, life in small diners and campsites, when he was just another guy cruising through with no story, no dead parents, had been harder than he expected. He had been dropping a coin into the slot of a press-a-penny, cranking the wheel and choosing his image, when he was supposed to be taking his finals. He should've been in a room with graduated seating and chairs with the swiveling desk arm. He should've squeaked that arm down over him like the safety bar on an amusement ride, cracked his knuckles, and set three sharpened pencils perpendicular to himself. He preferred when things were perpendicular, though he wasn't sure if that was a visual or auditory preference. He never liked the word "parallel." *It sounds snooty, preppy, too good for the other lines,* he thought.

The canyon, with its irregularities and sunken verticality, seemed off-putting, like a fallen cake. It was something that could have been perfect, but had not worked out. What had been a great expanse of rock, or ocean floor, a plane of infinite axes, was now a mathematical mess. Even pressed into a penny, he could feel its incongruities.

After his fifteen minutes as a tourist, Danny had gone back to the car in the visitors' lot. He had assembled a bologna sandwich from the contents of a small cooler in the backseat. It was his fourth day on the road. He had at least two weeks before they would expect to hear from him, four or five before he'd need to see them, eventually making his way back north to the house.

He sat facing sideways on the backseat with the door open and his feet on the ground. His forearms rested on his knees, as if the effort of holding up the sandwich with both hands was too much. He'd been feeling that way recently, that the small things were tiring. He could hike a mountain or fuck a girl, no problem (or, at least, the two times he'd done it there hadn't been a problem), but parallel parking exhausted him, as did washing dishes or getting dressed. During the last cold snap of spring, he wore his duck boots all day, every day, sleeping with his shod feet hanging off his single bed. That meant wearing the same pants as well, being unable to get them off over the boots.

The school counselor had encouraged him to fuck those girls. He hadn't said it like that, but that's obviously what the guy meant by, "Maybe you should just be young, let loose, allow your guard to drop."

So Danny took his prescription and he tried. First with his RA, who had been practicing her best shrink voice and poses on him, the earnest nod, the crossing and uncrossing of the legs. And then with his roommate's girlfriend one morning when, having waited until her boyfriend left for class, she simply climbed out of one bed and into another. Her pure ballsiness was so impressive. He couldn't help himself.

Neither hookup led to anything. The roommate moved out a few weeks before Danny left. He wanted to believe it was because of the girl, but he knew it wasn't.

Danny hauled himself out of the pool, convinced Libby had finally given up. His knees ached from squatting for so long. He walked the perimeter of the pool, stepping over a fallen log woolly with lichen. He heard a screen door slam back at the house. It was late afternoon, someone would be getting dinner ready soon, pasta with pesto, mozzarella, tomatoes. They all ate what they always ate here. There were no diets, no new foods. Wasabi peas, a gift from a friend over for a drink, had been unceremoniously rejected as the friend's boat pulled away from the float.

He thought how the raccoons must treat this pool like a buffet. They must crouch anxiously on their branches waiting for the sun to go down, then come to sit on the edge of the pool. Dangling their little rodent feet in the imaginary water, they hold corncobs in their claws and suck out the roots of every kernel.

He had managed to keep his road trip a secret, but he wasn't sure how long he could keep it hidden. His brother and sisters always wanted to hear about school. They were still young, or on the young edge of old, and still nostalgic for their college days. They wanted to live vicariously, and he just wanted to live with them. He wanted to be able to smoke joints with them. He wondered what they'd been like in college, dancing on tables and playing I Never. Gwen, the second oldest, was the only one he had seen do that kind of thing. Plenty of joints had passed between them. But Gwen was like a river, and rivers don't get old, they just keep going.

And now she was pregnant, barely. But it was already changing her. He could see it in her face. He didn't want to consider the loss of one more Willoughby, even a proto-Willoughby. He could talk around whatever doubt Gwen had. But it made him nervous, how careful she was being, avoiding terms, looking the other way, slouching. She was not one to swallow words. He knew it was his fault. She looked like a dog who had stolen something out of the trash, because he probably made Gwen feel like she was throwing something away. As if it belonged to him. Like uncle-dom was a valid form of ownership. He felt like a jerk. *Who asks their sister to have a baby she doesn't want?*

She had the gift of always knowing what she wanted. All that certainty of hers usually made him envious, but also filled him with admiration. She would not slink away to the Grand Canyon in a leased Subaru. If it were her, she might not have told their siblings she was leaving, but only because she would've decided between her house and the gas station, not because she was afraid of what they'd say, afraid that they could convince her not to go. She would've just sent postcards: "Oh, by the way, I've dropped out of life and I'm riding the rails, sailing around the world with a Rastafarian band, selling handmade dolls at the base of Kilimanjaro."

Gwen would have liked the Grand Canyon for about five minutes. She would've driven right by and blown it a kiss on her way to a motel with cable and a pool. Danny still cared about what he would say to people, people who would suspect him of taking a trip instead of exams and not going to see the Grand Canyon, blowing off the blow off. That is what Libby would think. Danny refused to even consider what Tom would think. Of a whole semester's tuition down the drain, of incomplete grades on everything, of being a five-year senior, or worse, never making it to senior year at all. Tom would have things to say about all of it. Long, drawn-out things that would be said across a large, empty dining room table as they sat in hard dining room chairs, while Melissa whistled like a fairy tale in the kitchen. Tom would have things to say.

Danny kicked fallen branches into the pool, scraped quilts of moss up with his shoe, kicking them toward the pool's edge. He wanted to dig down through the pine needles and weeds. He used his heel, chopping at the dirt. He got down on his hands and knees, pulled and scratched. He pushed and dug. Rocks went over his shoulders, sticks flung to the side. *I need a shovel,* he thought. An osprey flew over, crying and circling, her nest nearby. Danny sat back on his heels; he watched her circle, this mother eager for him to move on. She flew low out over the water, glared at him through the tree trunks.

If his mother had been here she would have understood about school. After their father died, she did what Danny had done; she had run away. Technically, she stayed, and everyone else left. Danny wished he had that luxury. She stayed in the house well into fall, something they'd never done. She never talked about why or what she had done in that time. The others were a gossipy mess over it, clucking over phone lines. Gwen imagined her mother and Remy carrying on a clandestine affair. Libby thought that she must have been writing their father's biography. Tom believed that whatever she was doing was ridiculous and that she needed to be with her family in a safe, urban environment with central heating. Danny stayed quiet on the subject. Speculating held no interest for him, which only convinced his sisters that he knew something.

Danny knew, without being told, that she was watching the water, watching the light change over it, because in the water there was life and hope and time passing, a union of all things. Because her husband was scattered in that water, and she wanted to watch him slide over the backs of seals and foam at the keels of schooners and dash against rocks that they had walked on together. She spent a month and a half saying good-bye.

Danny's father had died the summer after his senior year in high school. He had to leave Outward Bound three days early; they dropped him off at this house. His family was on the float waiting for him. They sat there among their bags and cried together.

Danny could see the water winking through the trees. The plastic bag in his hand, empty and twisted, was like a rope. He imagined it was a wet towel. He turned back toward the house. The pool, he thought, could only be restored in his memory, a memory that wasn't even his own.

Libby's words started to filter through the trees. She must have been calling for a while.

"Jesus, Dan," she called from somewhere near the house, "you're off the hook. Now stop hiding in the woods. We've got to go get Melissa."

FOUR

Tom

July 2

That night Tom found Melissa because she couldn't stop giggling. *Like a child,* he thought, *she can't play the game right.* The closet was tucked under a balcony in the corner of the great room by a seldom-used side door. A forgotten place. Melissa was sitting at the bottom of the closet full of tennis rackets and foul-weather gear.

After dinner, once the sun went down, they had decided to play Sardines, one of Danny's favorite games, and Melissa agreed to be It. The goal was to find her and hide with her. The last person still looking had to be It in the next round. This usually ended up with six people standing in a bathtub shushing each other behind a moldy shower curtain. But she had chosen a good spot. He couldn't even see her when he first opened the door, though he could hear the soft nasal rumblings of suppressed laughter.

"You're worse than Kerry," Tom said. "How old are you?" He quietly moved a pile of tennis rackets and some ancient snowshoes. He sat down beside her, cross-legged. She was cursing herself for giving away such an excellent location. He told her in a whisper where the rest had headed—Danny upstairs, the girls down the back hall—it would be a while before they circled back. He was catching her giggles.

"Don't you start," Melissa gave him a shove. He pushed her back, and she pulled him close, slung her legs across his lap in an effort to move them both farther into the corner. They were nestled behind a few yellow slickers hanging from pegs, and Melissa lined up boots in front of them to try to hide their feet.

"Smart thinking," he said.

"Not my first time," she said.

On their third date, both of them just barely out of college, Tom and Melissa had sat in the dark. Bare legged on an itchy blanket, they had watched a movie at the Hatch Shell. *Notorious.* Cary Grant punched Ingrid Bergman in the face in the first ten minutes of the movie; the audience roared at the inappropriateness, at the absurdity of a man seeming to take care of a woman too drunk to drive by knocking her out in one punch, KO.

"She'll have to fall in love with him now," Melissa had whispered.

"Once she punches him back we'll know they're soul mates," said Tom.

"The worst thing I've ever done in a car is puke," said Melissa. Someone a few blankets ahead shushed them.

Tom whispered, "I killed a cat with a car. Not on purpose."

She wrapped both of her arms around one of his and put her chin on his shoulder.

"It was a driving lesson, and the neighbor's cat was asleep under our car." Tom had had to stop talking for a second. "It made a sound." He had watched his father get out of the car and look underneath. His face pale, he opened Tom's door. He had said, "Why don't you head back to the house." He hadn't wanted Tom to see, to even know.

"My dad tried to hide it from me, but I wouldn't leave. He said it was a cat. *Was* a cat. He didn't say, it's Pickles. The neighbor's cat I fed sometimes. The cat who preferred to sleep on our front steps. I couldn't bring myself to look under the car. I just started to cry. It was a few weeks before my seventeenth birthday. He told me, it's not your fault. Then he got a towel and pulled out Pickles and wrapped her up."

They were whispering so close it was as if they were alone in the dark. The screen was the moon rising. Melissa pushed a tear off his face with her thumb.

"I never wanted to drive again," said Tom. "He had the bundle in his arms. I asked to hold it, and I unwrapped the towel by her head, kissed her. She was so soft. My father said he'd take the cat home to the neighbors. I said I wanted to. She was still warm. He walked beside me with his hand on my back. I couldn't even talk when they opened the door. He told them he had been the one driving." Sometimes Tom forgot that he had ever loved his father. Tom kissed Melissa's forehead. "I've never told anyone that."

"Once at a summer camp, when I was four, I killed all the class pets," Melissa had said. "I thought I was helping them."

Tom laughed and what had begun to fall apart in him came together again.

"I just thought the turtle should be free so I shoved it under a gate into a field." Melissa pushed both hands forward close to their blanket.

"Where it probably died of thirst?" Tom patted her knee.

She grimaced and shrugged. "Then there was a hamster that seemed really hot, and the kiddy pool was right there. And then the goldfish was just gluttonous. That one was barely my fault."

"Karmically speaking, we're not in good shape." Tom hugged her to him.

"We should get a cat, to redeem ourselves," she had said. They'd adopted their dog two weeks later. Melissa had named her Mukti, meaning freedom from the cycle of birth and death.

Now, in the dark of the closet he reached for her, grasping gently up her arm to find her face. He let his hands frame her face, pulled gently at her earlobes, kissed her. She moved into his lap, kissed back, led his hand underneath her shirt. He wrapped his mouth around the tendon between her shoulder and neck, the soft slope that dipped into the hollow above her collarbone. He bit her slow and hard, and she sighed, pressed herself deeper into his lap. They kept kissing, moving, hands and arms, turning their heads, first this way, then that. She turned in his lap to face him, wrapping her legs around him. His hands went under her shirt up her back. Her skin like water. She leaned back and then forward, pressing her forehead to his, both of them breathing hard.

"Why can't it be like this at home?" she whispered.

He exhaled sharply out of his nose. *She's so quick to kill the moment.* Whatever had been building went flat, and they were just playing a stupid game.

"That's why," he said and slid her off his lap.

She always wanted to pull it all apart, dissect it, put pins in it, put it under glass. She wanted to bring someone else in, a team, even. She talked about therapists, doctors, even third-party participants, like some kind of porno. She said she'd try anything. He believed it, too, all those ex-boyfriends, the one girl at boarding school. She still talked to some of those people. There was the filmmaker with the huge cock, Gigantor; the white boy with dreadlocks, who discussed the motion of the ocean (the voiced cliché hurt him to think about); the heroin addict with the Rottweiler; the alcoholic bed wetter, known as the Elf (an admitted low point for her); the Irishman whose name was either Ronan or Roland, she could never quite tell; the tattoo artist (she still talked to him); and the writer (the occasional e-mail).

And then him. Him in a long line of strange, deranged freaks who'd defiled his pretty wife in ways that he wished he didn't know. Christ, she'd tried things that he had never thought of. At first all her experience was thrilling. *Dating a slut is great,* he told himself: no inhibitions, no judgments, his mundane fantasies happily tried, refined, perfected, bolstered by her own ideas, her flair for the risqué. He wanted to believe that.

But after their children were born there was a lull in things. While she healed, while they adjusted to being parents, to no sleep and no energy for each other, something happened. It was so small. The turning of a page, the whisper of paper, the hush of a finger down a fresh sentence. It was imperceptible at first. And things seemed fine, fine for years. Until she started to complain. And then he saw that it was not fine. That she was changing, or his response to her, as she claimed, was changing.

He saw her in two ways, both as a woman who'd spent years fucking other men, and then as a woman somehow separate from her sex appeal, purely maternal, a woman who spelled words out for children, who strangely had started baking her own bread, whose hair had gone coarse and dull like she lacked vitamins. Her breasts hung from her chest, joggling lasciviously when she brushed her teeth. How many men had grasped and kissed and chewed and sucked on those beautiful, ruined breasts? Not ruined, exactly, but tainted. You were supposed to fuck sluts, not marry them, he realized. He was tired of trying to blot out all those other men, his own just another flag, and hardly the biggest, planted on a littered mountaintop.

There in the dark he was sweating. His clothes felt too tight. His knees hurt. She was always demanding that he talk. "Just tell me," she would say. "Whatever it is, just say it out loud." *Where to even start? I resent your past. They've* invited *me to take a leave of absence from work. I caught Buster jerking off to cartoon porn. Who invented cartoon porn? You aren't mine anymore. We are too broken. All of us.*

He still loved her, her thoughts, her jokes, her voice, her lips. There were days when her body seemed unchanged from their first night together, and that was almost worse. Her body lying to him like that. They still found each other under the blankets, across the dark plain of their king-size bed. But less and less. When she asked why, he couldn't exactly tell her. He couldn't say "because you have ruined your breasts twice, first with men and then with babies, because there's no space for me, your past is full, your future planned." *I will stay in my cold corner of our too-large bed,* he told himself. *This will not change, this mattress, this torn spot of wallpaper by the table; this will stay, and I will forever be able to satisfy my pillow, desperate only for my sleeping head.*

Tom cried there in the dark closet. He couldn't satisfy her. Someone else had to. If he could fuck her mind with his mind and leave their bodies out of it. That was what he always wanted, pure mind fucking. *The body makes it all base, all so rife with potential betrayal. She knows this, ask the Elf, she lied to him.* She said she loved him as she backed away from the bed with plastic sheets. "You're wonderful, I'll be right back." She tells this story, laughing, a cautionary tale, a commiseration with their single friends. She has been there. And he? He was only in the closet with his wife, who wouldn't be his wife much longer.

Melissa had her arm around him, her forehead on his shoulder.

"We haven't told the kids. Nothing's set in stone," she said. But they had been over this too much to turn back. He couldn't find his footing; he was being pulled away by the force of this current. He loved her still. But he had already consulted a lawyer, three actually, informational interviews, screening them as he had the prospective nannies for their children and prospective specialists for his mother. The first was too bloodthirsty, used to shouts and refusals exchanged across a conference table. His watch seemed to have rates instead of hours. The second's office smelled of canned minestrone and instant coffee; Tom almost expected to find carbon copies and electric typewriters on the lone receptionist's desk. The last, somber and straightforward, like a funeral director for the royal family, was the obvious choice. As Tom left the office, the lawyer said to just leave the retainer with his assistant. Suddenly it was done, before he had even meant to do it. The current was taking him out. But Melissa wanted to keep trying. Which, to her, meant therapy. She wants them to go, together, separately, everything. She keeps talking about outlets and support.

"Things could change," she whispered, "if we work at it, if we get some help."

"We're out of options," Tom said. "People go to therapy to get divorced."

"Well, then, if we're getting divorced, why can't we go to therapy?" asked Melissa.

"Because the job is done; you don't go to a doctor for an appendectomy if you've already taken it out yourself."

"This does kind of feel like amateur surgery."

"Which one of us is the amateur?" Tom whispered. They were still trying to keep their voices down.

"I'm just kidding. It's all awful; nothing about this feels good. I just thought we could use support." They couldn't see each other in the dark of the closet; she put a hand on his knee. He moved it away.

"Say what you mean. You really want *me* in therapy."

"We need both. Together and separately. We need to figure out what is our shit together and what is our individual shit." Melissa slid closer to him. He could smell the suntan lotion on her skin.

"So it's all shit." What did she even want to save then?

"Maybe getting a diagnosis would be helpful." Her hand was back on his knee.

"Is there a medical term for slut?"

He felt Melissa twitch and then shift deeper into the closet, away from him.

"There's one for depression"—she stopped whispering—"clearly professional help is in order."

"That's what lawyers are for," he said.

"Jeez, just kill me now."

"Look, I'm doing the best I can." Tom's whisper was growing louder, more raspy.

"Really? Because it feels like you're not even trying." She sounded tall and bright, even in the darkness.

"You think if we fuck more everything will be fine."

She leaned close to him; he could feel her hair brush his arm.

"I think," she whispered, "if we fuck at all we might have a chance in hell." She said this into his ear, her breath burned.

There were footfalls in the great room. They stopped talking. Someone was coming. The door opened and a hand pushed the slickers out of the way.

"Ah!" said Libby before flinging a hand over her mouth and craning her neck to see if anyone was on the balcony above. She then stepped quickly into the closet and squeezed between the two of them.

"I can't believe we all forgot to check this closet. Nice choice, Melissa."

"Thanks." She looked past Libby at Tom, who reached forward to pull the door shut, putting them all in darkness.

"Where are Danny and Gwen?" asked Melissa.

Now that Libby was hiding with them, now that he couldn't have her, Tom wanted Melissa alone, back on his lap, her face between his hands. He wanted to answer her questions.

It's not like this at home because I am afraid. Because if I don't leave now, you will beat me to it, because if I fuck you the way I want to, I will disgust myself, you, the memory of my mother. I'll be no better than he was.

He could smell the wine from dinner on Libby's breath. She elbowed Tom to move over, giggling at the clatter of a tennis racket to the floor. Footsteps on the main staircase. Ten bucks says it's Gwen. And there she was, opening the door and pushing past the raincoats, not even reacting to them, as if she knew they were in there all along.

"Shhhh," she said. "Dan's in the rug room; he heard me coming down the stairs."

They were silent, holding their breath, pressed together, hot skin and the cold rubber of raincoats. There was nothing. Nothing. And then the sharp tap of a Ping-Pong ball on the paddle, fast, tap tap tap. The door yanked open. There he stood, paddle in hand. "Alright, everybody out of the closet. Libby, you first."

"Very funny, loser," said Libby, stepping over the boots and fallen rackets.

"Poor Danny Boy, always last," said Gwen, patting his cheek as she stepped from the closet. Tom gestured for Melissa to go ahead. She moved to the doorway and reached back for his hand. He took it. *I'm sorry*, he mouthed. The others had gone toward the bay window, out of sight. He pulled her back into the closet. Kissed her.

"I don't know why," he said. "I wish I did." She made a fist around a lock of his hair, shook it gently, and rested her other hand on his side. Then she let go, went to join the game. They were already counting.

FIVE

ANOTHER SUMMER

From the porch, the Willoughby children can hear the water. The tide turned now, coming in, slapping and gulping at the drums of the float, a sloshing in its belly, and a soft kissing of the rocks down on the beach. The wind is slack now. Not like this morning, when the blue twilight, the birds' usual hour, was overtaken by wind funneling the oak leaves white and flattening the long grass of the meadow. So loud it woke them, lying in their beds, the nursery facing east away from the water, and still too loud in the trees. Now the wind is slow, the flag hangs loose on its pole, a handkerchief about to be dropped. Out in the thoroughfare the jammers are floating in on a breeze. Five sails and a streamer off the bow mast.

"Cattle boats," their father says. So full of tourists, they line the deck. Their motor is on too, maybe the sails are just for show, but that's fine. It's a good show.

The pine has overtaken the smell of seaweed as the tide covers the rocks' slippery skirt. When the wind is gone, they hear the white-throated sparrow calling, *Sam Peabody Peabody Peabody*. All sleepy and melancholy in his minor key, summer is short, he sings, it is already fading, even as fireworks bloom and motors buzz and lobsters head to warmer waters. Honeysuckle snakes up the steps, making them think their mother is wearing perfume.

The thunder of the jammer loosing its anchor to the harbor floor comes across the water fast and jumbled.

"Must rattle the ice in the tourists' cocktails," says their father.

Then there are big motorboats, all tinted windows and gleaming plastic, white and black like office buildings or getaway cars.

"Fornicatoriums," their father says. The children laugh, though they don't know what he means. They watch him scratch his back on the porch posts, like a bear, a bear with a beer in his paw. To them he is as strong, as furry. They wonder when they will have summertime lunchtime beers. Their mother shoos it away.

"Will put me to sleep," she says.

"Exactly," their father says.

He lays low in the Adirondack chair, feet on the wide rail, a crumb-strewn plate at his heels. He pulls his hat down to his nose, holds his beer on his belly, listens to the jammer's anchor tumble up, done with their lunch too.

The children saw a rabbit out by the pump house yesterday. They want to catch it, not catch it, but see it again, lure it to them, just to be close to it. Tom says they could stuff it, add it to the collection of heads in the great room. The other two look incredulous for a moment, then disregard him. He is pulling their leg, telling tales. He is no bunny killer. Libby decides she'll take no chance, though. If necessary, she is ready to step between brother and bunny, take a slingshot's rock to the chest, tell on him, on everything she has ever seen him do that could be considered suspect. Gwen sees her sister's thought, sees her defiance spread across her face like so much fire on a dry California hillside she has seen only on the television. She pats her sister on the head, gives her a smirk, a he-can't-fight-us-both face. The forest sizzles and pops its last, and Libby's face is black trunks and blue sky, a frown and a hopeful furrow.

The thoroughfare changes color nine times while they stand in the trees behind the pump house, shushing each other. Their mother sits on the wide white railing and watches the water, having already removed the half-finished beer from her husband's sleeping hand. She drinks the rest and watches—slate, violet, ashen, smoky, smudged, mossy, white, silver. The sun glares from the other side of storm clouds, and, for a moment, the town and the water go white. The wind picks up.

"Southwesterly," she whispers. And the water in the cove goes black, the pebbles of the cove's beach washed-out gray as the boathouse beside them.

She heads through the house, the dining room, the kitchen, pushes open the screen door from the top where it sticks, calls them. No response. Whistles sharply, once, a short burst so as to not wake her husband. With waving hair and knobbed, scuffed knees, they tromp high-kneed through the long grass, still humped and curved from a morning storm.

"It's blowing up out there," she says. "The rain's coming." They nod, Libby keeping an eye on her feet; a twisted ankle last summer makes her wary. Tom looks out to the water at the side of the house.

"Southwesterly," he says. Gwen stays behind, walking arms out, like a mother duck, hustling her bairns along, *stay together, head to the porch,* say her wiggling fingers.

"We should wake your father."

"The rain will wake him." Gwen giggles, a streak of the devil in her always. The beer is still unfinished in their mother's hand; she leaves it just inside the soapstone sink and doddles Libby off to wake their father.

He will hold her over his belly, saying, "You'll do for an umbrella, a bit wiggly, but dry enough."

She hates this. Feels his hands sink into her flesh too hard, holding her up above him; it hurts, but she laughs, and he doesn't understand and she can't say. He doesn't know his strength or her weakness, her softness. He can't balance her right.

The storm is almost upon them now. The water goes from slate to a deep viridian that makes the trees seem brighter, more yellow in them, and the sky goes dark and steely, gunmetal, twilight hours early. They pull the cushions off the wicker porch furniture, their father doles out pillow after pillow to tiny waiting arms. Their mother holds open the door, motions for her husband to move the chairs under cover, annoyed that he drags the old wicker chairs, doesn't lift them the way she would.

The children tear around the rug room, cards out, the window seat lifted to reveal piles of board games. Tom, at the fire, carefully crumples newspaper, builds a teepee of kindling on top of it.

"Get me a log, Bibs." He waves Libby toward the woodpile.

She drops her deck of cards on the table; slippery, they slide to the very edge. Gwen lounges on a chaise, pretends to paint her fingernails, lists game after game they could play, but dismisses each one before the others even notice. She will decide the game, and they will object. She will say, "I suggested that one, but we decided it was too slow, too few players, too long, too hard for Libby, too easy for Tom; this is the one we'll play."

Now the fire is lit and the game—Parcheesi—is laid on the rug, all while their parents whisper harshly in the kitchen about the proper way to move porch furniture.

The rain comes. It is quiet and there is tea and the turning of pages and the rolling of dice. Their father plays. Thunder, not an anchor, vibrates in their chests, in the window frames. Gwen sits by the window when it's not her turn, watches for lightning, no fear. Their father lets out a whoop, sending two Parcheesi pieces back to the start. Libby and Tom groan in unison.

"He cheats," they say. "Gwen, come from the window, we need a witness."

~

Tom hears his parents one night. At thirteen he is no longer in the nursery with the girls, no longer lies next to Libby when she whimpers in her sleep, no longer fetches cups of water in the night. He is downstairs now, down the back hall off the kitchen, the glassed porch with a brass bed that his mother says is fit for royalty. It's his father who says it is an old-lady bed.

He hears her first. Early, before the birds. The black, shagged limbs of the pines around his room go prickly and yellow in the sudden light from the kitchen window. He hears the pull clink against the bare bulb. He hears the whine of the cabinet in the pantry, tea and cookies. The water sloshes fast and tinny into the kettle and the stove snaps to light itself. His mother's bare feet pad the painted floor; he hears her go from the sink to the back door, to the pantry, to the bottom of the back stairs. *Is she looking for something?* The kettle thinks of whistling and the stove clicks off, and he knows the tea is steeping and she is at the kitchen table, her feet on the rung of a chair. He hears her breath stutter out of her; he knows that sob. Libby cries like that, labored inhales and exhales. *Like an asthmatic,* he thinks. Though he knows no one with asthma. He pulls back the blanket, tugs it from its hospital corners, and wraps it around his shoulders. Sitting on the step of his threshold he leans against the closed door and waits.

Tom sits and whispers, "Please, birds, wake up, please let it be four fifteen, let the sky lighten, birds, please start singing."

He has never thought much about the birds and their chatter, about *Sam Peabody* or the towhee who tells you to *Drink Your Tea.* Now he craves their soft first flights, from low branch to low branch. Their songs will fill the nursery, and his sisters, for a moment, will be awake too.

Scarlet leans into the steam. Her stuttering breath brings it in and then pushes it away. Her hand encircles the mug but doesn't touch it, the mug too hot. And nothing seems worse, which makes her breath harder to move. Sometimes it just stops all together. The less she breathes the more she cries. The window is ajar, and the breeze through it chills her, blows right across her shoulder blades, making her press her elbows to her sides. She wishes for her bathrobe, but she can't close the window, for closing the window would mean moving her hands, and she wants only to hold the mug.

Gwen is still in the nursery, but Scarlet knows it is in her, too, the strange realization that beds could be for more than sleeping, and certainly should be far away from one's siblings. Their mother sees only Libby, with her tanned skin and downy hair, like she was born from the warm summer hay of the meadow. Scarlet has forgotten what beds are for.

Her husband, their father, thumps and bangs down the stairs, not at all like it is the middle of the night. The stairs creak under his feet, under his shushing slippers, shush thump shush thump. He stands in the doorway at the bottom of the steps, his hands grasping high on the doorframe like he's ready to launch himself into the room. But as with most of his entrances, he flags, hesitates. He tucks his wide chest under shoulders and slides past her to the fridge, cracks and shuffles an ice tray, and slides back to her side. He slips two cubes into her tea, and she turns to him quickly. But the ice has already softened at the edges and he has turned away.

She starts anyway. Who needs his help, she says, all venom and whisper. He robbed her of something; that it isn't right, that the tea should just cool on its own and then she can hold the mug. Now the mug is still too hot and the tea too cold.

Even the way you drink your tea is oppressive, says the roll of his eyes. She misses it.

He wants to make her more tea, but it is too late, her moment for tea is lost. He hates that she robs him of every opportunity to be close, to do something nice for her, and she hates that she can't get near him without him ruining things. He hugs her too hard. He does that to the children too, she sees it in their faces. And she knows that he has found someone to hug as hard as he wants. She doesn't know that he brought another woman here once.

The woman from the other island, he brought her here when his family was in their winter home, back for a wedding that he couldn't tolerate. He brought her to the house and let her touch the animal heads, something he hated anyone doing, but he let her. He laughed with her when she broke a wineglass.

"My wife will ask about that." *This woman is building lies as she stands here separate from me. Her presence is a new lie I have to tell.* But he didn't take her to her house, buzz her quickly over the thoroughfare, a fast ride of slap and spray. Instead, he took her to a room, the last room down the back hall filled with mothballs, and pillows that didn't make it back to their rightful spots when they opened the house. She told him her hair would smell of camphor for weeks. He said that she should be happy; she would repel bugs. It was black fly season.

PART II

SIX

GWEN

July 4

On the Fourth of July they always ate lobsters. Gwen looked forward to this feast all year. The decadence of it all was not lost on her. Remy had come by that afternoon and dropped them off, while Gwen and Libby lay on beach towels on the float. Too numb and sleepy from lying in the sun most of the morning, they hadn't even heard the boat until it bumped up against the float.

"Hello, Willoughbys," said Remy.

"Hey, Remy. Hey, Maddie," said Libby, looking up at the caretaker and his daughter standing in their boat.

Remy pulled their spare trap up from the water, where it was tied to the float, while his teenage daughter, playing stern man in yellow waders and a tank top, sorted out five shedders. They exchanged a few pleasantries, or tried to, with Remy's response always being "Suppose so" or "That's the truth."

Gwen and Libby looked at each other quickly in shared awkwardness and guilt, lounging in their bikinis while Remy's daughter, muscled and mud smeared, had just literally brought their dinner up from the bottom of the harbor. As the boat putted away to join the circles of other lobstermen chugging from pot to pot, Gwen and Libby shook their heads and laughed. It was just part of being summer folk, embarrassing themselves like that in front of the locals.

Gwen had always wished Remy had a son. She loved lobstermen. The way they talked; the way they looked in short sleeves and waders, hauling on lines; the way they watched her motor in too fast to the town dock before throwing the thing into reverse at the last moment.

"Gonna drop an engine one day, Gwen. That ain't no sports car."

"Yeah, but it sure drives like one," she'd say with a wink.

She liked the way, after spending an afternoon anchored in a cove with a lobsterman, she'd smell of salt and mud, streaks of it up her back, down her legs. She didn't need to go in the cabin like the local girls; she'd do it right there on the engine cap, on the pulpit. To them she was spoiled and beautiful and on the fast track to nothing good. They'd say this to her, as she led them up the back steps. "You're nothin' but trouble." Despite her leaps off the ferry tower, her drinking with the locals on someone's boat, bringing those locals into her house, her bed, she knew she'd always be a bit of a joke, a bit of a legend.

That evening, Tom and Libby stood in front of the soapstone sink full of lobsters and seaweed. Melissa hid out in the rug room, taking refuge in a crossword. Gwen was beside them at the stove while Danny sat at the kitchen table messing with an old tape deck. The whir of the deck fast-forwarding changed pitch with the varying strength of the ancient motor. Libby and Tom argued. They reminded Gwen of their parents, of their parents before Danny came along. It was silly and sad, but also soothing.

"You must get the water to a rolling boil and then drop them in," said Libby slowly, as if giving instructions to a caterer.

"No, you have to start them off in cold seawater, then bring it to a boil. It's the humane way to go," said Tom.

"Are we cooking lobsters or are we euthanizing them?" said Libby.

Gwen laughed as she changed one large pot for an even bigger one. Libby, so straightlaced, could always be counted on for the unexpected zinger.

"You got an opinion there, G?" said Tom.

"Nope, I'm just the sous-chef. I do as I'm told, though I don't think it matters if you use seawater or not." She wasn't about to get involved in their age-old lobster fight.

"Of course it matters," Tom and Libby said together.

"Why don't you hypnotize them?" Danny suggested. Tom and Libby ignored him. Gwen picked up a lobster from the sink and brought it over to Danny, setting it next to the tape recorder.

"God, this isn't even the right pot." Libby stormed out of the kitchen and into the pantry. They heard the rattle of pot and lid, the crunching of paper, and the skittering of kibble across the painted wood floor.

"Why do we still have dog food?" said Gwen.

"Aw, Beardsley," said Danny. He stuck out a pouted lip. Gwen mirrored him.

Tom tried to convince Gwen of his system; she nodded, an expression of utter seriousness on her face.

"Just like frogs, if you throw them into boiling water they jump out. If you put them in cold water and slowly bring up the heat, they won't even know they're being boiled to death." He lowered his voice and leaned toward Gwen. "She's being such a child, always wanting to have things her way. Half the time she acts as if we're all guests in her house. Like she's the hostess in charge of who sleeps where and which boats can be used on what days, and how to cook—"

But here was Libby again, marching forth with the largest pot. Handing it off to Gwen, she pushed up her sleeves and gripped the rim of the soapstone sink as if about to jump into it. They continued to snap back and forth, "They'll cook unevenly if you put them in one at a time," "But you'll run the risk of overcooking them if you start from zero." Libby pulled a beaten and stained copy of *The Joy of Cooking* down from a wooden shelf and held it open toward Tom. He rolled his eyes; he had seen that page dozens of times. Gwen wished she had popcorn. She sat down next to Danny, holding the pot in her lap like a great oval cat.

"They're really channeling the B.O.B. on this one," she whispered.

"She went for the cookbook too early," Danny whispered back. "She should've built up to it."

"Lobstermen don't use cookbooks, Libby," said Tom.

"So now you represent the masses for us? How nice. I'm glad you can keep us in touch with the people, Tom. Are those Teamster loafers you're wearing?"

Libby spent six weeks a year in this house, cooked lobster at least twice every summer. She had complained to Gwen for years that Tom thought he understood the task better. That he was somehow more in touch with this place than she was. Gwen thought it was hilarious that it all mattered so much to her sister. Cooking lobsters and tying up boats; how hard could it be? As long as you didn't poison anyone, and the boats were still there in the morning, job done.

"How is cooking lobster a class issue?" Tom demanded. Gwen had seen this fight many times before, but it was always different. Like a photograph of the same spot at different times of day. Maybe she should go back to photography. It was all so much simpler—click, capture, done. Painting was visceral, all emotion and misunderstanding. Maybe that was why she resisted acrylics as her medium, too much mess. Watercolor gave her the strokes without the heaviness, the colors without the texture of the medium itself, though certainly still visceral.

The rest of them couldn't see the picture they were part of, except Danny. She sometimes thought Danny could see through time, deep into the universe to some dark star. He was still a kid, after all, and kids have magic and vision. She watched Danny as he held the lobster upside down on the table, balancing on the tripod of its head and claws. Danny slowly rubbed its green back, and its flapping tail calmed and its claws relaxed. He smiled up at Gwen and she took the now limp lobster from him and placed it on a bed of seaweed in the sink.

She heard the tape deck click, Carole King suddenly sounding bright and strong through the kitchen for a second. Then Danny stopped it, the music replaced with a whirring. Gwen took sticks of butter from the freezer and stacked them on the kitchen table. *Just keep things rolling.* Libby slammed a saucepan down on the stove, and Tom leaned on the counter watching her and aggressively bit his nails. Danny pressed play again, more Carole, then click and whir, then play again.

"Dear God, Dan, just play it or don't," said Gwen as she took the lobster pot from the stove and shoved it at Tom.

"I was just hoping there was something else on this tape. Guess it's this or *Godspell.*"

"*Godspell,*" said Tom and Libby together.

Tom grudgingly left to fill the pot with seawater. When he returned Gwen stood in the kitchen doorway. Gwen was too hungry to wait for them to decide how to cook dinner. She took the pot from him, water sloshing, saying, "We got it from here. You're in charge of cocktails. I'd like a Shirley Temple." While the water boiled Gwen and Libby watched the lobsters stumble and clunk in the sink. Danny spread the inside of a baguette with garlic and butter. Carole King felt the earth move.

The five of them sat at the dinner table. At first there was just the cracking of shells as everyone tucked into their plates. Gwen wished that Kerry and Buster were here. One of them usually got full, or lazy, partway through the meal. She always sat between them.

"Let me crack those claws for you," she would say, taking a small toll for the service. Or even better, one of them would be on a humanitarian kick and wouldn't be able to stand the thing on their plate looking at them, and she would end up with an entire second lobster. She would scavenge anyone's plate; she was not squeamish or picky—legs, tail fins, even antennae, like gnawing on fishy Twizzlers—she ate it all, the tomalley, the roe. If she could chew up the shell she would have. Gwen twisted the tail from the body of her lobster and let the liquid drain into the Royal Copenhagen punch bowl in the center of the table. The bowl was one of the few pieces left from their parents' wedding china.

"Ewww, gross, it's throwing up," said Tom.

Libby had said this as a kid, a visceral reaction that she always had despite adoring lobster. And now it had to be uttered whenever someone drained their lobster—it was automatic, a compulsion, like the second half of "Shave and a haircut."

Melissa was not a natural with her lobster, but Gwen admired her commitment. Having grown up in Ohio, seven hundred miles from the coast, Melissa hadn't had proper lobster until she was in college. Once Tom started to bring her to the house, she became a true convert. She'd tear into her dinner, using both hands, always changing into a ratty T-shirt before dinner.

"You're in my favorite outfit," said Gwen.

"It's my full-body bib," Melissa explained. A scattering of shell bits lay around her plate. "I came up with this system when the kids were little. Bibs are inefficient, and what is a shirt, if not a full-body bib. This way, I can just toss it in the wash when I'm done. Easy." Melissa was practical in all the best ways.

"Really you should patent the idea, just put a lobster on it and a slogan, and you'll make a million selling it on Route 1 next to those lawn ornaments of the lady bending over showing her bloomers. You know, classy," said Gwen.

"Like, bibs are for shrimps," said Libby. "T-shirt bibs are for lobsters."

"No, it's got to be catchy. Get it?" said Tom. The table let out a collective groan.

"It should be something like: 'Get Boiled,'" said Danny. "You know, like you're getting wasted on lobster."

"I like Tom's idea," said Melissa. "The shirt would read 'Catch it!', and the tagline can be, 'For what misses the bib.' Although that sort of makes it sound like an STD."

"A delicious STD," said Gwen.

"But, really, how is it different from a regular T-shirt?" asked Tom. "Aside from the marketing."

"God, Tom, how is a stick up the ass different from a dildo?" said Gwen. "It just depends on how much you enjoy it." Gwen saw Libby put a hand over her mouth as if willing a sip of wine not to come out of her nose. "I'm just kidding, T. I know we can't make marketing jokes around you. Besides, I'm sure someone's already beaten us to the full-body-bib punch. Bodybibs.com."

"Probably. I'm sure ass-sticks.com is taken too," said Tom. "You've got to get those domain names early if you want to control your brand."

This degenerated quickly into a contest for who could come up with the most ridiculous domain name possible. Eventually the conversation circled back to the age-old question of making, but always forgetting, to eat the salad with their lobster dinner. Gwen felt salad was just a distraction.

"I think now is as good a time as any to talk about our finances," said Tom.

"Leave it 'til later," said Melissa quietly. She reached a hand toward him, but he sat back in his chair.

"I don't think talking money is really how our forefathers wanted us to celebrate this day," said Libby.

"Booze and lobster, on the other hand . . . ," said Danny.

"Those are basically the building blocks of any good nation," said Gwen. She and Danny clinked glasses across the table. Maybe she could fend off the topic; maybe they could derail Tom.

"I'm not saying we need to balance our budgets, but I do think we have some decisions to make," said Tom. Libby refilled everyone's wineglass. Gwen didn't have one. Tom tried to wave her away.

"I'll just top you off."

Gwen watched Libby wink at Danny. Gwen had a low tumbler full of iced tea and mint, which she hoped looked like a rum cocktail.

"Melissa, how is Kerry doing at school, is she still going to tutoring or has that stopped?" said Gwen. She twisted a claw from her lobster and snapped it open at the knuckle.

"This is her first year without it. Dyslexia's a bitch, but she's figuring out her strategies." Melissa used a tiny fork to dunk a sliver of meat into a butter dish.

"There is one piece of our inheritance that we haven't nailed down," said Tom. Even the subject of his own daughter wouldn't deter him.

"That's an unfortunate choice of words," said Melissa.

"It's time for us to consider selling the house." Using a cracker, he crushed open his claws but looked up at each of them as he talked. "I know this is tough, but we need to be realistic."

Libby and Danny looked at each other. Gwen had known this was coming. Tom wasn't one to hide his feelings or string them along, but she had been hopeful. Hopeful that he would be too busy, too distracted, to bring this up now. Hopeful he would give them one more summer before they had to lose something else, or struggle to keep it.

She was tired of struggling. She wanted a true vacation, one from her struggles, her decisions, her insecurities. She wanted to be the reed in the river, rooted but flexible. Here in this house she would not be washed away by questions, here was a still point while the rest of the world drifted by: the torn roster for a 1959 Ping-Pong tournament tacked to the wall in the great room, the winner one Edmund Muskie.

The black-and-orange battalion of the Social Registers from 1943 to 1972 sitting, frayed and mildewing, on a shelf beside a jar of dried sea urchins.

"I love this place"—Gwen waved her lobster tail—"and I can't imagine someone else having it, but how much would it cost us if we split it? How much would we be spending for however many weeks a year?"

Tom looked slightly shocked. *Good.*

"That is exactly the type of practical question we need to be asking ourselves," he said.

Gwen could see Danny crunching up his napkin and then smoothing it out only to crunch it up again. *Stay cool, Dan.*

"It could be more than just a few weeks," Libby suggested. She had barely begun her lobster, still sucking on its legs. She had the reverse philosophy of Gwen. Libby liked to be the last one to finish, as if by virtue of being last she could actually eat more lobster. This infuriated Gwen, one of the few ways Libby could truly get to her. Libby savored her lobster while Gwen perched at the edge of her chair, a vulture on a dead tree.

Their mother's chair at the end of the table was empty.

Tom sat in their father's chair at the head of the table, a heavy chair with thick, wooden arms and a woven seat. He rested his elbows on the edge of the table, holding up his lobster-covered hands, looking a bit like a freshly scrubbed surgeon, afraid to touch anything. His lobster fully dismembered on his plate.

"Bibs, I know you love this place. Look, you've put more work into it than any of us. But you can't afford this on your salary. Danny's still got a year of school left, and we need to pay for that—"

"I can handle the tuition on my own," Danny objected. "I don't need you guys to pay my way." Danny was mashing lobster bits into his potato with a fork.

"Shut up, Dan." Gwen sighed. She was hunched over her plate, coming up for air with each sentence. "Mom left some money. Your tuition is covered. Don't scare them, Tom. The house is its own issue." And then she went under again, miniature fork in hand.

"Take it easy, G," Dan whispered across the table at her. "Shellfish isn't good for everyone." Gwen narrowed her eyes for a moment but said nothing. No one else seemed to notice. *No one is wrecking this lobbie for me. Not Tom. Not Dan. And not this goddamn baby.*

"What you all need to figure out is what you can each afford," said Melissa. "And if that's enough to keep it up." Tom looked at her for a moment, his wife sitting next to him. Her plate was a pool of lobster juice that periodically sloshed over the plate's lip. *Good thing she's got her shirt bib on,* thought Gwen.

"I think what Melissa means," he said, gesturing at her as though she were a showcase, "is maybe we could pull it off—maybe—but, for me, for us"—he looked at Melissa here—"the sacrifice isn't worth it. We've got kids. College tuition on the horizon. We've got other places we need to spend that money. You really want to dump all your inheritance into this house, Dan? Even if it will only buy you a few more years?"

"Hell, yeah, I do," said Danny, grabbing a fistful of paper towel off the roll that sat on the table and wiping his hands. "You might be pretty comfortable sitting at the head of the table, Tom, but switching seats doesn't mean you're in charge."

The table was quiet, the cracking of shells ceased for a moment. Gwen cheered silently in her head. She wasn't sure she had ever heard Danny speak to anyone like that, let alone Tom. Danny looked pale and shaky. He dropped his fork, then picked it up. He scratched at his arm.

"Can I please just eat my lobster and then make any life decisions after dinner?" said Gwen, raising a hand to them as if to wave away an unsatisfactory dish.

Libby, who'd finally begun working on her claws, was struggling with the cracker, turning the lobster around on her plate, flipping it over, and then back again. Struggling, Gwen thought, to find the most efficient and yet time-consuming way to dismember her meal.

"Who has a knife?" Libby asked. Tom, sitting to her right, took her lobster from her plate, and with merciless efficiency, broke off both claws and the tail, drained the juice, and put the pieces back on her plate.

"Ewww, gross, it's throwing up," whispered Danny.

"Christ, Tom, you gonna feed it to me, too?" said Libby.

"Well, I knew you'd just end up spraying me if I let you wrestle with it any longer." Tom got up and went into the kitchen.

Danny and Melissa started talking about wine versus beer as the correct pairing with lobster.

"He treats me like a goddamn kid," Libby whispered to Gwen. "He's got his own kids; he can act out with them. Of course, they'd rather be home with Grandma, who can't keep their names straight. He's always stepping over the line, taking the boat without asking, leaving the lights on at night, referring to Patricia as 'your friend.' Like a blind old man. She's not my fucking friend. She's the woman I fuck. Important distinction."

"Maybe if you actually told him that, he might be able to make the distinction more easily," said Gwen.

Tom came back in with the saucer of lemon wedges. Gwen, tipping the last of her empty shells into the Royal Copenhagen bowl, took a lemon wedge from the saucer now at the center of the table and began scrubbing her fingers with it.

"We're not going to decide this in one night. Melissa's right. Much as I loathe the idea, maybe we all need to do a little math. Nothing," Gwen said, looking pointedly at Tom, "is out of the question. Let's all relax and enjoy our vacation. No matter what we decide, this"—she pointed into the bowl—"is not the last lobster we'll eat in this house."

"Fair enough," said Tom. "I appreciate you not wanting to make any decisions lightly, but by the same token, we need to consider the timing. We need to keep in mind good selling markets, investment strategies, school vacations, personal days. You name it. And the sad thing is, there are not an infinite number of days that we can be here together, make decisions, sign papers. Some of us actually want to retire someday."

"We sold the sloop already," said Libby. "I think that should be enough for now. Let's just take this one step at a time. Boat by boat."

"This is bullshit. Why are you all pussyfooting around him?" said Danny. "Look, a decision has been made, Tom. You've been outvoted."

"Dan, that's just not practical. We don't even know if we can afford to keep it. Imagine what we could get for this place. Imagine what having that kind of financial security would be like," said Tom.

Gwen already saw it in Danny's face. *Don't do it, Dan.*

"I don't have to imagine. Libby's got an offer for three mil sitting in her pocket. And we're saying no."

"God, Gwen, you told him?" said Libby.

"Was I not supposed to?"

Libby rolled her eyes.

"An offer?" Tom looked at Libby, who looked at her lobster. "Why is this the first I'm hearing of it?"

"It's not the offer to accept, Tom," said Gwen. "It's some developer who would just bulldoze the place. I know you don't want that."

"No, of course not. But you know what I do want? To send both my kids to college. I want to give them the same debt-free education that we spoiled brats had. God, you three don't even know how lucky we are. You want to say no to that money? You want Kerry and Buster living with me 'til they're thirty because they can't afford rent on top of student loans?" He was on his feet now. "Fine, then just give me seven hundred thousand dollars, and this place is all yours. You want to exist in your own walled-off little world, the three of you? Go right ahead.

You'll be buried alive in this place." Tom slammed his napkin down on the table.

"Tom." Melissa looked at her husband. "Loans can be paid back. We can work this all through. Libby's right, you've got what you need for now." She stood up beside him and put her hand on his arm. "If this guy wants the house, I'm sure there will be a whole slew of people just like him."

"It was a handwritten note," said Gwen. "Who knows if the guy was serious or even sober when he wrote it."

"There's one way to find out," said Tom. He went into the china closet between the dining room and the kitchen, and returned with the rotary phone, its cord trailing behind it. He set the phone on the table next to his place and held his hand out to Libby. "The note, please."

"Tom, you can't be serious," Gwen said. Libby didn't move, but she looked at the sideboard. Tom followed her gaze, walked over, picked up her wallet, and opened it. The note was wrinkled and missing a corner. Tom dialed the phone, the sound of the rotary spooling out each number. He didn't look at any of them.

"Voice mail," he whispered. "Yes, my name is Tom Willoughby, you made an inquiry about our house on Vinalhaven. If you'd like to come and take a look at the place, we can discuss this further. We will be here until the twelfth. Again, this is Tom Willoughby, w-i-l-l-o-u-g-h-b-y. Thank you." He hung up the phone. His color matched the lobster shells.

"Way to go, Tom, very respectful," said Gwen, shaking her head.

"You are unbelievable," said Libby. Had she not been elbow deep in lobster juice, Gwen thought Libby would've stormed out. "Danny is right. You're not in control here. No matter what you think. You can't do anything without all of our consent. Being the executor doesn't mean anything," said Libby.

Danny was silent, staring at his plate. Gwen was fairly sure he was crying. Melissa slid her napkin under the edge of Danny's plate and stood up next to Tom.

"None of you need to make this decision now," she said, rubbing Tom's back absently. "You shouldn't. Tom. Scarlet has only been gone for six months. You don't need to lose this house in the same year. Give yourselves some time."

This is how it must go at home. Melissa always talking him down, defusing his prickly, wired heart. Tom sat down. Melissa did too. He nodded. He reached for her hand.

"Sorry," he said. "I just think this is an opportunity we need to seriously consider. I need us to. I need things too." He coughed and scrubbed his nose for a second.

Libby bent over her lobster in concentration, working out the tail fins like loose teeth.

"We'll think about it, Tom. Everyone's opinion matters," Gwen said, looking at Danny. "We'll make this decision together."

Danny started to eat his baked potato fast, breathing heavily through his nose. The only one who'd wanted a potato, he'd cooked it in the microwave right before dinner.

"I like how the potato soaks up the lobster juice," Danny said to Melissa, trying his best, "like a poor man's shepherd's pie, but with lobster."

"A rich poor man," said Melissa.

Tom leaned back in his chair, sighed. Libby held her lobster tail pinched in her fingers and dunked it liberally in the butter dish. Gwen watched her as usual, poised on her gnarled branch. Soon they would be done with dinner, and she could hide from this decision, from all decisions, in the dark of the porch, while the boys set off fireworks. Maybe it was time for a real cocktail.

SEVEN

DANNY

July 4

It was dark. They had waited almost too long, the neighbors' weak fireworks long since faded from the sky. Their smoke was somewhere over Rockland now, mixing in with the city-funded pyrotechnics. Danny and Tom stood together on the float facing the house, both with hands on hips. Danny bent down and repositioned the colorful tube in a coffee can half filled with sand. Tom shook his head, pulled the thing from the sand or pushed it deeper. Back and forth. Danny couldn't believe he had to stand next to Tom, to follow his instructions.

"Insert stay firmly in fireproof foundation," Tom read.

Danny found that each direction did its part to remind the reader of the fireworks' ancestral origins, coming off more like a koan or a haiku than anything remotely instructional. Danny was more of the light-it-and-run-like-hell school of thought. But for Tom it was always a slog, always take-it-slow and let's-just-go-over-it-one-more-time.

This wasn't rocket science, not exactly. It was mini rocket science, much like Libby's Easy-Bake Oven, passed down to Danny in some hope of reversing centuries of gender profiling. He had used it as a parking garage for his fire engine collection. No, this rocket, like the oven, would not live up to its full-size version. It would fly but not terribly high.

"Point it out more. You don't want it on the roof," said Danny.

"I can manage this a little better than Dad," said Tom.

During Danny's fifteenth summer, his father, all heft and stiff knees, clambered out onto the roof from Libby's porch to stamp out an errant firework in a muddy gutter.

"Lucky he didn't blow his foot off," said Tom.

It's an overgrown sparkler, not a land mine, thought Danny. But he kept quiet. He had plenty of experience watching Libby say the things he was feeling, and Gwen do the things he was afraid to do. He knew it was not worth fighting Tom on much. Particularly since emotion and sentiment seemed to have no effect on him. Maybe Tom was a robot. Maybe Scarlet and Bob got him as a baby prototype, My First Kid.

Snap, the lighter, fizz and flare, the fuse. The two of them running up the ramp, ducked low, but high-kneed, looked like burglars.

This first one fizzled with a shrieking whistle, but without a light. Catcalls from the porch. The women enjoying themselves up there, leaning back in wicker chairs, moving from wine back to cocktails.

"Gotta try harder than that, boys." Gwen.

"Yeah, Washington wouldn't have seen much glory by that light." *Melissa, such a nerd sometimes,* thought Danny.

"You're thinking of Francis Scott Key," called Tom back toward the porch.

"Just blow something up," shouted Gwen.

They tried again. Approaching slowly in case something hadn't gone off, in case it was a live one.

Danny pulled the spent cracker from the coffee can, and Tom slid a new one from the package. Up the ramp, they watched the thing whistle by in a stream of light and plume in the sky. Then the booming crack that was delayed and the umbrella of sparks, yellow, faded to green as it slid down the sky like so much electric rain.

Great whoops and whistles from the porch. More. Again.

"Make our ears bleed." Gwen.

They went through four more; one with the whirling dervishes of "The Five Spangled Banner"; one with concentric rings, "Let Freedom Ring-a-Ding"; and two more different shades of Queen Anne's lace, "Lady Liberty."

There was a pause as they assembled the finale. Tom had these and more lined up along the float, perpendicular to the slats to be sure that none slipped through. Danny liked that. Together they weeded and traded, paired and grouped. Pantomiming reminders of different shapes, explaining that the star-covered ones were always blue, the ones with gold foil on the tips were yellow with an orange finish, with silver, yellow with a green finish. Back and forth.

"Tom," Danny said—swapping out the Whistling Dixie for the booming Cannons of America—"we need to keep the house."

Tom sat back on his heels, holding the paper-wrapped explosives across his knees. "'Need' is a strong word."

They had turned off the dock light, for a better view, and with the light of town behind him, Danny couldn't tell if Tom was looking at him or the house.

"Sometimes if you want something enough it becomes a need," said Danny.

"That's called obsession."

"I love this house, Tom." Danny didn't want to say it, but he couldn't help it. "When you were little, you guys had each other all the time. But for me, with you guys away at school, I only really saw you here. This is our house, you know? I understood when Mom sold Archer Avenue. Dad gone, us away. But here? We're here."

He could feel the tears coming, blocking out the right words. He never liked to cry in front of Tom. Brothers were supposed to be all slaps on the back and what's the score and look at those tits. Or at least this was what Danny imagined brothers to be. He wasn't sure, since he hated organized sports of all types and had never once heard Tom use the word "tits."

In fact, Tom seemed to exist outside of sexuality. Unlike Gwen, who had no problem airing her lobsterman obsession in front of the entire family, often barking like a wild dog in the middle of the night. She'd feign modesty in the morning, saying that Kyle or Patch or whomever, just needed some encouragement. Gross, hilarious and gross. Even Libby with her maternal smell and quiet hands, had the hottest girlfriend Danny had ever seen. He knew that had to mean something. Libby was cute and smart, but he knew it took more than that to hook a girl like Patricia.

Poor Melissa, poor cute, nerdy Melissa, who was probably a heartbreaker in college. Before Tom. She still was, really. She kept everyone going with her questions and her earnest nods in response. She'd taught Danny how to make crystals from sugar when he was young. Tied his bow tie at Gwen's wedding. She whispered in his ear at their mother's funeral, words that stayed with him, words that settled his heart more than Gwen's "This sucks" or Libby's "You were her favorite, and you're our favorite."

"What an adventure she is on," Melissa had said. "She and your dad." He liked that. That the two of them were loaded down with gear, buckled and strapped and cramponned and goggled. No, that wasn't it. They were on the deck of a sloop in sun hats and boat shoes, loose billowing cotton shirts that the sun shone through. His mother at the tiller leaning out to starboard, watching the telltales. His father at a winch cranking in the spinnaker, with a good strong wind from the south.

He could be sailing too.

This was his moment to tell Tom: "Didn't make it to the end of the semester, old man. Could've used a term off. Get 'em next year."

"I'd like to stay here the rest of the summer," said Danny. "Maybe even into the fall. I need some time up here. I'm sure Libby will be here until at least mid-August."

"Well, when does your semester start?" said Tom. *Enrollment is often required to start a semester,* Danny thought, and he had not yet registered. He'd have to take quantum physics and golf. The reject classes.

"I'm not feeling so great about school these days."

"Not happy with how you finished the semester?"

"Yeah, not really. I kind of took some time off." Danny cringed there in the dark. There were some grumblings from the porch, a call to pause for bathroom breaks. Girls, always peeing.

"What do you mean, you took a break? When? Did you withdraw from your classes? Did you get your tuition back?"

Danny was on his knees facing the house. He felt as if he were in a church, the float and pier were the nave, and the porch its altar. For a moment he was praying.

"The add/drop period is only the first two weeks of the semester. And withdrawal is only another two weeks after that," said Danny. *Amen. Let it end there.*

"And when did you leave?" Tom sounded like a doctor taking vitals.

Danny could practically hear Tom counting days in his head, adding up costs of meals not eaten and books not read.

"In May, right before finals."

"Can't you just make up the exams, then? I'm sure there are contingencies." The relief in Tom's voice was the worst part. "I could call your professors." Tom put one knee on the ground and rested an elbow on the other, as if about to sketch an attack plan in the dirt.

"Well. I left in May, but my attendance record wasn't exactly stellar before that." Danny rolled a bottle rocket back and forth between his palms, feeling his calluses catch on the paper label.

"I don't understand? When did you stop attending class?" *How many clicks behind the enemy are we?*

"Sometime in March maybe."

"Have you talked to the bursar's office? Did you take a leave of absence? Did you tell anyone anything before you left?" *How's your ammo stock, C rations, radiation shots?*

Danny dug the tip of the bottle rocket into a callous on his hand. He just wanted to sail away.

"I just figured it was too late. Once they've got your money, they don't exactly like giving it back."

"Yes, Dan, that's called nonrefundable tuition. It is supposed to be an incentive to go to class." If the water had been warmer Danny would've happily slipped silently off the edge of the float and paddled out into the darkness.

He hadn't even attended enough classes to be considered a student in them. Danny did go a few times in the beginning of the semester. He had even taken notes. Notes on how his English professor was single-handedly reviving the suspender; on the correlation between girls' exposed underwear, tags lapping at the back of their jeans, and class participation. But he'd never established a clear pattern.

He had been that weird guy you'd see on the first day of class and never see again without knowing why. He would wash his hands for twenty minutes, picking each fingernail clean, before deciding that he was, in fact, too late to bother going to class.

His knees hurt from kneeling, but he didn't want to stand, he didn't want to appear at all confrontational. Dinner had drained him of all the fire he had. He had nothing left but wet coals smoking and hissing inside him. He wanted to set off the fireworks and run up the ramp, all the way to the porch and finish his gin and tonic next to his sisters.

"That's disappointing, Dan."

Tom stood up and walked to the edge of the float, looked out toward the town, toward the moored boats that would give feeble honks of their air horns, for the few fireworks set off. There was a darkness in his voice, just like their father. Rarely, only at times of true peril, had

Danny heard it. Like when, at age nine, he took out the Whaler alone. When, in their hundred-year-old wooden house, he left a candle burning in his bedroom.

"Gwen's right. We can't make any decisions about the house right now," Tom said. These disturbingly foreign words, "Gwen's right," made Danny nervous.

"Have you talked to the girls about this?"

"Not yet." Danny heard Tom make a surprised humph.

"But you should know that money, it has to go to school. It's earmarked. There isn't much left. Maybe enough for now, but a few tuition increases from now? I don't know. Think about that, Danny. Think about what it is that you truly need. What I think you need—"

Danny jabbed the bundle of rockets into the sand-filled can, lit them, and then grabbed Tom by the wrist, pushing his older brother up the ramp ahead of him. He couldn't listen to any more. They ran up the path, Tom now pushing Danny ahead of him, up the steps, and onto the porch.

"Jesus, Danny, that's how you blow off your hand or end up with a glass eye."

Melissa came through the screen door. Tom stopped talking. She turned and shouted back into the house, "Hurry it up, ladies. The Wonder Twins couldn't wait."

Their finale was already bursting over the float. The fireworks squealed. Someone had cleared away his gin and tonic.

"Dan," Tom said, "tomorrow we will make some phone calls." Danny thanked God for bad cell reception and rotary phones.

EIGHT

LIBBY

July 5

After she washed the lunch dishes, Libby went up to her porch and found Gwen topless, basking like a bird, arms out, on a white towel. The glare from the towel and the white railings imprinted on Libby's eyes, and with each blink, she saw the negative image of her sister's silhouette. A white bird in a black sky. Libby took off her shirt and sat leaning against the house in her bra and shorts.

"Where is Miss Patricia?" Gwen asked, not moving or opening her eyes. Gwen was one of the few people who always rolled the *r* and gave the *c* the sibilance that the Spanish pronunciation required.

"She's back in Boston," Libby said. Her legs were perpendicular to Gwen's; if Libby pointed her foot she could touch Gwen's calf.

"Bibs, she can be here when we're here. I love that lady."

"I know. I'm just . . . Anyway, she had things to do."

"You still think Tom doesn't approve?" Gwen rolled onto her side and propped her head up on one elbow. "I hate to break it to you, but we all saw this coming. If anything, he's just jealous that you can get a hotter chick than he can."

"She always jokes that, in Segovia, she's no one. But in Boston, she's a goddess." Patricia was all beauty and passion, not just for sex, but for everything. She was more like Gwen in that way, sumptuous and slow in her enjoyment of things: escargot, the swan boats, the curve of Libby's stomach. Next to her, Libby felt clumsy and awkward, all slapping feet and pathetic breasts.

"She should be up here for family time," said Gwen. "Next year, no excuses."

Libby kicked softly at her sister's leg as Gwen rolled over. Gwen shared a not-so-ample bosom with Libby, but on Gwen, Libby thought it looked svelte and trim and somehow more sexy. Maybe it was because Gwen never wore a bra—"What's the point?"—and wore those tissuey tanks with dangerously wide armholes. Though today her breasts had a plump quality, not bigger exactly, but somehow more ample. Libby in slinky tops felt exposed, simultaneously slutty and unfeminine. *Like a dyke.* She kept her hair long to offset that impression. Still, she wondered if there wasn't something in her skin that let everyone know, an undertone of cerulean or magenta.

Patricia was an administrator at the nursery school where Libby taught. At school Patricia was the only one in heels or tall boots and knit dresses or jeans tight enough to flood her heart with blood, like high-style compression hose. If Patricia was fire in the classic Spanish sense, Libby was water, boat, sea, breeze, house—in the WASP sense. Lesbian or not, Libby refused to even use the term. She didn't call Patricia her girlfriend, but Gwen did. She didn't call herself a lesbian, but Gwen did: "If you've only slept with women, you're a lesbian." There had been one man, though, a boyfriend of Gwen's, which Libby, of course, never mentioned to her sister.

"Patricia wants to move in together," said Libby as she picked up a pair of pine needles, joined at one end like delicate tweezers, and pulled them apart. She found the idea stifling. Her space, her home, her identity—all would become linked to someone else. Linked to someone so beautiful and loud people stared at her on the street, someone who inexplicably wore a bra to bed (actually there was a totally irrational explanation Libby preferred to ignore about a grandmother's old wives' tale and voluptuous Spanish flesh).

"Watch out, your excitement might be contagious," said Gwen. "She's smart and funny and she cooks. How bad could it be?"

"It's just the accent," Libby said. "She's really not that clever."

"Everyone is a sucker for an accent," said Gwen.

Libby managed to see both ends of the spectrum simultaneously. Patricia was sophisticated and totally exasperating, and Libby was at once mesmerized and annoyed by her.

Gwen rolled a pinecone toward Libby; the porch was scattered with them, like beer cans on a public beach. The pinecone wobbled in an arc and stopped a foot short of Libby's leg. They both closed their eyes and let the sun grow hot on their skin.

No, she wasn't ready. Maybe there were other women out there, other men. Not that she wanted anyone else; she simply wanted to be able to extract herself easily in case she did. But the idea of life without Patricia made her feel sick, congested, her ears blocked, her olfactory nerves deadened. Life without her would be a perpetual flu.

It was Libby who had stepped forward, put herself on what she imagined was a long government roster of women who fell in love with women. The list of women who fuck women was too long to maintain; women's colleges skewed the data. Three years before, at a play, Libby had held Patricia's hand. She was the one who reached out first. It was not like her. She was someone to wait, to let things develop, to give things space to breathe. On the day of her high school graduation, Libby's mother had told her that she stood back from life, that if she weren't careful it would go right by and she wouldn't even know what it tasted like, smelled like; it would just be a breeze and then gone. So

Libby had made moves before this, to be sure that life, one small corner of life at least, grazed her hand, her lips. Later, she realized her mother hadn't been telling her to find Life, but to find a certain acceptable lifestyle.

Libby chose to take the version of the advice she preferred. She hoped for experience, for vibrancy, but didn't believe it was a thing that could really happen. Or, rather, she knew that it could, just not to her. She could flip a switch in her living room, and the desk lamp would come on, but she couldn't explain how electricity worked beyond an explanation that would suit her three-year-old students: it is made in a station and travels down the wires to your house, but you don't want to waste it. *Don't waste it,* she had thought, with Patricia's hand in hers. *Don't let this current expire in an empty socket.*

Days before the hand-holding, she had felt a current, a small charge rush through her feet. While Patricia was at lunch, Libby crept into her office and, something that shamed her like masturbation or childhood shoplifting, she picked up the lavender sweater hanging over the back of Patricia's chair and pressed it to her face, inhaling deeply. It smelled like honey and musk. A charge swept through Libby and brought the arches of her feet up from the soles of her shoes.

So it was then, standing in the dark of the theater, after the curtain fell with the stuttering sound of applause all around them, when Libby had slid her hand into Patricia's. Months later, she asked Patricia why she hadn't been clapping. Why had they stood with the rest of the ovation, neither of them clapping, like the still spot of a stone beneath rippling water? The play was *Twelfth Night,* and some of its magic must have swept over the seats, over the little orchestra, and down the broad aisles to Libby's fingertips. She wrapped them first around the corner of Patricia's hand opposite the thumb and then slid them into the small bowl of her palm. Patricia's fingers closed over hers, then opened as she slid Libby's fingertips between her fingers, just there, pressing Libby's rings down.

"Is Patricia coming up in August, then, with the rest of your crew?" said Gwen.

Libby opened her eyes, but everything was white and blurred at its edges. She picked up a pinecone, bent her knees, and let the pinecone roll down her thighs into her lap.

Patricia was supposed to have come with her to Maine for this trip, but after Libby said she wasn't sure about moving in together, Patricia told her to go alone, to have a trial separation, to take her space and see how it felt.

It felt like home without her mother. Which she had expected to be liberating in some way, but it felt beautiful and sad and lonely. Libby shaded her eyes.

"Maybe. I don't know."

"Do you want her to come?" said Gwen.

"She asked me the same thing." Libby let the pinecone roll down her calves so it tumbled into Gwen's side.

The cedar shingles dug into Libby's back. She crossed her legs and leaned forward, resting just her fingertips on the hot roof. The grit of the asphalt roof, the sticky flecks of pine sap and eddies of sand, made her long for a beach chair. Something else to add to her list. On the main porch the Adirondack chairs her father had liked best were warped and cracked; those would need to be replaced too. Now, they were closer to driftwood than furniture. Libby leaned against the wall again, but the shingles felt sharp and seemed to move with her. She turned around, facing the wall cross-legged, and pulled at the shingle. It came off in her hands, like an artichoke leaf.

"Uh-oh."

"You broke it?" said Gwen.

Libby started to shove the shingle back in place, but the one above fell out too.

"Shoot!" Libby.

"Stop trying to fix it." The two of them moved to the far side of the porch as if being close to the wall would cause more fall apart. Gwen pulled her shirt on. Libby went to her closet and came back with a small ladder. She had recently installed smoke detectors throughout the house. Apparently, Scarlet had planned for them to all go up in flames. Libby opened the ladder on the porch next to the wall and climbed up to peek over the roof. Her breath sucked in sharp. The roof sloping down away from her toward the bay windows was pocked with missing shingles, leaving shiny black patches, like gaps for missing teeth.

"It's not just the walls," Libby said from the top of the ladder. She climbed down and Gwen climbed up.

"Oh, shit. I'm no roofer, but I'm pretty sure there aren't supposed to be holes," said Gwen. "Could we just stuff umbrellas through?"

"That might be more of an art installation than a repair. I'll call Remy and get him to come take a look. Maybe it can be patched."

"Lots of patches," said Gwen, coming down the ladder. "Now I want to do an installation of houses made out of umbrellas. You are totally a conceptual artist."

"That's what happens when you hang out with three-year-olds all day."

"I don't think Tom needs to hear about this." Gwen picked up the shingle from the floor of the porch and waved it at Libby.

"The shingle that broke the camel's back."

"I'm worried about him," whispered Gwen. "Last night was nuts." They both sat down on Gwen's towel.

"Be worried about us. He wants to sell this place out from under us," said Libby.

"It's not just last night. He's been off lately," said Gwen. Gwen leaned against the porch railing behind them; Libby tapped her shoulder and shook her head, no longer trusting that anything was as sturdy as she had thought. Gwen nodded and scooted forward so she could lie down instead.

"He keeps showing up at my place with Scarlet's urn," said Libby.

"That's just 'cause I won't let him leave it at my place; I don't care what her will says," said Gwen. There had been so much nodding, so much reassuring at the end, Libby hadn't realized what they'd agreed to.

"I didn't think we'd actually trade off. Who does that? But he wasn't going to take no for an answer," said Libby.

"Not from you, that's for sure," said Gwen. Libby thought they ought to be wearing suntan lotion. But she wasn't willing to go look for it.

"We could figure it out, right? We could retire poor old Remy, once he fixes the roof. That would save us tons. And we could do some repairs ourselves."

"Don't look at me. I make art. I don't do anything that involves power tools, or safety goggles." Gwen laid an arm over her face and peered out at Libby from the crook of her elbow. Libby imagined Gwen wearing a tool belt full of compact umbrellas, washi tape, X-ACTO blades, palette knives, tubes of matte medium, and vintage postcards.

"No, we'd make Dan do all the hard stuff. He's young. He can take it. I just don't want Tom to think he can make any executive decisions." Libby started absentmindedly cracking her knuckles.

"Don't get all worked up. Tom is just Tom. He's in his own world with Melissa and the kids. He's so bogged down by life, it's amazing he can even breathe. He needs this place just as much as we do, maybe more. He needs a place where he doesn't have to be perfect. I mean, besides his Chinese Gambling Parlor," said Gwen.

Libby laughed. She loved it when Gwen talked about Tom's fictional life of debauchery and deviancy.

"Or his Bunny Ranch."

"You really think it's all talk?" said Libby. "You don't think he's serious?" She started to line up pinecones next to her.

"How serious is a voice mail, really? He is exercising his man-of-the-house role. It's machismo in action. He doesn't realize it's the ladies who have always been in charge." Still lying down, Gwen passed her pinecones from the far side of the towel.

"For better or worse. At least as the new guard, we'll be more enlightened." Libby's pinecone lineup became a small pyramid.

Gwen reached out and squeezed Libby's foot. "Love is love, baby. Scoot."

Libby leaned to one side, and Gwen pulled out the towel and wrapped it around herself and stood up. "I'm ready for a swim."

Libby felt hot and nauseated. She blamed Tom, as if his wishes had somehow invited this threat into their lives. The simple existence of the offer was dangerous. It was an unlit match in a hayloft. The idea was sickening. She needed to purge it from herself.

"Maybe just a quick dip," said Libby. She would extinguish the match before it could even strike. She would drown the idea in the frigid sea.

NINE

TOM

July 5

In the gravel parking lot of Schooners they stood in front of the house car, a dusty jeep that lived at the house all year long, rusting quietly under the oak. Gwen sat in the car, facing out of the open passenger-side door, her feet hooked on the edge of the frame.

"This is why you can't rush me," she said.

"You are responsible for your own person," said Tom. He couldn't believe that she still pulled this kind of absurd behavior. After her practical comments about the costs involved in keeping the house, he hoped she was growing up, but turned out she was still a child who needed him to bail her out. Just like when she bounced a rent check, or three. Tom had two children, and they were more than enough (wonderful, actually, if only Gwen were more like them). He turned his back to the car and took a deep breath.

"I'm not a toddler." Gwen.

He turned back to her and gestured at her bare feet with both of his hands. "You forgot your shoes."

Gwen wiggled her toes.

"I'll go in," said Libby, "sit down, take off my shoes, and pass them off to Danny, who'll bring them out here to Gwen. Easy." She said this slow and saccharine. Gwen tried not to laugh. Libby shoved Danny toward the restaurant as he took a photo of Gwen's bare feet.

"I love this." He grinned.

Tom rolled his eyes and followed them into the restaurant while Melissa waited with Gwen. A harried waiter waved them at an empty table, and they sat down. Tom watched Libby slide her shoes out from under the table toward Danny.

"The swallow is in the nest," she whispered.

Danny winked, bent down, and hooked her Keds onto his fingers.

"I will take my leave of you, madam." Danny put the hand with the shoes behind his back and made a small flourish with his free hand.

"I'm going to the head." Tom got up, not wanting to hear another word. *Why do they make everything a game? Libby thinks of herself as the host here, but she's barely better than the other two. Well, at least she has a career.*

In the bathroom Tom splashed water on his face, trying to wash the heat out of his skin, out of his cells. In the mirror he looked puffy and mottled. *Maybe I should stop eating salt. Maybe I should move to Costa Rica and open a turtle farm. I can be the surly owner who sits under a palm tree and bottle-feeds baby turtles or gives them lettuce.* Tom didn't know much about turtles. He could remind tourists that there is no escaping reality, that sea turtles are going extinct even when you're on vacation. *Someone has to be practical. Someone has to save the turtles while everyone else is getting a tan.* This is, he was sure, what his siblings didn't understand. Life meant being practical, moving forward no matter what. It meant keeping your grades up, introducing your "friend" as your girlfriend, it meant wearing shoes to restaurants, it meant working until midnight if that was what it took to polish the social media platform presentation. Why didn't his boss, Linda, understand that? Apparently, staff can't "be pushed so hard." Why was he the only one who had to push himself?

"No one should be calling their assistant at three in the morning to go over account stats," Linda had said. "Take some time off and spend it with your family. It's important to be with them at times like this." This had been his boss's carefully worded kiss off. Tom understood. Linda didn't want him there. All his devotion to that company, and she decided how he should be mourning his mother. No thought to what the clients might need. What he might need.

He needed to get back to work. It had been a month, and he was spending his days in a Starbucks in Lexington where he could answer e-mails with no fear of running into anyone. Really, he just sat at his computer and thought about how he had failed his wife. Even if her failures were more obvious; it was his; it was him. He was trying his best to hate her, because his love felt far more toxic. And then he'd think of his mother. And then he'd be crying in the Starbucks bathroom crouched beside a stainless-steel toilet bowl. Work. That was his thing. But Linda refused to tell him how long this "break" would last. What kind of alimony could he pay with no job? What about health insurance? Melissa's part-time editorial work wasn't exactly going to pay the bills.

It had been six months, almost seven, since their mother had died. Tom tried not to keep track. He wished he could wear a black armband. It seemed far more civilized than the pathetic arrangement of carnations from his assistant, who was apparently a tattletale. Melissa had understood, at least. She hadn't asked him questions or given him sympathetic looks. She just kept the kitchen sink scrubbed clean the way he liked, had the kids do their homework in the dining room where he could watch their books get dog-eared and highlighted.

He came out of the bathroom and, without intending to exactly, slammed the door behind him. Half the restaurant turned in his direction. Eyes down, he headed back to the table. Gwen was there, and everyone already had a drink but him.

"I wasn't sure what you wanted." Melissa pointed at her wine. Tom shrugged, caught the eye of the waiter, and ordered a whiskey. Libby looked at Gwen for a beat. Normally, Tom didn't catch this, but today he saw their eyebrows go up, saw the corners of their mouths crinkle slightly, then nothing.

"Yes?" he asked them.

"It's awesome to see you cut loose a little," said Gwen.

"Well, we can't all be on perpetual spring break." He tilted his chair back on two legs and held on to the edge of the table with both hands.

"Maybe make it a double," said Danny quietly. Danny unrolled his silverware from his napkin and put the knife and fork on opposite sides of his plate.

"You know what, let's all have a whiskey," said Melissa. She patted the table with both hands as if she had struck upon the ultimate solution.

Libby started flipping through the wine list, a small, rigid binder. Schooners had been slowly moving up on the scale of sophistication. When five years ago they had started using tablecloths, Bob had walked into, then immediately out of, the restaurant.

He refused to enter until Danny popped his head out of the door and said, "Dad, they've got gelato now!" Bob had turned on his heel and headed into the restaurant. "Well, we can't let the children down."

Scarlet had turned to Tom and said, "Apparently we're having ice cream for dinner."

Libby passed the wine list to Tom.

"Let's just get a bottle," said Tom.

"Or two," said Melissa.

Tom could feel the whiskey traveling along his limbs, drawing everything closer to the floor. It was small, but all he needed. He left the wine drinking to the rest of them. The whiskey acted like a scrim. It gave just enough separation between him and them that he could stop worrying about their stupid choices. Instead, Tom watched Danny push his hair out of his face as he explained cannabinoids to Gwen. Gwen unabashedly ate the bread off of Danny's bread plate as he talked. Danny passed her more butter. Libby recounted to Melissa a face-off with one of her students: "He literally said, 'but it's my body, my body.' What do you say to that? You're right, your body is your own, be empowered, be protective, but also stop drawing all over it."

Tom held Melissa's hand under the table. He wanted to pull her onto his side of the scrim. He wanted to take her to Costa Rica with him. They could be co-owners; they could teach the turtles to catch grapes in their mouths. But that would mean telling her he didn't know when he would be allowed back to work. That would mean telling her what he's been afraid of for most of their marriage. It would mean acknowledging what she has told him. It would mean confessions and therapy and tears and there was no way. He just needed to get back to work. They just needed to separate.

The check lay on the table, and Tom picked it up instinctively. Sometimes he would experiment, giving his siblings a minute to swoop in. There was never any swooping. But then again, the minute he had started earning enough, he'd always picked up the check. He reached into his back pocket. His front pocket. He patted his chest pocket. The back pocket again. He excused himself and went out to the car. Tom emptied the glove box, the well in the driver's door, the pocket behind the seat. Nothing. He had forgotten his wallet. He could see it on his dresser, waiting for him to finish his bath, to comb his hair and run his belt through the loops. He kept checking, but he knew it wasn't there. *How could I have done that? How?* Tom went back into Schooners and sat down. He whispered to Melissa that his wallet was back at the house.

"Shit, I didn't bring mine." She cringed. Melissa turned to the others. "Who brought their wallet?"

They had the look of kindergarteners asked to read a clock, on the spot and clueless. Blink. Blink. Then they all began digging through pockets and bags. Then shaking their heads.

"Maybe we can come back tomorrow with the credit card, or call it in when we get home?" said Libby.

"I'm ready to wash dishes," said Danny, pushing up his sleeves.

"Dine and dash," said Gwen.

"They know where we live, Gwen." Tom. He knew she was kidding but just couldn't—

"I'm sorry to bother you." A man, not much older than Tom, was standing at the head of the table.

"I couldn't help overhearing, and I would love to treat you all to dinner." He had curly blond hair cut close and a square chin that brought to mind regattas and lacrosse, like maybe he had just come from an alumni event at Colgate. Tom looked at him, stared for a few moments. Then quickly shifted his gaze to the tablecloth. *No. No no no.*

"That is so thoughtful, but we couldn't," said Libby. "I'm sure they'll let us come back with it later."

"You're the Willoughbys, right? I insist. I knew your parents. Jeremy Aldridge." He held out his hand to Libby. She shook it and introduced each of them around the table. Tom didn't look up. *Why? Why is he here? Why is he talking to us?*

"Do you live on the island?" Gwen asked. Tom picked up the bill off the table and drew it into his lap.

"Every summer my entire life."

"Oh, so Ned is your dad? You've got that great place on the other side of Tiptoe Mountain," said Libby. Tom didn't want to know any of this. Not his name, not his house.

"Is Evan your brother?" Gwen asked. She shifted up in her seat.

"Cousin. Ned is my uncle." Jeremy Aldridge rested his fingertips on the edge of the table.

"So you're just a freeloader." Gwen.

"Exactly, which is why you should let *me* get you dinner." Here Jeremy Aldridge scanned the table. Tom held the check tight in his

hand, until his fingers ached. Wet footprints on the porch, in the dining room. *No.*

"No, thank you, we've got this." Tom looked only at the man's chin
as he said this. *I don't want to know the color of your eyes.* He pushed back
his chair with a screech. As he walked out the door, the check still in
his hand, he heard the man say to his siblings, "I'm sorry to hear about
your mom."

Out the door and over to the small bridge above the cove, Tom
leaned out, letting the wall dig into his stomach. *The last time I saw
that man was the last time I loved my parents.* He threw the check into
the water. He spat after it. He walked back to the jeep and got in. With
both hands on the steering wheel, his arms were straight as if he were
about to take a sharp curve. He turned on the AC until it was icy. It was
all he could do not to drive away, drive and drive and drive.

Melissa knocked on the glass. Tom unrolled his window.

"It's okay to forget your wallet."

"Let's go. Get in." He motioned to the front seat.

"Gwen already called shotgun."

"Of course." Tom rolled his eyes.

Melissa got into the back, squeezed in the middle between Libby
and Danny as they hopped in on either side. Gwen slid into the front
seat like an oily queen. Her feet were up on the dash before they even
pulled out of the parking lot. She was still wearing Libby's shoes.

"That was one smoking gentleman," said Gwen. "I don't know how
I missed that one."

"You dodged a bullet," said Tom. He pulled onto the main road. He
would've scuttled a hundred ships to keep that guy away from his sister.

"You didn't let him pay for dinner, did you?" said Tom.

Gwen put her hand to her chest. "What kind of WASP do you
take me for?"

With each passing car Tom lifted four fingers from the steering
wheel in an automatic island wave.

"They can't see you in the dark," said Gwen, her feet now pressed to the windshield.

"That doesn't mean I should be rude," said Tom. Really he couldn't stop if he wanted to. It usually took him an hour on Route 1 on his way home to stop waving to every passing car. It was a locational Pavlovian response. Car, wave, car, wave. Gwen unrolled her window and turned up the music.

Tom needed the windows up, the AC on. He wanted to feel the cold swirl around his feet. He wanted to retreat from his skin, deep into his body to get away from the cold. The island would recede, and he would be somewhere deeply internal, sterile, the inside of a conference room in a distant hotel, fluorescent lights and wall-to-wall carpeting.

All that flubbering wind drowned out their words. Tom put up all the windows.

"I've got the AC on," he said. He wanted their words. He wanted to push Jeremy Aldridge's face back under the surface.

His name is Jeremy. He's a good swimmer. No.

"Dan, have you talked to Gwen and Libby about last semester?" Let Danny fall on his sword. *I'm sorry, but please, Dan, just this once.*

"Did you know," said Danny, "that alligators can decide if their babies will be boys or girls? They look around at their alligator community and see what gender they need more of, and boom, they make more of that gender. Reptile genetic modification." Danny slapped the back of Gwen's headrest for emphasis. He was practically in Melissa's lap.

Tom wanted to apologize to him. *I know it's not fair to put you on the spot until we've made arrangements, decided how to proceed with school. But . . .*

"Clearly, they need to lobby Congress," said Gwen. She turned to face Danny. "Can't you see it, an alligator in a three-piece suit lumbering down the aisle to the Senate floor."

Suddenly they were deep in a world of genetically modified, super smart reptiles running for office.

Tom's knuckles hurt from gripping the steering wheel, and he flexed the fingers on one hand and then the next. Why had Melissa sent him up a day early? Or was she just putting off the inevitable? Or was she getting him out of their house? Was he going to lose both homes this year? He only wanted this one gone. This house had to be sold. Had to be. *Get the fuck out of my house, Jeremy.*

It was dark as they drove empty sections of North Haven Road, with the dotted yellow line and the dim arc of headlights ahead, then lost around a curve. Tom looked over at Gwen. She leaned her head against the glass and watched the sky as they drove. He hoped she would fall asleep; she always looked happy when she slept. Instead Gwen gave the constellations her own names: Perseus, King of the Druids; Androcles sitting in the mouth of his lion; Isis holding the severed head of a missionary. She begged Tom to turn off the headlights, just for a second.

"We can stop," was his completely reasonable, in fact, accommodating, solution. No, not good enough, never quite close enough to the edge for Gwen. Danny agreed with Gwen.

"Light speed in the darkness," said Danny in a guttural death-metal growl.

"Nocturnal birds in a dark forest," said Gwen, going Goth. She rambled, and it made Tom tired, made him acutely aware that he did the driving while she sat there with her feet on the dash, singing along to the radio. He reminded her that without headlights there would appear to be no road.

"Yes! Does the road exist if the lights are off? It's a philosophical exercise," said Gwen.

Yet again his sister, his thirty-six-year-old sister, was demonstrating the mental development of an adolescent. Even at twenty-one, even being of an entirely different generation than the two of them, Danny usually, this past semester notwithstanding, had more sense than she did. But still Tom tried. On the next straightaway he gave her five seconds of what Danny called "Total Blackout." But he saw a car stopped by the side of the road at the bottom of a rise, and as it pulled back onto the road, Tom flipped the headlights back on, and the expansive sky and boundless forest closed in on them again into a narrow tunnel of night driving, black and white.

And in that tunnel on the side of the road, they saw it.

The deer was huge and reclining, as if in some medieval tapestry, head held high, legs folded primly. But the backdrop was not a flat expanse of flowers curling in on themselves, just blackness. The deer was panting, mouth agape, tongue lolling pink. Red. It was in Technicolor. It stared straight at the aurora of their lights with the glossy green eyes of the night forest. There was a huge gash on its hindquarter that moved from its knee over its hip to its belly. Her belly. As full and taut as a horse's. The torn red flesh and white of sinews looked wet and utterly wrong.

Tom jerked the wheel slightly but recovered quickly when he realized the thing wasn't going to move.

"Poor thing," said Melissa.

He kept driving. His neck itched. His ears popped. He didn't think of the road or the car or the deer. He thought of the first time he saw Kerry asleep in her incubator, looking more like a wild thing than a baby, curled up under the nurse's hand. Her eyes fused shut, covered in down, sleeping in a box like a newborn puppy. He thought of Libby, who was the baby until Danny came along. Libby, years before, all feather-limbed and barely in double digits, sinking fast to the bottom of the cove. Things about to die.

"Gwen, call 911," he instructed.

"Stop the car, Tom," she said.

"There's nothing we can do."

"Stop the car."

Tom drove past the doe. A muffled noise came from the backseat.

"Stop the goddamn car, Tom." She said it quietly, sitting forward in her seat, no seat belt, facing him, one arm stretched along the dashboard, her hand close to the wheel.

"It would be dangerous and pointless for us to stop." He looked at her. Her eyes were like the deer's, not wild with fear but black and unyielding.

Danny pulled himself forward between the front seats. "I'm gonna throw up."

"Pull over," said Libby.

The brake lights lit the trees behind them as they came to the shoulder, then the reverse lights lit them low and white, like a dropped flashlight in the woods. Tom came within twenty feet of the thing. The doe struggled to stand. She tried to shift herself in their direction, to face her death, and in doing so, in one last expression of bravery, of instinct, save herself. Tom had felt this diving in after Libby, the moment the water hit his chest. The water, cold enough to make him gulp for air, was at most fifty degrees. That spring he had failed the YMCA lifesaving course when he almost drowned trying to tread water without using his hands. But he had thought, *I swim, she lives; I breathe, she lives; I live, she lives.* He told Melissa that story when he realized he wanted to be a father. When he realized he wanted to be brave. Sensible and brave. He and Libby had never talked about it. He wasn't sure she even remembered.

Gwen got out of the car, the hardscrabble of the shoulder crunching under her feet.

"We'll just wait for the police," Tom shouted after her. He needed to find his phone. He needed to catch his breath. His chest hurt. He felt cold and not the way he wanted to. Danny was already on his hands and knees heaving into a stand of ferns. Libby was rubbing Danny's back. Melissa sat in the open door looking after her. Tom, sitting in the driver's seat with his seat belt still on, heard Danny mumble something about lobster rolls. Gwen laughed.

The car doors were open, and the car's insistent dinging, requesting closed doors and seat belts fastened, drowned out most of Danny's words. But Tom could still hear his voice. Then Danny's tone changed. Something in it went quiet and into the back of his throat.

"Tom?" Libby called to him. Tom had visions of the deer hurtling toward his sister. He'd heard of animals' crazed instincts and power in their final moments. *What if she charges?*

The seat belt recoiled as Tom jumped out of the car. Gwen's purse lay on the ground. She leaned against the trunk of the car facing the doe. In her hand she held something thick and heavy.

"Jesus Christ, Gwen, a gun?" said Tom. "Where did you get a gun?"

Melissa jumped out of the car and stood behind Libby, peering over her shoulder.

"You're a vegetarian," said Danny.

"Our mother grew up on a farm," said Gwen.

"Not a munitions farm. Is it loaded?" Tom.

"She got it when the Boston Strangler was loose, used to sleep with it under her pillow," said Libby to Melissa. "I thought she got rid of it."

"Can I shoot it?" asked Danny.

Gwen ignored them all. "I'm going to shoot it."

Melissa whispered to Libby, "How do you forget your shoes but remember your gun?" Libby put her finger on her nose.

"Jesus Christ, I've been driving with a loaded gun in the car? How many laws does that break?"

"What about the right to bear arms?" said Danny, looking at Tom. "I thought you were into that."

"I'm not a Libertarian." Always ribbing him for voting Republican. Lincoln was a Republican.

"Holy God, both of you shut up," shouted Gwen, looking over her shoulder. "We are going to do what needs to be done here."

She walked forward in the glow of the reverse lights and stood between the car and the panting, bloodied deer. They could see its mangled hindquarter clearly now. Its clumped fur. The deer's eyes glowed a quick iridescent flash in her shadow. From fifteen feet away, Tom could hear Gwen whisper something to the doe. "I'm sorry."

Gwen lifted the gun and held it steady with both hands. Her feet were together, and she looked as if she were about to say a prayer, or take a bow. And then flash flash, crack crack. The animal slumped over.

Shaking, Gwen got back into the car, leaving her purse in the dust of the roadside. She found Tom's phone and was talking. Melissa and Libby got back in the car and seemed to be comforting Gwen, rubbing her shoulders as she spoke into the phone. *They are all insane,* thought Tom. Danny and Tom looked at each other over the roof of the car, listening to Gwen. "North Haven Road just before Murch's Brook, not in the road, off the road, on the shoulder . . ."

"She's probably the leader of some underground sect, a militia of underappreciated artists," said Danny. "I should've seen this coming." He started to laugh, but it devolved into a grumble. Danny got back in the car, a hand on his stomach.

Tom, walking to scoop up Gwen's empty purse, thought that the stand of ferns looked particularly appealing. He wouldn't mind purging himself into that green fringe. But instead he had to swallow it down.

TEN

ANOTHER SUMMER

Gwen is eleven years old. She stands on the covered portion of the front porch. A cut on her bare leg births a thick drop of red. She is in the shadow, watching Libby play with dolls in her tin dollhouse. The blood begins to make its way down her leg, slow and steady. Gwen stands there while her parents are on the other side of the screen door.

"I can't keep her tied to the house like a dog," says their mother.

"You could try watching her, telling her what she can and can't do," says their father.

"She's your daughter too."

Back and forth they go, while Gwen stands there and the blood slides into her shoe, wet sneakers, no socks. Where had she left her socks? Her pointed anklebone sends the rivulet around and down. Drops from the sea still cling to her ankle. Her clothes are wet, her hair matted in thick strings that send salt water down her back, slow through her cotton shirt. The blood is dark on her leg; the cut is starting to sting. It hadn't hurt, but now the wind brings it sharp to her attention.

"Did you know what she was doing?" her father asks.

"The locals jump the tower all the time," says her mother. "I didn't know that *she* did it."

Libby keeps playing. Maybe she can't hear them, maybe because it is not about her it doesn't matter. Gwen wants to play with her, but she is afraid to move. Sitting would make the cushions wet, playing would make her seem unapologetic, though she isn't sure exactly what she has done wrong. She assumed they already knew. She has been jumping from the ferry tower for two summers now. Some kids jump a beat or two after the ferry leaves the dock, when the water is still roiling, still oily and flat in spots, and frothy and churning in others. It only pushes you under the dock for a second, then sucks you back out again. At first she had done it only when the ferry was gone and the water quiet. But she watched the older boys, locals only, do it as the ferry left. She has been working up to it all summer, and today was her victory.

She climbed the green metal ladder as the automatic grated ramp went up. As the ferrymen slipped wedges under car wheels, she shuffled out onto the catwalk, and as departing families stopped waving good-bye to their friends, their summer island, she jumped. She was stirred in the pot of black soup, she thought, brought up and pushed down, a bobbing carrot nub. She swam against the current as she'd seen those boys do, and then rode it in swirls, a moment under the dock, sharp rock against her thigh, just above her knee. She emerged, climbing up the ladder that curved to an end on the thick wood ties of the dock, those blocks of wood that weep black oil in the heat. She emerged dripping in her bathing suit and shorts. She wore the shorts on purpose, not wanting to look too much like a girl, too slim and frail up on top of the tower, like a diver or a weathervane. She emerged, and they cheered for her, the first summer girl to have done it.

"I can't follow her, drive five miles an hour behind her bike," says her mother.

"You can lock up the bike," says her father, "you can take her with you, you can be sure she's hanging out with kids who won't force her to risk her life."

She doesn't want to touch it, but the cut wants to be touched, washed, dabbed with alcohol, flooded with peroxide, smeared with Bactine and covered with a Band-Aid, a big one that looks like a small bumper sticker. She's earned a big one. Her feet are starting to feel sticky, not slick, in her wet shoes. She takes four steps, slowly, backward toward the stairs, and goes to sit on the top step.

"Please stay on the porch," her father calls through the door. She is bent, about to sit, and his words make her freeze, assess how "on the porch" this second-to-top step is. She sits. Here the sun comes in under the overhang. Here the gray wood is hot, even through her wet shorts; it warms her.

Back and forth they go.

Libby comes over and sits beside her, looks up at her big sister.

"You're bleeding." She is the first to notice. "I'll get you a Band-Aid." From inside, there is a smash, a shattering. They both move down a step.

"Well, if you weren't on that damn boat all the time."

"I need to get away from you, from this."

The girls move down another step. It is their mother who is breaking things. She goes for their wedding china first. Gwen figured it out earlier this summer, watching her mother furiously hunting through the china closet for the right dish to throw. But even this is better than what comes.

They cry. Her parents, the adults, cry. Together, holding each other. They sit on the floor, on the landing of the main stairs, on the edge of a guest bed, on the rail of a porch, and cry together. "It shouldn't be this hard," they say.

And then they drift away, and it is quiet again for months. He drifts to his boat and she, to her books, and they are apart. And the three of them, Tom, Gwen, Libby, leap off ferry towers, and jump from higher and higher ledges at the quarry, and fling themselves from the dock. Trying to fly away, up high enough to become birds, to swim away deep enough to become fish. But Libby, in her life jacket, Libby standing at the top of the swim ladder too afraid to jump, she keeps them there. She is too small to make the change, and they are too big to leave her behind. Tom is off on his bike now, riding over the low hills and through sharp turns. Soon, he will journey on boats, not bikes. Soon, he will have his way out.

The girls move another step down until their feet touch grass and rock. Gwen whispers in Libby's ear, and on the count of three, they run for it. Down, down the path, down the pier and the ramp, down to their own float. Libby trails her life jacket behind, always waiting for her at the bottom of the steps. She is golden, with a great orange streamer against the green trees. Once on the hot planks, Gwen buckles Libby in, and they jump. *I will wash this cut in the sea, give the blood back to the hungry ocean that tried to take it from me.* They splash and laugh. They hear the screen door slam. They are in for it now.

Their mother comes and stands at the edge of the pier under the limp flag. She stands with arms crossed and watches them swim, determined not to let them drown, not to let her husband accuse her of being a bad mother. She doesn't have the energy to haul them out of the sea, to spank them, at least Gwen, as she deserves. She doesn't want to talk to them, or him, or think about all her failings, as they have been so conveniently listed for her in the last half an hour. She watches her children swim. Though they have paused and hang with little fingertips from the edge of the float, peeking up at her. She gives them a wave, tells Gwen that they will talk about it later, which means not at all. And they both know that. So they splash and squeal and scamper in and out, up the ladder and down again, up and lofted over the edge of the float.

"Mom, watch this, are you watching, Mom? Watch, look, look, look at this, wanna see something? Mom." Gwen does a cartwheel off the end, while Libby watches, all adoration. Libby then hangs off the ladder, one hand and one foot loose, and then drops herself in. Gwen cheers wildly for her sister. "Again, again," she says. But before Libby has a chance, Gwen is back up, taking up their mother's attention, a handstand at the edge and a backspring into the water. Their mother sees a cut on Gwen's leg she hasn't noticed before. The next time she surfaces, her mother asks, "Is that a cut on your leg?" Gwen looks at it as if she has never seen it before.

"I guess," she answers.

Their mother calls them both out; it is time to start dinner. Their little lips are blue. Many calls and much counting later, the three of them come up the steps, and in the sun there, her mother looks carefully at Gwen's cut, crouches down, puts her hands on either side of her leg, gently pushes at the skin around the cut.

"This is deeper than I thought," she says, "Inside."

They leave Libby at the tin house once more. She cannot leave the porch alone, and her mother knows that is a rule she, unlike her sister, will not break. Their father has disappeared. Probably on the south porch hiding. Libby will find him; their mother smirks, happy that his peace will be interrupted. She takes her daughter, her misbehaving daughter, into the bathroom and sits her on the closed lid of the toilet. Peroxide fizzes in her cut. She squirms, her eyes water. Then her mother dabs it with a dry washcloth, smooths Bactine over it, and seals it all with a Band-Aid. As she's smoothing the edges of the bandage, Gwen puts her arms around her mother's neck and rests a cheek against her forehead.

"Thank you, Mama," she says. And her mother thinks, *This child is still mine.*

ELEVEN

GWEN

July 6

The setting sun shone over the thoroughfare, lighting the sails of the ships coming home for the night; it streamed in the kitchen window. Though the view was good, Gwen hated to cook dinner, to be sequestered in the kitchen, to miss even one night of leisurely cocktails on the porch. But Libby's laminated cooking schedule could not be ignored. It was their turn. Gwen wondered how their mother managed cooking every night, every summer of their childhood. The light shone in Gwen's eyes and made it hard to see things on the west wall of the kitchen, the bucket in the soapstone sink, the flame under the steamer pot she had just set to boil. The sun brought the temperature up in the room, as if they were roasting chicken for dinner, not simply steaming mussels.

"Just sit there," said Gwen. "Your job is to keep us company."

"I could at least set the table," said Melissa.

"It's not your night," said Libby. "You should relax. Danny can do it; it's his job anyway."

"He might like an excuse to get away from Tom. When I left them on the porch, they were both staring at a schooner, not talking. Not even making fun of the tourists."

"See, you're much better off here with us," said Gwen. She was wondering about Danny. He seemed to be skating around the edges of the house. She thought of him forever camped in the rug room on the wicker chaise rotating between books and cards. But this trip she kept seeing him disappear up the road, or into the woods, not all the time but enough. She wondered if he was getting stoned and didn't want to tempt her in her condition. Or maybe he was doing something worse, though she couldn't imagine what that might be. If he was shooting up, he'd never leave the house; if he was doing coke, he'd never have left the city in the first place. Maybe there was a girl, someone pulled to the edge of the paved road waiting for him to emerge from their dirt track. Whatever it was, he couldn't keep a secret from her very long.

The mussels were in a bucket in the soapstone sink. Gwen put the bucket at the center of the kitchen table, and Libby set two bowls beside it.

"So what is the order of operations here?" asked Melissa.

"How have you never done this before?" asked Gwen.

"I don't do fish. I'm afraid of poisoning everyone."

"I've already washed them," said Libby. "Now we just need to weed out any bad ones and pull the beards."

Mussels had been their mother's specialty, and she had passed it on to them, the girls, teaching them to scrub and pull and tap. Then she would turn them loose to carry a beer to their father, to pass the cheese plate to guests on the porch. She would finish cooking alone in the kitchen, the windows wet with steam.

"Sounds like we're testing fake Santas or something," said Melissa. Gwen had already worked her way through six mussels. She enjoyed mindless tasks like this. She excelled at stuffing envelopes and filing. It was a moving meditation, like grocery shopping or folding laundry.

Simple tasks gave her all the satisfaction of doing something with her hands, accomplishing a goal, but with none of the pressure of actually creating something. She found such things to be the perfect break from drawing, deliciously mindless. When things got tight, when she hadn't been assigned any classes at the adult ed center for the fall semester, hadn't sold any work last summer, she'd taken a temp job. By the time she couldn't take another day of fluorescent lights, they'd offered her a full-time position. She had tried not to laugh. Then, on her last day, she filed drawings of naked women standing on desks, scaling filing cabinets, basking in the glow of a flaming photocopier.

"Like so." Gwen took a mussel from the bucket, gave it a sharp tap with her finger, like she was playing a particularly sticky piano key, yanked off the stringy bit of fur that hung from the flattened edge of the shell, and then tossed the mussel into one of the bowls.

"Then what's this for?" Melissa pointed to the empty bowl.

"The rejects, the ones that don't close up tight when you tap them," said Libby.

As they tossed the mussels on top of one another, the shellfish ticked together like walnuts. What looked like stone sounded wooden and brittle. She wished she could pause this cooking party and take out her watercolors and paint the bucket and bowls, the menacing blue-black of the mussels, their grained shells pocked with the occasional barnacle.

"They're so prehistoric," said Libby.

"More mystical, like black magic," said Gwen. The place where voodoo and Norse myths might collide, the ridged fingernails of a sea witch.

When the bucket was empty Gwen and Libby stood, each with a bowl in her hands.

"I'll get the boys to dump these," said Libby, heading out the door. Gwen took her bowl to the stove and checked the water.

"Almost there," she said. A watched pot. She put her hand to her belly. Then shook her hand like she wanted to wake up her fingers, realizing that they were dreaming. They were betraying her, resting there like that, searching for some seismic sign.

"Have you talked to the kids?" she asked Melissa. "The house still standing?"

"They haven't managed to tie up their grandmother and make a break for the border yet. They're too lazy to do anything really terrible."

"I wish they were here," said Gwen. "But it must be kinda great to take a break from Mommy duty."

"Yeah, but life is so much easier now. It's when they're little that you really need the breaks. Now they spend half their time in their rooms with headphones on. I tried to convince them that they could do that here, but they couldn't bear the idea of spotty cell reception."

"I don't know how you did it, two kids, two years apart. How did you have a life?" said Gwen.

Libby came back in and followed Gwen to the fridge. Gwen passed butter, lemons, and berries to Libby. Melissa sat at the table, slowly spinning a glass of wine from its base.

"I didn't, really. Your old life sort of disappears, and you create a whole new one that has some of the old stuff and a lot of new stuff. It's very phoenix-from-the-ashes," said Melissa.

So it burns, and you are a magical bird singed and caged.

"You handled it well," said Gwen, "Trapped in the house all the time. Parenthood seems more like being an ex-con, only you have to nurse your parole officer." She had dated the dealer who lived across the street from her, and she referred to him as The Felon, though he had never been convicted of anything. Their relationship consisted of smoking spliffs on his front steps and making out. Eventually things regressed into more of a straightforward business arrangement. Spliffs, yes, kisses, no. That was as close to a life of crime as Gwen had ever come.

"Guess that makes me a corrections officer," said Libby. "Maybe I should get my kids little striped suits for the dress-up box. Men seem to think relationships are so much work, when really it's the baby that's the real ball and chain, not the wife."

"See, Bibs, a wife wouldn't be so bad," said Gwen.

"We're talking about babies," said Libby, "not wives. I've got fifteen kids every year. I don't need a wife too." Libby distributed each item around the kitchen, the berries to the sink, the lemons on the table, the butter beside the stove.

"Maybe just a wedding, then, for the presents and the dancing and the champagne," said Gwen. She stacked sticks of butter into a mini pyramid.

"I doubt her parents would want to foot the bill for a wedding when I won't even let her move in." Libby rinsed the berries in the soapstone sink.

"Who says she gets to be the bride?" said Gwen.

"Why won't you let her move in?" said Melissa, tilting her head a bit to one side.

"I look crappy in white."

"Does Patricia want kids?" said Melissa. Her glass had grown frosted from the chill of the wine.

"She wants cats."

"Well, you definitely can't let her move in, then," said Gwen as she went to get the butter dishes from the china closet. "Just make her live in her car, in your driveway, with the cats."

"Gwen, are kids on your agenda?" said Melissa. Libby snorted.

Gwen was happy to be standing in the china closet, to have her back to the door so Melissa couldn't see her face. She didn't keep her own secrets because she was a terrible liar. She had embraced that quality by being brutally honest; *if the truth is all over your face, why not say it.*

"It's just not my idea of a good time," she called over her shoulder, trying to sound distracted and nonchalant. "Maybe all those years of babysitting poisoned me against the idea. It seems like a two-man job." *It's hard enough when you get paid to do it. What happens when it costs you?*

At seventeen she had spent two weeks in Hawaii with their neighbors, the Sheldons, and their three kids. For weeks leading up to the trip, she'd had stress dreams. A school of sharks would be waiting under the crest of a coming wave as the three Sheldon children frolicked in its shadow. She liked the kids, but with each wipe of a wet cloth digging between tight fingers, with every curled ear she massaged with suntan lotion, she had thought, *motherhood is horrible.* At night, she would find the waiter who had served her deflowered drinks at dinner. In his room between the ice machine and the transformer she would collapse on his single bed and ask how we had all managed to survive past infancy. He massaged her pruned hands that had held the youngest Sheldon afloat for most of the day.

"In Hawaii children are raised by the sea," he had told her. She wondered if that wasn't true of herself and Tom and Libby. Danny had had parents, had her. Gwen thought of her father holding Danny as they rode the ferry, her mother pointing out porpoises.

She rummaged through the closet, rattling stacks of plates, even though the butter dishes were right in front of her, hoping the subject would change. Then Gwen went to the stove, unwrapped the frozen sticks of butter, and let them thud into a saucepan, then she slid the cleaned mussels into the steamer pot.

"The best kids are other people's kids," said Libby. "The ones you can just give back at the end of the day."

"Is that true of other people's boyfriends, too?" whispered Gwen with a smirk. She'd almost said "other people's wives" but stopped herself. She could tease Libby about Tim but never about Riley. Even so, Libby looked shocked.

"Tim Sherman was real cute," said Gwen.

The three of them hung out for a few weeks one summer, going sailing on the Charles, drinking forties on their back porch. After a party one night she had stayed behind to hold the hair of the hostess and asked Tim to drive Libby home. Gwen knew exactly what would happen; she figured she didn't like Tim enough and maybe Libby did. In fact, Libby had never liked a guy before or since. Tim had broken up with Gwen the next day. Neither of them had said anything, but Gwen knew. He was a good kid, a safe guy for her sister's first hetero time.

At this point, Libby, red from the collarbone to the hairline, was intently rinsing berries, again. It had never occurred to Gwen that Libby might have thought she didn't know. Hadn't they joked about this before? Libby left the berries dripping in a colander in the dish drainer.

"And he was the love of my life." Gwen sighed, fluttering her eyelashes. Libby twisted up a dishtowel and snapped it in Gwen's direction. Gwen moved next to her for a moment and kicked her foot up and smacked Libby's butt and then went back to the stove.

"Anyway, I agree with Libby. Other people's kids are the best. I'm madly in love with Kerry and Buster," said Gwen. She filled the butter dishes with hot water from the electric kettle to warm them. No one wanted congealed melted butter.

"Really? I hate other people's kids," said Melissa. "My kids *are* amazing."

"Bibs, I forgot to add—"

With a wet hand Libby passed Gwen the white wine from the counter, the redness now receding down her neck, just a speckling, like she had hastily applied sunscreen. Gwen splashed wine into the pot, then pointed the neck of the bottle at the lemons scattered by the edge of the sink.

"Since Tom is anti-lemon, I'm going to leave it out," said Gwen.

"We can just give everyone their own wedge. Melissa?" said Libby, pointing to the lemons on the table. Melissa stood up, eager for a job. She went to the counter, stared at the magnetic knife strip for a bit.

"Check the block to the left," said Gwen from the stove. Libby pulled a cutting board from the shelf and put it on the table.

"Just berries for dessert?" said Libby.

"Naked berries? Please." Gwen went to the pantry and produced cream from the fridge, a stainless-steel bowl from the freezer.

"So smart," said Libby. They had made strawberry shortcake last summer and ended up with soupy butter instead of whipped cream because the heat in the kitchen kept the cream too warm, too watery to whip.

When she was a kid, Gwen's parents were the storm. But then with Danny they didn't lose each other; there were no houses or boats or china whirling perpetually around them. After Danny was born, she remembered them, her parents, curled together in the rug room on the chaise. They had always liked to sleep when it rained. To nap together. Like cats. They became something impossible—parents who couldn't get enough of each other. Then again, hadn't it always been that way? Before, they couldn't get enough of each other's tears, and then, they couldn't get enough of each other's space and time. They hung on each other, like middle school couples on the school bus, with a desperation, as if at any moment someone would tell them they needed to stand three feet apart, tell them to fornicate on their own time, call them into their office to explain how they were making people uncomfortable with their affection. All of which had happened to Gwen during seventh grade.

"The hardest part of the kid thing," said Melissa, "is losing the life you had with your partner. You can get back a lot of what you had by yourself. Well, after the first year. The first year is a fucking tornado."

"Particularly with Kerry. Jesus, that shit was ridiculous," said Gwen.

Melissa had practically lived in the NICU, Kerry asleep on her chest, the size of a twelve-week-old kitten. She and Libby had alternated days taking care of Buster, picking him up at day care. On weekends Gwen went to the hospital and held Kerry, gathered her tiny, splayed legs and arms to her body and cupped her head as she lay in her incubator. Gwen would go home, but she wouldn't even make it inside. She'd sit on her front stoop with her sagging purse on her knees and smoke cigarettes.

"But at least I got to recover, got to sleep at night. That was the upside. Skipping the last trimester definitely made recovery easier too. But leaving her there every day, not knowing. That was hell."

"I don't know how you made it through," said Libby.

"Tom got through it," said Melissa. "I just followed him. One day I refused to go to the hospital, knowing that every day there was only a fifty-fifty chance she would make it. I felt paralyzed. And Tom put me in the car and drove me to the hospital. At a stoplight he said, 'If she goes today, at least we got to meet her, to have her for a few weeks. Even one day is worth it.' He was the strong one." Melissa arranged the lemon slices on a plate. "Strange to think that was twelve years ago. We talk about it sometimes. He doesn't even remember that day. He remembers the bills."

"I remember holding Kerry when she was just home from the hospital, and you had gone somewhere. I spent the whole time watching her breathe; I was terrified," said Gwen.

"She did have a tendency to turn blue. You'd have to give her a little shake."

"God, no wonder you guys never had a third," said Libby. She poured more wine into Melissa's glass and then her own. Libby held the bottle toward Gwen, but she waved it away.

"Maybe with dinner," Gwen said. Libby looked at the wine bottle for a moment and then put it on the table.

"The more kids, the more you end up losing track of each other. I didn't want to compound the problem," said Melissa. Gwen and Libby exchanged a look. Melissa often complained about Tom. He kept his briefcase under their bed. In the middle of the night Melissa would hear the thunk of the latches opening as he searched out his blackberry. He insisted that their children's friends call him Mr. Willoughby. Usually, though, she told these stories while sitting next to him, rubbing his back. This was new.

"Your parents somehow managed with four," said Melissa. "I have no idea how they did it."

Maybe their parents were an aberration, their love and their success as parents with Danny. Maybe the real truth was children ruin things. Maybe it was the three of them that made their parents that way. But then what was Danny? How could three destroy something that a fourth could save?

"Well, they did it in shifts," said Libby. "It's not like they had all four of us in the house at once. Besides vacations, Tom and Danny have never lived in the same house at the same time." *Maybe that's the trick, not too many. Maybe it's all mathematical,* Gwen thought, *maybe prime numbers are the key to success.* Families of three or one. But not two, not her alone with a baby; she didn't want to burn the kid's dinner while she dreamed about glory days smoking spliffs.

"Too bad, both those boys could've used it," said Melissa.

The boiling water rattled the lid on the steamer; Gwen turned the heat down a touch, looked at the clock.

"They would've killed each other," said Gwen.

"You're the only person Tom can stand to live with," said Libby. "I couldn't live with anyone, except for maybe Gwen."

Gwen ran the eggbeater, and Libby sat at the table with Melissa. When the noise stopped, Melissa said, "Tom's definitely better than some of the roommates I've had; at least I don't have to put my name on my food. And I'm certainly not his idea of the perfect roommate. I stay up too late. I load the dishwasher wrong. I have to sleep with the room pitch black, and when he gets up to pee he trips over the laundry basket because he can't see. He says I'm a safety hazard. Half the time, he sleeps in the guest room because he's afraid he'll break his neck."

"Get him a flashlight and tell him to shut the hell up," said Gwen. Living with her ex-husband, Reed, Gwen had felt like she woke up in a mausoleum. Was this where Melissa was, entombed within the blue walls of their house? Was she living on wine offerings and dead leaves? *Tom must know better,* Gwen thought, *than to leave his wife alone in an empty bed.*

The unplugged beater in her hand like a gun, Gwen walked through the china closet to the dining room and called toward the open porch door for Danny.

"Dan, table, please."

She was tempted to confront Tom right here and now: "You aren't fucking this up, are you?"

Through the window she could see her brothers sitting on the porch each reading a book, two sweating cocktails on the table between them. She imagined them as old men living together in some dust-filled apartment. Maybe they wouldn't be so bad together. They seemed to know how to coexist. But she and Libby and Danny had great plans to retire to Florida and glue tiny shells on lamps that they'd sell on the curb. She waited as Danny slowly turned down the corner of a page, read a last sentence, and put the book down, before going back into the kitchen.

Melissa was slicing strawberries; Libby was peering into the steamer.

"I think these puppies are done," Libby said.

Then Melissa gasped, throwing the knife onto the table like it burned her. She gripped her left hand to her chest.

"You okay?" Libby and Gwen said together, moving close to her.

"I can't—" Melissa shook her head. "Just leave me alone a second." They stepped back, and the tears came down Melissa's face and blood came from between her fingers, smearing on her shirt. Air hissed through her teeth as she stood there frozen. Gwen hurried down the back hall and returned with a dusty first-aid kit from the seventies. She opened it, and the plastic hinge broke off. Libby grabbed a roll of paper towels and pulled off a few sheets as Gwen began to unpack the kit onto the table.

"Let's just see how bad," said Libby, easing Melissa's hands away from her chest. Libby covered the bleeding hand with the towels, and Melissa sat down. Libby held Melissa's hand to her own chest so that Melissa looked as if she were raising her hand to ask a question. *Libby is the one who should have a baby,* thought Gwen. *She has the partner; they have a family to expand.* Libby hadn't been very maternal as a child; she carried her first doll around by the hair. But now Libby was the one who tied shoes and changed diapers and understood the difference between Dora and Diego. *Libby is already more of a mother than I am,* thought Gwen, *no matter what she's avoiding.* Gwen already had her foray into motherhood, giving Danny bottles and baths and suctioning snot out of his nose. How many times in life did you need to do those things? Libby looked at Gwen, eyes wide, prompting.

"Melissa, don't you wish Libby had brought Patricia?"

Libby rolled her eyes, and Gwen shrugged. If Libby wanted distracting conversation, she couldn't get choosy.

"I love Patricia," said Melissa, looking everywhere but at her hand. "I really do. She's the prettiest woman I have ever seen in real life. You should marry her, Bibs. She obviously makes you happy. Marriage isn't for everyone; it's risky, but she brings out the best in you. How many couples can say that?" Melissa looked out the window at the oak tree.

"Maybe I'm just not sure this is my best," said Libby. She snuck a look at the cut, tilted her head from side to side, an it-could-be-worse tilt.

Holding gauze and tape, Gwen moved to stand next to Libby. She mouthed the word "stitches." Libby shook her head. Libby rested her head on Gwen's shoulder for a moment, and Gwen squeezed with her free arm.

Once Melissa's finger was bandaged and she had been plied with Tylenol and whiskey, Libby doled out the mussels into shallow bowls. Gwen took a baguette from the bread box, a little stale but perfect for soaking up the juice. The cooked mussels sat on the kitchen table, their sharp little beaks open, exhaling steam.

At dinner Tom scootched his chair next to Melissa's. He opened each shell for her, speared each mussel on a small fork, and handed it to her. She held her bandaged hand on top of her head, like she was keeping a hat from blowing away. *Maybe I'm wrong; maybe things aren't that bad between them.*

TWELVE

DANNY

July 7

Danny played Ping-Pong with Gwen in the great room, while Tom stood beneath the balcony on the east wall staring up at the discolored beams. Libby had gone for a walk up the road, to "touch pavement." Meaning she would go all the way to the paved town road, one mile each way. The rest of them had opted to stay home. Still too early in their trip for earnest exercise, Danny had explained. At least that was what he had meant by, "Hell, no." Once Libby passed the bend in the road, Danny felt as if they were teenagers left home alone, or when someone leaves you alone in their dorm room. Gwen immediately wanted to play the most cutthroat game of Ping-Pong possible. Tom began inspecting the house. Danny wondered how long Tom would wait to announce to their sisters that he was an academic failure. What was he waiting for? Maybe Tom thought it could all be fixed, that the girls shouldn't have to worry about Danny's fuckup. He couldn't bear them worrying about him anymore anyway. At least Gwen was easy to distract.

Danny sent shot after shot sailing over the table into a new corner or cobweb. The ball skittered under masts that were pushed against the long, low step of the stage. It wasn't actually a stage, but an alcove with diamond-paned windows just under their parents' room. Its raised stone floor and lower ceiling set it off from the rest of the great room. The whole space was like the bow cabin in a cruising boat. The cabin that his sisters always shared, while Danny had to sleep in a berth across from the galley, smelling the kerosene and cod all night long. Danny always thought this alcove cast the rest of the house as a great schooner. Each summer they embarked on an epic voyage, a transatlantic crossing, rounding the Golden Horn, skirting the Falklands, the Maldives, the Faroes. When they sat on the porch, he saw them all sitting on the deck of a steamer, or a jammer, depending on the weather.

His next shot sailed over Gwen's shoulder and bounced up the wood step to the stones of the stage. Gwen bounded after it, and caught the ball in midbounce. She didn't even ask if Danny was ready; in one fluid motion she stepped up to the table and took her serve. He tried to chop the ball, as if instead of a paddle, he wielded a hatchet.

"Dan, quit trying so hard," said Gwen as she picked up another rogue shot from underneath the child-size pool table. "You're wearing me out."

"I'm trying to master backspin. You've got to give it some snap, you know?" Danny flicked his paddle forward.

"It might be a more effective strategy for you, if you ever actually hit my side of the table."

She sent a fast and low serve over the net that just nicked the table, before sailing behind him into the dining room. "Like that," she said.

Danny had learned Ping-Pong from Gwen, but she had conveniently left out the secret to backspin, which she used against him mercilessly.

"You're a shark," Danny said, retrieving the ball for the hundredth time from underneath the dining room table.

"I sleep too much to be a shark. And I believe that was the game point. Tom, you wanna take over?" Gwen held her paddle out toward her older brother.

His back was to her as he looked up to the ceiling. Danny didn't want to play Tom. He'd rather bounce the ball on his paddle. He knew that was unfair. Tom just approached everything like an assignment, like there was a secret instruction booklet that only he had seen, and it was his responsibility to Do It Right. Danny wondered if Tom's manual was one large volume divided into different chapters and headings, or if he had many volumes, thousands, like a Time-Life Book collection: *How to Tile Your Bathroom or Kitchen*; *How to Alienate Your Children*; *How to Belittle Your Brother Under the Guise of "Encouragement"*.

"Where's Melissa, I need a decent opponent." Gwen said this more to Danny than Tom. Melissa was a shrewd Ping-Pong player. Danny couldn't deny that.

Tom continued to eye the ceiling.

"Napping," he said. "She sleeps almost as much as the kids. Teenagers."

Danny thought it was funny how Tom said that, as if his kids were so old; Buster was only fourteen and Kerry, twelve. She wasn't even officially a teenager. Really it was Tom who seemed old. Funny that Tom had been Danny's age when he got married. Danny couldn't imagine getting married. Danny could barely imagine what tomorrow would look like, maybe toast for breakfast, or cereal from those mini cereal boxes. Danny could commit to cereal, but not the big box, just a mini one.

"See this crack," said Tom. "It runs all the way across the beam. How it's widening at the top? That's bad."

Gwen went and stood beside Tom. He pointed to the stains that wormed along the plaster and across the beams. Danny paced slowly from the edge of the Ping-Pong table to the short passage that was populated with a slew of slickers and fleeces between the great room and the dining room. He bounced the Ping-Pong ball on his paddle and listened. He felt the house rolling on the waves.

"The place has lasted this long," Gwen said, and patted Tom's back. But she stayed there and looked.

"I don't even know what this would cost to fix." Tom motioned to a crosspiece on the low ceiling beneath the balcony. "This beam is just cosmetic." Then he turned around and pointed to the four large beams, two vertical, two horizontal, that ran up the height of the two-story room like masts. "But those are structural."

From beneath the archway between the great room and the dining room, Danny could see the stain Tom was pointing to. The long yellow plumes spread the length of the vertical beams, and in the center of those plumes, cracks.

"Let's get someone in here," said Danny. *Engage the pumps, dump the ballast, break out the wax, the duct tape.*

He wedged the ball under the paddle on the table and walked over to Gwen and Tom. The three of them stood beneath the center beam, staring straight up. Danny had spent his childhood wishing he could walk on those beams. He thought about cracks in the bones of this house, in the ribs of this room. The balconies around its edge were great arteries, his parents' bedroom the driving heart.

"The cost would be prohibitive," said Tom, "replacing the roof, and then the rotten beams." Tom, so willing to let the place lose gangrenous limbs, to suffocate under its own rot.

"Plus, by now I'm sure Libby is in love with the water stains," said Gwen. Gwen and Tom snuffled. *At least Libby wants to keep the place alive,* thought Danny.

Tom left the room and came back with a broom in his hand. He climbed the stairs to the long balcony that ran the length of the room. Holding on to a pillar, he climbed up on the railing.

"I don't mean to be critical, but whacha doing?" asked Gwen.

In his free hand Tom held the broom, his hand near the bristles.

"Testing," he said as he stretched the broom up toward the ceiling. "If the leak is squishy that means it's new, but if it's dry and crumbly that means it's old."

Danny looked over at Gwen. She had told him about the holes she and Libby had found in the roof. He didn't want to tell Tom another thing.

With the broom handle, Tom clunked and knocked at the portion of the pitched ceiling he could reach, looking like a disgruntled downstairs neighbor.

"Tom, I wouldn't—" A large flake of plaster dropped to the floor. Tom quickly brought the broom down.

"So what does that tell you?" said Gwen. There was a strange crunching noise. Tom stepped back to the floor from the railing. Another jagged piece of plaster fell, the size of a dinner plate. Danny and Gwen shuffled backward toward the stage. A crack opened in the ceiling, and a continent of plaster lowered at one end like a ramp, showing the lath like bones underneath. Then the continent cracked and fell directly on top of the Ping-Pong table, covering the entire thing. A cloud of dust billowed toward them. Gwen and Danny turned into each other to cover their eyes and mouths.

"Fuck me," said Gwen. Tom pounded down the stairs.

"You guys okay?" He brushed dust from Gwen's hair, from Danny's shoulders.

"How much asbestos do we have in our lungs now?" said Danny.

"Don't worry, there is nothing fireproof about this place," said Tom.

From the stage the three of them looked up at the ceiling. Danny could see small lines of light around the lath. The house was shedding its skin from the inside out. Dust was settling over everything, giving the animal heads—bucks, moose, a boar, a fox—a gray tinge, aging them.

"We need to clean this up before Libby gets back," said Tom. "This will be too much for her."

"I told her we needed umbrellas," said Gwen.

Tom ran up the stairs and came back with the broom.

"Could we patch this up and paint over some of that?" Danny waved his hand toward the other water stains. The three of them moved to the bottom of the stairs.

"It needs a bit more than a patch, Dan," said Tom.

"What's your real estate golem going to think about this?" said Danny.

"One disaster at a time, Dan." Tom looked up. "Why Scarlet didn't do anything about this, I'll never know."

"She didn't have the B.O.B. here to motivate her," said Gwen. Three years without their father had made Scarlet reluctant to take on much.

Danny thought Tom wanted the place to be a mess, an unsalvageable mess. He wanted it to be the fucking *Titanic*. Maybe Tom wanted them all to be a mess so that he could swoop in and save them, or at least look that much better standing next to his siblings at funerals, uncles and cousins saying, "You've turned out well."

Gwen had turned out as they expected; Libby too; and Danny, they all seemed to just forget he existed, or that he ever grew past the age of four. "You can't possibly be in college," they had said. Funny, they were half right.

"Bibs won't want a quick fix," said Gwen, sitting on the dust-covered stairs. "She'll want a full restoration, a historic preservation, make it the way it was when we were kids. I'm sure if she could, she'd put wallpaper back up in every bedroom."

Danny stood at the bottom of the stairs. *Does this make Tom want to sell it more or less?* thought Danny.

"Only Bibs's room ever had wallpaper," Tom corrected her. "The rest were always painted."

"No, the nursery had that diamond pattern of buttercups. You don't remember that?" Tom stood in front of them, absently sweeping dust into a small pile, creating a little clean patch.

"You're confusing this place with Archer Avenue; that place was covered in wallpaper."

"You just forget because you moved out of the nursery first."

"Maybe it's just 'cause he's old." Danny.

Gwen shook her head sadly, whispered, "Early onset."

"You two are the ones killing brain cells all the time." Tom put his fist to his mouth and made a series of sucking, slurping noises.

"Have you *ever* used a bong?" said Danny.

"There's proof," said Gwen. "Even Scarlet and Dad's room had wallpaper; you can still see it in the closet."

Tom turned and they all looked up at the window of their parents' bedroom, which opened into the great room above the stage. Danny loved that window. He'd always thought that the slim diagonal panes added to the whole Heidi's-grandpa's-house look. One pane was cracked. Their mother had been a Ping-Pong wizard, and in a victorious frenzy she had sent a ball flying up into that window. No one had ever mentioned repairing it. Just like no one mentioned checking the closet for wallpaper. Danny had no intention of going into that room. Even the crack in the glass was too much to look at. He scratched at a fresh blister on his palm, ran the soft tip of his index finger against it. He could think about the blister. He could think about how his skin was just layers of molecules ready to peel away and disappear into the ether.

Gwen came down the stairs, stood just behind Danny, put her arms around him, and rested her chin on his shoulder. She was a good three inches taller than her little brother, and Tom was even taller than she was, both of them giants like their father. At twenty-one Danny still felt like the baby. He would never outgrow them. Even his license still had the great red mark on it, "UNDER 21." Though now that wasn't true. It was his only legal ID, since losing his passport this past spring somewhere between Scranton and Ensenada. And now it lied. As if the world was conspiring against his growing up. *Stay small,* the world whispered. Even his doctor was in on it. "I'll give you the quarter of an inch, but you just aren't five eight."

"Dan? Remember when you were little, how you got scared at night up here?" asked Gwen. "You used to come into my room to look at the lights from town."

"You'd tell me what each light was and what it meant."

"That was a game that Scarlet taught me and Tom. We'd sit on the end of the float after dinner, after Libby had gone to bed, and try to figure out every light."

Danny looked over at Tom. Tom had leaned the broom against the wall. He had always assumed that somehow Tom and Gwen lived separate lives as kids, like mini adults, standing in the doorways of their separate rooms in feetsie pajamas, waving cordially, but never inviting the other in.

Tom gave Gwen a pat on the shoulder. "That's true," he said, "but now they have those horrible new floodlights on the ferry landing. You'd think they were expecting the QE2. Maybe that's what Scarlet was hoping for, that the QE2 would pull into port and take her away." He looked out the bay window, over the water, to town. Tilting her head back so Danny could see her face, Gwen made a what-the-hell-is-he-saying expression that Danny had seen before, often.

"I think Scarlet was living the dream," said Gwen, "eventually, anyway." She squeezed Danny's shoulder. He was the dream.

Tom picked up a magazine, wiped the dust from the cover on his pant leg, and headed toward the dining room and the door to the porch. "Sure, an elaborate fallacy created by her subconscious, or her conscious mind, depending on the day," he said, and left the room smacking the rolled-up magazine against the heel of his hand. "You guys can handle the cleanup."

"Tom?" Gwen called, but they heard the screen door smack shut. Again, Gwen turned to Danny and grimaced.

"You'd think her dying would've chilled out his irrational anger," she said.

"That, or turning thirty-eight," said Danny.

"Maybe he's just mad she's not here to fight with."

"That drama queen," said Danny, "maybe he's just in withdrawal. They hadn't had a good blowout since my seventeenth birthday. Are you seriously still allowed to storm out of parties after you're thirty?"

"He didn't come back for poor Melissa for two hours. Just forgot about her completely. That lady is a saint." Danny was drawing lines in the dust with his toe.

"I can't even remember what he and Mom were fighting about."

"Insurance. Because that is *such* an emotional topic." The two of them broke down into a small laughing fit. When they heard Tom drag a wooden chair across the porch, they laughed harder. Scarlet hated when they dragged the furniture around. But then Danny didn't want to joke anymore. Laughing made him feel like he was too deep in his body, too far away from his skin. He coughed from the dust.

"I feel like I haven't seen you in forever," she said. "Finals must've been a bitch."

"Yeah, it's been tough." He leaned into her for a second. "I need some water."

"Oh, crap. She's back." Gwen pointed out the window to the back-yard. "Flee the scene!"

THIRTEEN

LIBBY

July 7

From where they sat on the porch Libby and Melissa could see Tom at the wheel of the Whaler. He'd just come back from a jaunt, and tied the boat up, but stayed where he was, looking out toward town. The women were in matching Adirondack chairs, their feet propped up on the rail, books lying facedown in their laps. Melissa wore a hat, and her legs looked pale and veined next to Libby's, which were tanned from hours working on boats and clearing brush from the edge of the wood for the past few weeks. Melissa looked delicate and magical, Libby thought, like a lily or some thin, exotic cat. So unlike her own seasoned self, the salty dog with the tennis body, her hands a little too rough for the country club but too lithe for the lobster boat.

"I can't believe that those idiots broke the house. I was only gone for an hour."

"At least they tried to clean up," said Melissa.

"'Tried' being the operative word." Libby glanced over her shoulder at the bay windows. Through them she could see the hole in the ceiling, a dark patch with pinpricks of light. It made her strangely happy. *No one else will want it now.* The risk of the offer had been buried under ancient plaster.

"At least it's not raining," said Melissa. Libby would rather the house become a mud pit then a fleet of condos.

"Tom has been obsessively listening to NOAA to make sure nothing happens before we can get it fixed," said Libby. Remy would come tomorrow and start putting it all back together. How much could a roof cost?

"See, he's not such an idiot. It was on our second date, when Tom told me about you."

"Really?" Libby scratched the top of one foot with the arch of the other.

"He talked about his little sister, he said he always used you as an example in meetings: 'Would my little sister like this ad, would this make her buy it,' like you were the everygirl. I expected you to be in college. And then when we first met, you were only fifteen."

"That's surprising, considering Tom thinks he's in a generation all his own. I wonder why he told you about me. Gwen would have made the better story."

"There was something incredibly sweet and vulnerable in the way he talked about you. It was the reason I went out with him a third time. I'd planned to end it at two dates, but . . ." Melissa looked down at her husband sitting in the boat as it pulled at its painter, adrift but tethered.

"Lucky for us you saw something," said Libby, leaning her head back on the chair and closing her eyes against the sun. "I hate to think of the kind of person he could've ended up with." There had been a few casual girlfriends before Melissa, the kind who either oozed all over their mother, trying to make a good impression, or the kind who would attempt to become Libby's best friend. Both were equally depressing to watch. Melissa always seemed just interested in Tom. She was kind and thoughtful and polite, but clearly felt no pressure for anyone to like her. And so, they all loved her.

"So when did you know that he was the right one for you?"

Libby figured that with someone like Tom there must have been a sign, a large manila tag hanging from the back of one of his shirts, like a forgotten dry cleaner tag, that read, "Your Soul Mate." *How else could she have known?* She wished it worked like that, that everyone came with a tag. Life would be so much simpler with labels like "Friend," "One-night Stand," "Work Acquaintance." She could avoid so much confusion, so much trouble, trying to turn one thing into something it wasn't.

"You mean besides the first time he brought me here?" They laughed.

"I think this place is Patricia's favorite thing about me too."

"Shut up. That girl would walk over hot coals for you, Lib. She's probably already done it."

Two years ago at the Omega Center.

"Pretty crazy talk on the Fourth, about the house," said Melissa.

Libby could practically feel Rafe Phillips's hot breath on her neck.

"We just keep the ship afloat. As always. Fix the roof." Libby jabbed a thumb behind her toward the windows and the great room and the Ping-Pong table now covered with a drop cloth to catch the constant dust that sifted down as the wind changed. "At least it's early enough in the season we should be able to get it done this summer. So my inheritance goes back into the house. Where else would it go? Tom might be ready to cash out, but that's not happening." Libby switched the cross of her feet on the rail, the backs of her bare heels clunking the wood emphatically.

"You know Tom and I aren't always of one mind, right?"

Libby wanted to kiss her, not in a romantic way, in a thank-God-I-have-an-ally-on-the-inside way. She reached over and squeezed Melissa's forearm.

"This place is beyond money. It's a natural wonder. There is no market value for that," said Melissa.

"Just three million." Libby said it quietly.

Melissa took off her hat and smacked Libby in the chest with it. "Don't even say that shit out loud. Denial is a very real strategy with Tom. You've got to be careful or he'll have you all packed up and on the next ferry."

"And then you'd have to divorce him." Libby said this with a chuckle. Melissa put her hat back on and sank back into her chair.

"Actually, our trips up here always made me feel closer to you guys than to Tom. He retreats when he's here. Like the way he is when he looks at sailing charts. Like he's already out on the water thinking about channels and harbors, even when he's sitting there with you on the porch."

"I know," said Libby. "Most of the time he's out on the water. Dad got the Whaler when Tom turned fourteen, and they went out in it all the time. Then, I guess, Tom hit puberty and it wasn't cool to tool around with your dad anymore. By the time he was sixteen he practically lived on that thing. But once he went to college he came up a lot less, and the boat"—she said this rubbing her hands together nefariously—"went to me."

"I won't tell him you said that."

"Sometimes it's better to keep him in the dark," said Libby. "Ignorance is bliss, right?"

He was better off not officially knowing about Patricia, for instance, better off not having his fears confirmed. And she was better off not being plagued by his fraudulent statistics about unmarried women dying young, about raising babies to be gay, about STDs, as if it weren't the mighty cock that was the fountain of burning, itching, and all things rashy.

Melissa closed her eyes and leaned her head back on her chair. The shadow from her hat fell dark over her eyes and nose, but the red of her lips seemed to be bleeding into her skin, blotchy like she was about to cry.

"You okay?" Libby asked.

"It didn't happen here, realizing he was the guy." She opened her eyes and looked down at Tom still sitting in the boat, working knots through a stray line. "It was one night, after your Aunt Kathy's fiftieth birthday, the night of that insane snowstorm with everybody house-bound. We were walking home through the snow, down Mass Ave. He didn't say anything in particular. We'd had a great time at the party. It was late, no one was around. The snow was up to the tops of our boots, and it was falling slow and straight, not that sideways crap that stings your eyes. We were gossiping about your cousins and which of the new girlfriends were going to last."

Libby could tell Melissa wasn't looking at Tom anymore, but out over the water, through seasons and years to streetlights glowing orange in the snow.

"He held my hand inside his coat pocket because I had forgotten my gloves. And I thought, life doesn't get better than this. That was it." Melissa shrugged.

Libby couldn't help wondering if life could be better—better for her, better for Melissa—though she was pretty sure that, for Tom, this was as good as it would get. Libby went inside now, the chill of the wood floor and the shadowy interior making her shiver. She got them each a glass of iced tea and carried them back out to the porch.

"Have you thought about talking to Tom about Patricia?" Melissa asked. She downed half her tea in two long swallows.

"I know which side he's on; I'm just not ready for a political debate. He'll want to talk me out of it, tell me it's a phase."

"He's not the most progressive guy in the world, I'll give you that," said Melissa carefully. "But he might surprise you."

"Yeah, I don't think surprises are his strong suit."

"He just wants you to be safe and happy. When we were deciding about having kids, he told me the story about you almost drowning at Bar Island. He said that was the day he realized he wanted to be a father. His paternal instincts just kicked in. He worries about you. At the end of the day, he's your big brother. Worrying's in his contract."

"Or his genetics," said Libby. "This is one of those rare times when he's way too much like Scarlet."

"She was definitely one opinionated lady."

"Is that a nice way of saying bigoted?" Libby snorted. "Patricia wasn't exactly her favorite person."

"Really? I always thought they got along well," said Melissa. "Two fiery ladies laughing and scratching. At Gwen's birthday they spent the whole time in the kitchen talking about remodeling bathrooms and costume jewelry."

"Limited exposure. That was the key with Scarlet. That and never bringing your business under her roof."

Melissa began to say something and stopped.

"Why would my almost drowning make Tom want a kid?" said Libby. "You would think it would do the opposite."

"Do you remember it?" asked Melissa.

"What?" Libby held a hand up to shade her eyes and turned toward Melissa. "Well, yeah. I just froze up, couldn't swim, and then my dad pulled me out."

Only ten years old, she had thought her father was kidding when he told her to get used to the cold, early-June water by wading in a tide pool. Like a baby. So she ran fast and hard, jumping from the edge of the whale-shaped rock that stuck way out into the cove. Libby had seen the water closing over her head, the floor of the cove so much deeper than she had realized. The water so cold she couldn't breathe, couldn't move her arms; she could only watch, looking up past seaweed and rocks, all browns and yellows and black greens, up to the surface— white, broken, and choppy. She saw the whale rock high and gray, she saw her father, in an arc, dive off of it. She felt the pull of the water against her as he swum her to shore, and the rough pile of the towel against her cold, blotched skin.

"Your father?"

"Yup, dove right in and saved me. Quite an exciting day." It had been humiliating. Clearly, she couldn't jump in like the big kids did, from rocks and floats and ferry landings. Frail and pathetic, she needed her father's warnings and savings. Maybe the universe had punished her for her pride, for her rebellion. This taught her she was better in boats than in the water, on top rather than in; skimming the surface, not plumbing its depths. She would leave all the jumping and diving to Gwen.

"Tom remembers it a little differently," Melissa said. "You should ask him about it."

"Tom, always the revisionist. He probably thinks I hate the water now."

"I'd think it would put you off swimming."

"Nothing could put me off swimming, just jumping in."

"Tom and I went skinny dipping here once. It was disgustingly hot one August, and you all were at some fair. We went right off the float in the middle of the day."

Libby sat up and looked incredulous. "Really? Tom? In the middle of the day?"

"He used to be different," said Melissa.

"God, I think of him as always being the same."

Libby stretched and picked up her book. Melissa looked down at the water, toward her husband still sitting in the Whaler.

That night was a bit chilly. They had their cocktails and hors d'oeuvres in the rug room. Tom and Danny were arguing in the kitchen over steak temperatures while Gwen and Melissa stared at the sunset through the arched window. Libby was laying a fire.

"Please," said Gwen to Melissa, "it would be so beautiful. Your curves against the arcs of the bed in the nursery. We'll take the sheets off. That ticking. Those old mattresses, the sagging, the buttons, the stains contrasting with your pale skin. It would be so French, in a sort of dusty garret style."

"Why not?" Melissa shrugged her shoulders up to her ears, and they stayed there for a minute.

"Oh, oh, great," said Gwen, obviously surprised Melissa didn't need more convincing.

"Have you ever posed for her, Bibs?"

Libby stood up from the hearth, the fire already catching. She dusted her hands on her pants.

"My entire adolescence. Her senior thesis was basically child porn." Libby had wandered from room to room in their creepy basement in Cambridge wearing nothing but a wreath of Christmas lights. Gwen had to order her to stop laughing so she could get the shot.

"You were seventeen; I wasn't exactly corrupting you."

"Have you ever posed for someone before?" said Libby. *Maybe Melissa had been one of those honor students who put themselves through school by modeling for the life drawing classes. What secret lives did Melissa live before Tom?*

Tom walked into the room with a drink in his hand and slumped down in the leather chair.

"Tom, guess what?" said Gwen.

Libby saw Melissa look at Gwen and slightly shake her head.

"How's dinner coming?" said Libby quickly.

"I don't care if we have freaking fish sticks for dinner. I'm done."

From the kitchen they heard Danny call, "It's cool, I've got this. Where's the fire extinguisher? Or a bucket of sand?"

FOURTEEN

GWEN

July 8

The nursery faced northeast, which meant to catch the light they needed to work in the morning. Early. So at seven they barged in and shuffled Danny off to Gwen's bed. His sleeping bag around him like a pelt, he looked like a cave man just ousted from his cave.

"The muse strikes," she explained. "No way around it."

"You're a jerk," he croaked. But he went, trailing his sleeping bag tail behind him. Gwen would've felt bad for him if she thought he'd stayed awake even five minutes after crawling into her bed.

After giving Melissa a few minutes, Gwen knocked on the nursery door and opened it a crack. "You decent, soon to be indecent?"

"As ready as I'll ever be," said Melissa. "Come on in."

"Nice outfit," said Gwen. Melissa wore a thin and faded hospital robe.

"From Brigham and Women's, when Kerry was born. The swag was all so baby-centric, I had to take something for myself."

Melissa sat on the edge of the cast-iron bed, its white paint peppering the floor around its legs. The sagging springs wheezed as Melissa crossed her legs. She leaned back on her hands while Gwen set up her materials: a small wooden easel; six tubes of watercolor of various sizes (three large: red, yellow, blue; three small: brown, black, white); and five brushes (one just a few bristles wide, something for fine detail; a fan; a large teardrop like the tip of a cat's tail; a smaller version of the same thing; and one with flat, wide-angled bristles). Gwen chose brushes not based on their intended purpose but on how the shape struck her that day. She saw the shape of the tool itself, not just the quality of its mark, as part of the composition. She used a plastic white plate, often used for sandwiches and chips at lunch, and the empty egg tray from the fridge as her palettes. Gwen looked over her work area—the heavy-tooth paper taped to the easel, the large jar of water on the bureau, which was so clear and would soon be clouded and then black—then said, "Let's get this show on the road."

Melissa slipped her robe from her shoulders and laid it tidily over the footboard of the bed next to her. Then she sat back down on the bare mattress that they had stripped after kicking poor Danny out.

Melissa adjusted the ancient down pillows beneath her head and shoulders. "No, the other way," Gwen directed, pointing one finger at her and another at the bed and then moving them over each other. Now, with her head toward the foot of the bed, she lay down, letting one foot dangle over the edge of the mattress.

"Perfect. You comfortable there?"

Melissa nodded.

"Good, just holler if you need a break."

Melissa scratched her nose, flexed and relaxed both feet, and then settled into the pillows and the trough of the horsehair mattress. After sharpening her pencil, Gwen began to lightly sketch in the curves of the bed frame, of Melissa's hip, of the heel of that dangling foot. This was always the hardest part, seeing the composition in her subject and deciding where to start on the page. But having a model was excellent motivation. A still life wouldn't care if she stopped before she started. A bowl of apples beside an old boot doesn't care if she had to have a snack and the smallest glass of wine and possibly a cigarette first. But with a model there was no room to stop, to judge herself. She just had to push through.

The light in the nursery was warm and gold coming in straight from the top of the ridge, shining in over the blueberries and the meadow, giving the whole room a sepia quality. Gwen sat with her back to the windows, the shadow from her easel falling across the amber wood planks between the two iron beds. They could smell coffee coming up the back stairs from the kitchen, and they could hear the soft murmurs of the classical radio station from Blue Hill. That would be Tom. She was happy to keep their little project from him. Gwen encouraged secrets, and in this case, it lent the scene that much more tension, that much more of a bordello flavor. As if just in the next room, removing his sidearm, was a young member of the French Foreign Legion back in his beloved city for just two days. Or better still, a poet whose wife, unable to put up with his self-loathing, kicked him out when he had writer's block. He would turn to lovely Melissa, his muse, his Venus rising from the mist of her dust-filled apartment, the froth of motes around her, her bare mattress a shell. Gwen wondered if Melissa had any real secrets from Tom.

"Do you hear from Reed at all?" Melissa asked. Gwen looked up from her canvas and let her eyes focus on Melissa's, not just on her subject, but on the person herself.

"The ex? No, we don't do that," said Gwen, circling her pencil in the air as if encompassing all that they no longer did. She had tried, but he wouldn't return her calls. Well, he returned one, to say he'd never return another.

They had been married on the dock, just a few days before the Fourth of July nine years ago. She had married Reed, the attorney from

Rochester, who promptly took her to DC. Their marriage lasted a total of eighteen months. Even Danny, at age twelve, had said she couldn't live in a coat-and-tie town like that. She assumed he saw the city as suited men going into polished white buildings, where great shining machines turned out something known as Politics. Machines that all looked like the printing press in the mint he had seen on a class trip. Although, Gwen had been twenty-seven when she was married; her image of Washington wasn't much different.

She had known Reed for a year and had some thought of helping him live out his thwarted creative side, being his muse so that he might feel connected to all the dreams he had sequestered, choosing law school over art school. She envisioned them as a balanced pair in a brick town house with a bright-pink door. She knew there was a problem when he refused to let her paint the door pink. She knew that she had fooled herself into thinking opposites could lead anywhere but opposition.

Reed had loved her spirit, her fire, all the things she wanted to inspire in him, but once married it became clear that they had each expected the other to change. She wanted to spend Saturdays posing naked for his figure-drawing hobby he occasionally fantasized about pursuing. He assumed she would turn her creative mind to more domestic ventures. That together they would renovate their crumbling town house, painting rooms that were "studies" or "guest" rooms in pale hues with convenient nooks for cribs and shelves for toys. But the house felt like a set piece to her, and then her life, their life, started to feel that way as well. The dust and billowing plastic curtains gave the place the feeling of a radiation quarantine. It was Silkwood, or Chernobyl, or the Eastern Bloc. It was only the suggestion of a home, like a black box theater. An armchair in a shaft of light was the living room, a skillet hanging from a hook and a bare wood table were the kitchen. She knew the renovations would end, that the place would become something real, and that a child could fill it all with light.

She knew a baby had the power. It had for her parents. It had the power to eradicate darkness from a relationship, to banish doubt and draw the two of them into the tightest of unions. But all of it—the union, the covenant, the oaths and promises and forms signed and gifts opened—they were all ropes around her, all pulling her deeper into some dark watery grave, no place for a baby. No baby deserved a pale and wavering mother, too long in the deep, too long underwater.

The whole city seemed to exist underwater, a place without color or air, beautiful and dead. And that, eventually, was how she saw her marriage, beautiful and dead. It took her eighteen months to swim to the surface, to turn on lights and pull back curtains, to dismantle the set and come home.

Her family actually seemed relieved when it happened. Even her father said to her simply, "Life is too short to stick with bad decisions." Tom was the only one who seemed surprised, or not surprised so much as disapproving. Marriage, Tom told her, was not a convenience that could be tossed aside because it felt hard; often what people saw as a lack of love, he told her, was just an abundance of laziness. Reed had told her approximately the same thing as she loaded her favorite chair into the back of her Civic wagon with two suitcases, a lamp, and a can of pink paint. He had stood there, his briefcase in one hand, keys in the other, stunned.

"You don't want me this way," she had said. "You don't want this pretend life."

"Don't tell me how I feel. I want you to stay. I'm not the one giving up. This is real. You're the one who wants a pretend life. This is work, and you're a fucking coward."

She drove three blocks away and sat in the car for an hour before she was sure she wouldn't turn around.

"This is dark, this is cold, but this is not nuclear winter," she had said to herself sitting in her car. But she saw their house frozen and bent under the rush of a nuclear blast. She knew that she wasn't a coward. She had done what he was afraid to do.

"I hear he moved to New York to focus on tax law," said Gwen. "Sometimes I think, God is really on my side, saying 'see, you made the right choice. See, tax law.'"

She had felt so sure of Reed as they stood together on the pier, as if the sea itself was presiding over their union. She didn't want to believe that certain types could not mesh. Or that she was any type of anything. And she didn't like to think that there were wrong choices. She never experienced what Danny called "Entrée Envy," when after the food arrives you want what your dinner companion has ordered. Nor did she have a problem putting a book down halfway through and never picking it up again. Life was too short for bad books, or even good books that you just don't like. That was Reed; he was *The Portrait of an Artist as a Young Man*, he was *The Waves*, he was *Infinite Jest*. He was Jasper Johns and Eva Hesse. Something she wanted to love but couldn't.

"Did you ever doubt your choice?" said Melissa. Gwen didn't hear her.

She had already set to work on the square of sun on the wall just above her subject, pulling out the white bars of the iron headboard from between her golden strokes. This was the room she and Libby had shared when they were kids. She and Libby.

"Gwen?"

"What?"

"Did you ever wonder, what if I tried harder, what if I did more? Did you doubt yourself?"

Gwen pulled her brush away from the paper, laid it across her knees, and shook out her hand. She thought of those three blocks, of how she stared at the stitching on the steering wheel and wondered how they sewed the vinyl on, what kind of machine could even do that?

"Not really. That's the beauty of choices, right? They're endless."

The letter she had written two months later went unanswered. He didn't want to run away to Bali and start a new life. He didn't want to become the friends they never were. He didn't want any of the options she gave him. All those doors painted on the envelope remained shut. Eventually, it was a relief. She never had to tell him about the baby. She never had to show Reed how much he had lost, or how much she had taken from him.

She picked up her brush and continued to work, thinking how afraid of regret she was when it came to painting, how each stroke was a potential mistake. Sometimes she just had to move ahead, jump into a cold pool instead of wading in, because if you take it slow there is always the risk that you will turn back, that you won't make it. She left a blank space she would fill in later for the black sconce on the wall, its two bare bulbs showing their caps of dust in the direct sun.

"I know you guys had your issues," said Melissa. Gwen rolled her eyes, like "issues" barely covered what they'd had. "But was there anything else, was there someone else?"

Gwen had been too sad for someone else. Who can you meet at the bottom of the sea?

"There's always someone else eventually."

The color on her paper was still so light, like a painting already faded from years in the sun. It was as if more color had ended up in the rinse water than on the page itself. She added more yellow from a tube to her palette, tried to resist the urge to dilute it.

With art there was no relief, but also no end, no way out. Doing it was hard; not doing it was worse. Her own way of working was dark and twisted, a path in a medieval wood that existed perpetually in shadow, all hooting owls and gnarled branches. Hard to navigate, the fear almost paralyzing. *But you can't stop here,* she would think. *Miles to go,* she would think. And yet there was no goal, there was no light in a distant window, there was only the path. She was afraid of never becoming the artist she was in her mind. She was afraid of making something good and then, in trying to make it better, she would ruin it completely. In every other part of her life it was easy to be fearless, but with a brush in her hand she flinched at every snapped twig on the path.

Gwen clinked a slim brush in the jar of clear water and made the palest pool of yellow, adding dots of red and brown to deepen it to a gold hue.

"Do you have any regrets?" Melissa asked. She wiggled the toes of her extended foot and rolled her shoulders.

"You need a break?" Gwen asked. Melissa shook her head and settled back into the mattress. Gwen began a different pool of yellow, much more red this time, the smallest dot of brown, and a large one of white, yielding a pale-peach tone.

"I'm not saying I never change my mind. Some choices are awful even when they're the right ones. I think when you listen to yourself, the right decision is hard to ignore. I mean, what is regret, really? It's just fear, fear of loss. Most people think that loss is avoidable. But I'm pretty sure it's not. You just have to ride it out. Like winter. Like people who move to California for the weather. They're leaving out of fear. And probably regret. I bet you money."

Gwen would've run to California after her split from Reed. She needed to thaw out. She wanted to fly from the pale-white eye of DC for the golden hills of the Marin Headlands, the pink walls of The Mission. But she couldn't face that much space between her and everything she was used to. After that lifeless house, she couldn't be in another place alone. So she went back to the red bricks of Cambridge, and it was a warm kiss on the forehead; it was her sister standing in her yard like a warrior holding pulled weeds by their greens, a severed head by its hair. It was Danny curled like a dog asleep in one corner of her couch. It was even Tom, dragging her to Costco to save money on salsa.

It was her parents too. Her father had been a jovial, sometimes distant king, crowned in a ring of pipe smoke. But once she was an adult, really once she was fifteen, he was her secret keeper. He would lean toward her when she was doing dishes after a family dinner and say, "Now what do we *really* think about this guy?" jabbing a thumb toward the dining room as if to clarify who he meant, her date, the yahoo with the wallet chain. He always wanted the truth.

Scarlet didn't often ask questions. Like she already knew all the answers. Once Gwen left Reed and was back in Cambridge, her mother would come over with a bottle of wine, salad niçoise, vine charcoal, and a kneadable eraser. Together they would sit quietly and sketch. Gwen stopped thinking of Scarlet as her mother when they were able to just be women, to just be artists together. Then things worked much better. Now Gwen had one less person to tell her secrets to, and one less person who already knew them. At least she was sure she'd meet them on the other side.

The sun rose higher, grew brighter, slowly bleaching out the sepia. The down on Melissa's earlobes, her arms, the sheen of her fingernails went from gold to white.

"What about that guy you were seeing, Libby said he's out of the picture?"

Gwen felt a wave of nausea. From her brush she swirled a black cloud into the jaundiced rinse water.

"Libby has high hopes for every guy. He was just a good time." She wished that he had mattered, that he was somehow unique and separate from the array that came before. Maybe if he were a lobsterman. A longshoreman. An explorer. The paddler of an ancient canoe, keeping the tradition alive. Even a gondolier. She wished there was more of the sea in his genes. At least he was a musician. Not that it mattered. In a few weeks the nausea would be eradicated and a new good-time man would be found. Maybe one that could lead somewhere. One who'd want a pink door.

"Do you have regrets? Some long-lost love you stalk online?" asked Gwen.

"Just the one I'm married to."

"He's the love or the regret?"

The door opened, and in walked Tom saying, "Dan, get your butt out of bed, Libby is making us dig that trench." He was waving a pair of work gloves. He stopped.

"Melissa." He said it sharp and quick, the way one calls a dog away from sniffing at the kitchen counter.

"Look how beautiful she is." Gwen waved at her painting. "I had to have her."

"Well, I guess you'll take your clothes off for anyone," he said to Melissa. Melissa sat up and stared at Tom but made no move to put on her robe. The two of them just looked at each other. Her skin was iridescent in the sun.

"Seriously, Tom, this is the guy you want to be? Grow up," said Gwen.

"I am the only grown-up *in* this house."

"How's that working out for you? Just because our lives don't look as picture perfect as yours doesn't mean—"

Melissa laughed.

Tom looked at her and shook his head, then turned back to Gwen. "While you're having fun painting pictures and sleeping late, the rest of us, and by that I mean *me*, have to get things done. Some of us have to pay the bills."

"No one asked you to be Atlas. We are perfectly capable of taking care of ourselves," said Gwen.

"Is that why you borrowed money from me in March? Is that why you had me pull Mom's plug? Because you're so capable?"

"You volunteered. Don't put your weird guilt on me just because you've hated her your whole adult life. For no fucking reason. What was the worst thing she did to you? Have another son? Poor baby. You should hear some of the fucked-up shit she put Libby through before you act like your life was so hard."

"I have to go dig a trench. Have fun masturbating." He walked out, slamming the door behind him.

"That's probably the first time you've ever said that word," Gwen shouted after him. She turned to Melissa. "I can't believe he's anyone's father."

"That's exactly how Kerry and Buster feel. What did Scarlet do to Libby?"

Gwen got up, opened the door, looked down the hallway, shut the door, and sat back down.

"Libby got the worst of it, but somehow ended up the most sane," said Gwen.

FIFTEEN

ANOTHER SUMMER

Now the sun down, dinner done, the water dazzles with waves of phosphorescence. The children lie down on the float on their bellies, stretching their arms into the water, waving them back and forth like the long fronds of kelp below them. They skim their arms just under the surface to see the lights slide over their skin, curl in on themselves as they pull in the opposite direction.

"The ocean is alive," they say. "It glows. So many little bugs, or are they fish?"

"It's full of stars we can wake up with our fingers."

"We are reaching into space to distant galaxies."

"Yes," their mother whispers from her seat on the end of gangway, its old wood wheels having rolled to the very front of their steel track. The float now just three feet below the pier.

"The sea is holding us up," Libby says.

"It resists gravity," says Tom.

"It's ruled by the moon," says Gwen.

"I'm an astronaut," says Libby, reaching her arms out into ocean. Her knees bent, her little feet floating in the air, long toes like her father.

"Yes," their mother says. Her voice is far away. He has gone for the weekend again. "Sailing to Brimstone," he said. He will bring them back the smooth black treasures that are the stones of another planet, without a mark and softer than the water that bore them. Smooth and black as space, as the water without the light, as the cove at sunset. He will come back, a pocket of his slicker fat and hanging low with the black stones. They have so many already. The walls, unfinished, showing their studs, are lined with them. Mantels and sills are humped and rowed with them. Tom uses one as a worry stone, rubbing it during exams. Gwen gives hers away to friends at home who believe that it is a piece of the dark side of the moon. Libby keeps hers, catalogs them, has a list, numbered, with a description of the stone, the date it was given to her, and the weather conditions under which it was found.

She has realized, living in this place summer after summer, that weather is important. It is like luck, or praying, but also like a game that one must know how to play, when to hold a card, when to lay it down in books. Help yourself first, is the rule of cards and weather. She knows there is more to it than this, but she is still learning. Boats need so much help, so much minding of the weather with boats. The wind up, her father would usually be down on the dock putting the Whaler on the outhaul, can't stay tied to the float. In a softer wind it could just be led to the leeward side, like a horse to a new stall.

Their mother is sighing on the edge of the ramp. Libby hears.

"I'm an astronaut," she says again.

"Yes, I see that," says their mother.

The older two go up, step past their mother as she leans to one side, not wanting to listen to her sighs anymore, but Libby makes her mother come and take their place.

"Lie down, Mama, on your belly," she pats the planks beside her. Her mother heaves herself up by pulling on the handrails of the gang-way. She squats down beside Libby, first balancing on the tips of her toes, then rolling down to her knees, then walking her hands forward to lower herself down. She can't seem to do much all at once, Libby thinks. Even this, lying down, is done in stages. *Adults,* she wonders, *so strange.* Her mother wags a hand in the water, keeping the other under her chin in a fist.

"I see," she says.

"No, no, both hands. This water," Libby explains, "is magic." Her mother needs to see. With four hands in, they wave in unison, and the lights trail their fingers.

"It's only like this here," Libby says. *Only here.*

She often sees her mother sigh at the house, stand in the middle of the great room, a gray, damp dishtowel over her shoulder. She looks for more dishes, but stops and sighs. She looks at the ceiling, rubs the toe of her canvas shoe against a spot on the floor, joggles the loose plate of an outlet set, inexplicably, in the middle of the floor underneath the edge of the Ping-Pong table. Libby is suspicious of her mother, of these lingering looks around the house, of a casual comment about new wallpaper in her room. Their hands go back and forth.

"Mama, you don't really want to change the wallpaper in my room. It is my new room. My room, no more nursery. I like it like it is."

The paper is like a fairy tale, each little scene a story, the boy finds the lost girl among the rose bushes in June. They skate together in January. In July the girl and her sister wear bonnets on their way to a picnic, small baskets dangle from their wrists. December there is a puppy in a box with a bow. April there is a storm that is no match for her sturdy umbrella. May there are blue ribbons around a small bouquet set in her lap as she reads her lessons. March there is a muff around chilly hands. This is a story that continues, she is still learning it, the months stretch on for years, above her porch door, the chimney, the bit between the light switch and servant bell that no longer works. Like a doorbell in her room. Funny that there was a bell and it is gone. She wonders what it sounded like, big and tolling, a church bell, or the buzz like the doorbell at her nana's apartment in the city. She wonders if the bell is buried in the meadow like an arrowhead. A relic, a treasure.

"The paper is stained," her mother says.

Her little hands are growing cold, but she washes them, agitating the little creatures.

"The paper is old and faded," her mother continues. "Let's paint it, simple and white."

This makes Libby cry. Simple, cover the stories of years with a great white storm? Blot it all out, bury it like a bell in the yard?

"No. No," she says.

Her mother sits back. "It is just wallpaper."

The tears come fast, Libby stands quick, no stages, just up. Her little hands bleeding cold water into her pant legs, her shirtsleeves.

"I love it, though," she cries. "I don't want it to change."

And it is this word that she holds on to. Change. It is this word that makes the tears come faster, the breath hiccup in her chest, her hair sticking to her face, her hands too wet and cold to pull the strands away.

"We're painting all the rooms," says her mother. "Ours is already done."

"Not mine. Not mine."

The word rings in the air around them. She is cold now, wet arms, no sweater. She is having trouble breathing, so much crying. *No more change.* Her father has been away most weekends this summer. He even has started traveling for work, gone for a week here or there. She sees him less, hears her mother's sighs more. This house is the place that is the same. Not the new school that she had to start this past year, where kids left her low and heavy alone on the seesaw. *No,* she would put her little six-year-old foot down. Wallpaper is where she draws her unsteady line. Wallpaper is a thing that can stay the same. Wallpaper in her big-girl room, her alone-without-her-sister room (though she is right next door, so no need to be scared in the night). Wallpaper. The calendar of a fairy tale.

"Fine." Her mother wraps her arms around herself, rubs her shoulders with her own wet hands. *Fine. Wallpaper.*

Her mother does not have the energy to fight this littlest of battles, with this tiny general aflame at her feet. *Fine. One room can remain stained and veined and peeling at the edges. It's one less room to do.* She has already started on the kitchen, painting the floor a bright yellow. Then the back hall and bathroom, periwinkle. The new color brightens things, but still there are things that can't be fixed. The hair was painted into the bathroom floor, a small twisted *J* of a hair. Something that she looks at each time she uses the room. Something she can't get away from. *Whose is it?* It is thick and wiry, not the downy plume that her two older children have started to bear, much to her dismay. *Is it mine? His? Someone else's?* This is not a question she wants painted into her bathroom floor, to ask herself before each meal, after her morning cup of coffee, between swims with a wet, sticky bathing suit drawn around her ankles. This is not a question she wants her son, who uses that bathroom most, to ask as he brushes his teeth, as he bathes, as he fills the compound bucket in the tub to aid in flushing because the chain tank stopped working last week. This uneasiness is not something she wants her children exposed to. But clearly, it is upon them too, a ringing suspicion that things are changing.

Let her have her wallpaper. That is one thing I can protect, one thing I can preserve. The rest I must fortify against, she thinks. For each time he leaves she pulls herself further away. Soon he will come home to an ocean in the rug room, a cold expanse across which she will be under a dim lamp with a dog-eared book. She will grow that ocean. If he must be in a boat, she will give him a great empty plane to sail through.

She hustles Libby sniffling up the gangway, the pier light a lonely bulb in a cage. She will leave that on. She still wants him to cross that ocean. To come home to her.

SIXTEEN

LIBBY

July 8

Libby noticed almost immediately. But she wasn't able to approach Danny for some time. Not until she kneeled in the flower bed by the front porch pulling up all violets that threatened to suffocate the peonies. Danny sat in a chair, his feet up. After each sip his beer bottle left a growing wet ring on the arm of his chair.

His eyes were dark, and he had lost weight since she'd seen him at Easter. It wasn't anything specific, but she saw the signs. When their father returned the summer she was ten, after he had left without saying good-bye, after weeks away sailing, he looked like this. Almost. He was gray and dragged. But there was a relief to him too—like a runner at the end of a marathon, or a passenger saved from some North Sea ferry disaster—the look of a survivor. The summer she was ten, she was still so young, still living in the tiniest details of things. She had noticed the scars on her father's wrists that he kept covered, one under a tight watchband and the other tucked beneath a long cuff. One sleeve rolled up, the other always down. But still pink ends crept from beneath the leather band, peeked out from the keyhole above the buttoned cuff. She knew what this meant. Had seen it in TV movies. The scars were the sign of something wrong that, thankfully, was past, moved beyond, healed over. Almost immediately she had put the sight of those scars away in some deep strange little drawer inside herself. It wasn't that she forgot it but that she chose never to think of it again. So that it became as far away from her as the moon, deep inside her internal universe.

Looking at Danny, the drawer had sprung open. With Danny there were no visible scars. She knew if it hadn't happened already, it was in the works. He was still running his race. He was still treading in those icy waters.

"Why don't you stay up here with me for a while, Dan?" she suggested. "You don't need to be anywhere, right?"

"Where would I need to be?" He said this drawn and slow, like it tired him to even think of obligations, of places or plans.

"School doesn't start too early this year?"

"School will start whenever I show up. It's convenient that way."

The day after they'd arrived at the house she had, on a hunch, called the registrar's office. Danny was not registered for the upcoming semester, nor had he finished the last one. This was the power of dead parents and the knowledge of a social security number. Having asked about matriculation, deferment, payment plans, correspondence courses, leaves of absence, she had solutions. And she had a deadline too.

She worked the ground with the cultivator, loosening all around the runners that snaked under the topsoil of the bed. Weeds, insidious, a disease. She eased the runners up, an explosives expert exposing a trip wire, found their noduled and gnarled core, and pulled it all forth, the circulatory system of death.

Danny took long drinks from the green beer bottle, the color of the sea but so much smoother.

"I think you should stay up here a few extra weeks, maybe Gwen too."

"What about your crew, aren't they coming up next week?"

"It's the first week in August, but—" She paused. She had not fully considered this. Danny and her friends in this place together? She had always been so careful to keep them all apart. The family in July, the friends in August. That was the deal. That was the only way it worked. She had tried to mix them once and had learned what Scarlet was *truly* capable of. But now, without Scarlet here, things were different. Things didn't need to be hidden or minimized. Her worlds could merge without repercussions, not including Tom, of course.

Danny was like one of her students. One left late in the afternoon, the early darkness of winter closing in. The blank curb, with no car waiting, the only thing staring back at him. As with any forgotten child, she needed to stay with him, or to keep him with her. *This house has the power to cure,* she thought, *I can't keep it all to myself.* Herself and her eight friends.

Though now it could be seven. Patricia, the eighth, would she come? Did Libby want her to? If Patricia came it would mean only that the decision had been made in Patricia's favor. It felt out of Libby's hands. And if she told Patricia to stay home, more accurately to stay out of her home, then her friends, those seven, would ask and discuss and accuse and berate and generally heckle.

Danny would, selfishly, be a shield. Danny would be a sad, dark river separating her from them. A new geological phenomenon that sprang up during the long winter, it would be unexpected and it would change the landscape of their vacation, one that had been the same for the last six summers.

"Maybe school can wait." She said this casually, tossing the strings of roots and blades of grass to the pile of detritus in front of her.

"I don't know, Bibs, some of those books, those ideas, might expire. Marx, Freud, Hobbes, they've been on the shelf awhile now; pretty soon they won't be safe to consume."

Always so cute, always the little smart-ass. If she could get him to stay, then she could get him alone. If she could get him alone in a boat, where they could really talk, she knew she could get it out of him. Where he'd been for the last six weeks, where he wanted to go, if he'd tried anything, started giving his possessions away, written notes? Did he have a plan?

Kelly Fern had an office on the back of the island. A man with the name of a flower, or a stylish purse, or a talk show host, was their father's age, would've been, and he was a psychologist. She could take Danny to him. Maybe Kelly Fern could explain how to mourn, how to keep going. Because what she saw, in the gray skin, in the sharp collarbone, was the deep void left by their mother. Like a door that had been left open, with Danny standing right in that cold draft.

"How'd school end for you, Bibs?" He scratched the back of one leg with the opposite foot.

"Good, it's always good at the end."

"When they can finally wipe their own butts, and tie their own shoes?"

"Butts, yes; shoes, no."

Good, because she loved them. Good, because they learned the schedule, and sat in their spots at circle time, and put away paints before nap, and washed hands after wiping said butts. They learned what she taught, and she loved them for it. But also just for them, for their words and songs and small feet. For five hot dogs wiggling in a frying pan, pantomimed with the wiggling fingers of one hand on the sizzling palm of the other. For the sly tastes of Play-Doh, homemade or not. For slow nudging of a halved grape toward one reluctant and satiated turtle. For questions like, "Why won't he eat it?" For declarations like, "My chin is an umbrella for my neck" and "I'm going to be a dinosaur catcher." Or the instruction that preceded bad behavior: "Miss Willoughby, just look over there (away from the activity), I'll tell you when you can look; just don't pay attention for a minute, okay?" Even the heart-breaking certainties that "Girls don't like dark colors" or "Boys don't have long hair."

Gwen, Tom, and Melissa were all napping. It was that time of the day. This left the house hushed and made Libby feel as if she and Danny were having a secret meeting.

"When are you and Patricia going to have a little butt wiper of your own?"

He never shied from questions. He got that from Gwen. His beer gone, he rubbed the wet bottle on the back of his neck, then brought the bottle's lip to his and blew across the top, sending a low moan, his own feeble foghorn, out into the sun of the afternoon.

"We aren't there yet, not even on that road yet. I don't even know if we'll get there." She had wanted a baby with Riley. She had wanted a lot of things with Riley.

Riley was her third girlfriend, the one just before Patricia. There were women in college who were more passing storms or breezes or great and powerful ideas, hardly what could be called relationships. Tiffany's upturned-collar-and-pearls name belied her actual tattooed-lesbian reality. Before Tiffany, Libby had just a few frenzied gropings in the common room after three a.m. Tiffany told her that women were meant to be together, goddesses on the mountain. And that men should serve simply as vehicles for fertilization, the sinewed arm that dropped grapes into their mouths. This was college.

Then there was Carmen, another woman who lived the opposite of her name, a buttoned-up writer who found the library to be the most erotic place on the map. Libby was constantly pulling up Carmen's tweed pencil skirt, bunching it around her waist while they writhed in a distant carrel in the geology section. Or pulling stockings down to Carmen's ankles, letting them hang accordioned from one foot. She laid Carmen back on the linoleum conference table in the basement closet that served as the office for the college lit mag. It was, as Carmen often said, steamy. There were no politics with Carmen. There was just Anaïs

Nin, Colette, bell hooks, and, in their nostalgic moments, even passages from Judy Blume's *Forever*.

And then there were years of no one special. After living with Carmen for a year, Libby felt that women demanded a kind of attention and closeness that made her skin dry, made her ears clog, made her lose her sense of balance and have to lie down on the couch with one foot on the floor to steady the room. Women came in every opening, through every door and window. Their belongings crept into drawers that had long been empty for the glorious pleasure of one uncluttered space. Their hair wove long strands into her sweaters, was brought gagging from the back of her throat. Not her own hair, no, these were great long red hairs that belonged to Carmen, then black waves that drifted from Patricia's mane. Patricia's hair, in its fullness, gave the look of someone perpetually turning her head, always a seductive bounce and sweep. Not lank and still like Libby's own. Libby couldn't even make a ponytail bounce when she walked. It hung stock straight like it was weighted at the bottom.

Libby's fingernails were black with dirt, the lines in her knuckles too, exaggerating the topography of her hands. A worm hung from the side of a small hole her weeding had created. She pulled it from the soil and placed it under the shady fronds of the day lilies she'd planted the year before.

"What about you, Dan? You want kids someday?"

"Only if I can sell them." *Feeling anything,* she thought, *must be hard for him. Has he loved anyone?*

Then there had been Riley. Riley with hair like August, dry, gold, and warm. She had loved Riley. Libby had brought her to the house one summer. Riley, who she loved so much her mother saw it in fifteen minutes, and saw her daughter wanting something no one should want. With Riley there had been something. She was the one. *The one that comes back in your dreams, that you are afraid to see, but want to more than anything.*

Riley was married, but wanted to see something. To try something that had been gnawing at her for years. Like a dying woman wanting to see Paris, Riley wanted to fuck a woman. They had started there. Just fucking. It began as the fifty-cent tour of Paris, a map and a croissant, just that.

It was in the ladies' room at the Ritz café, of all places, after tea. Libby had chosen the swank spot on Newbury Street because they would never run into anyone they knew there. Tea had seemed safe, a place to put things on the table, a wedding ring beside a miniature berry torte, a steaming teacup, a slip of milk, the slow turn of the spoon. Libby's slim ladies' watch made of gold links keeping an eye on the time; Riley had to beat her husband home. Forty more minutes still. Fingertips touched. The top of a foot, the back of an ankle. The check paid while they folded and refolded their napkins. Leaving behind a good tip and two linen swans. Libby knew how to do that.

A week later in their tour of Paris, they had moved from the double-decker bus tours, a straightforward overview, to lingering afternoons getting lost in the Louvre. They were lost in Libby's bed. Finally they planned the trip to Maine. They were going to play house in a flat on the Left Bank; for a whole week they were going to pretend to be French.

But after fifteen minutes with Libby's mother they were not in Paris. They were on the cold green waters of the thoroughfare, and Paris was far away, a heat wave killing hundreds.

The sun came through her straw hat in thin points. This hat had been their mother's. The light fell across Libby's face, and she could see the shadows move over the bridge of her nose; when she leaned forward, they moved over her arms, her gloved hands. She wondered if the sight of her in this hat, in this flower bed, was making Danny sad. He sat back in the chair, legs out straight, propped on the low rail, eyes closed, the sun bringing out his freckles. There was nothing for her to point to, nothing that he said. Only his weight. And the registrar's office. It was in the air around him, like walking into an empty room and knowing someone had just blown out a match or a candle, the trace of sulfur or tallow in the air. Here on the open portion of the porch, between the two covered areas, the sun was hot. He picked at something on the palm of his hand. She tapped the bottom of his foot with the spade, leaving a dark arrow of mud.

"Got a splinter?" said Libby. *This house loves to leave pieces of itself under your skin.*

"What? No, it's nothing."

"So, no girls I should know about? No one at school?" Or out of school. A possibility she hadn't even considered. Maybe this wasn't about their dead mother, the hat, the house. *Maybe he's heartbroken.*

"There are so many I can't keep 'em straight," said Danny, not opening his eyes.

Maybe not. Libby wondered if he was this way with Gwen, with women in general. *No wonder, no girls. Too bad.*

Libby stood up, and as she walked the tops of her tall rubber boots tipped from side to side like ringing bells, like green channel markers. She stepped over the lilies and the worm and into the aggressively bright patch of marigolds. Her mother had been trying to eradicate them for years now; Libby didn't know why. But if the marigolds posed some unknown threat, she would pick up the battle where her mother had left off. They smelled sour and left pollen tangled on the down of her arm.

Women were beautiful. Worth the time and effort. Men, with all their straight lines, were as intimate as an empty bookcase, everything out in the open. Women were curves and secrets and delicious melodies. As she walked, Patricia made a magical song, a downbeat, a quarter note, not so much bouncy as fluid. And breasts. That was the thing that made Libby feel sorry for gay men, no breasts anywhere. Not that she brought much to the table, breast-wise. But Carmen, Riley, and then Patricia brought forth cornucopias, a great feast set forth on the silver tray of lace and underwire, or better still in fresh sheets. This was something good, and kept her from pursuing the one or two men who asked her out, who called her in that desperate way men have when they can't see why they are being denied what they want.

"Where's your lady, anyway?" Danny asked, head rolled to one side so that his long hair shaded his face, one eye closed under the awning of hair, the other squinted at her. She kept digging, trying to find the edge of the fan of marigold roots.

"She had to work, couldn't get away."

Libby knew Danny didn't need to hear the story, to hear about another person he might lose from his life. Patricia was becoming more and more a part of things. A place for her at birthday dinners, at brunch. It wasn't anything she had planned.

Patricia had always flowed like a river, sweeping Libby right along with her, in a friendly way.

Patricia wanted to move in, flood her small apartment with stones and reeds and frogs, fill every available drawer, bring drawers of her own. And so Libby found herself drowning. She loved Patricia in a way that felt like drowning. Or the idea of losing her, in an effort to preserve some arbitrary order in her apartment, felt like drowning. And yet bringing her in, welcoming her, felt just as bad.

Libby's love for Patricia felt barely containable. She looked at this woman and wanted to kiss her shoulder, run the back of a finger down her temple, slide her ponytail between the ring of her thumb and forefinger. Libby loved that Patricia diffused arguments with friends, coworkers, even school parents with the simple words, "Well, I am from Spain." Mostly she meant, "Your stupid American customs are unimportant to me," but people interpreted it as, "You're the expert here, and I am simply a visitor." Libby loved that during their last faculty meeting she and Patricia had ended up giving a spontaneous presentation on the Reggio Emilia approach. Libby lobbed out statistics about student-led learning, while Patricia filled the whiteboard with a drawing of a plant-filled classroom lined with windows. It was essentially a continuation of a conversation they had started the night before. It had begun as a diagnosis/if-I-ran-the-zoo prescription for their favorite student, a kindergartener, who asked questions like "How did mermaids evolve?" and whose parents believed in the educational properties of first-person shooter games.

"You know we'd love to have her up here? Right, Bibs?" Danny asked. He had both hands up now, an impromptu visor. "That we're cool with that?" He uncrossed his legs and scraped the mud from the bottom of his foot on the railing. Libby had the urge to tell him to rinse it with the hose, not to scrub his feet on the railing. But she knew this was the hat talking, so she kept her mouth shut.

"Not everyone, I bet."

But she wasn't just talking about Tom. She was glad Patricia hadn't come, that she could sit in the dirt and postpone her decision, put it out of her mind.

"The only thing Tom cares about up here is if the Whaler's working. Keep her out of that boat, and you won't have a problem."

Danny didn't quite understand. He was in a different world from Libby or Gwen or Tom. By the time he was in high school there was the internet and cell phones, gay kids out at school. Then again, the summer he graduated, their father had died. Modern conveniences, technology, changing political climates—none of these could stop death. After their father's death, when Libby and Danny leaned against their mother and watched his ashes go into the sea, the ten years between them was nothing. The rest of the time, it was an ocean between them.

"Tom has issues with more than just the boat," she said. The house, her, lobsters, gays, Gwen, Medicare, mandated retirement. Now, with the offer, he had 3.1 million new opinions, new reasons to support his way of thinking. His politics and his life were all tangled together. She tried to keep things far neater.

Though maybe that worked better in theory. She sat next to a clump of marigolds, slowly digging around their roots. Here she was battling

Scarlet's floral demons. Maybe she should do the opposite, plant marigolds all over their land. Invite the demons in. But she kept pulling them up. Just like she kept coming to family dinners, to Christmases, to the Fourth of July weeks up here. But those lines were much easier to draw in the rest of her life.

Libby wasn't out at the school where she worked. The distance between her life with women and the life everyone assumed she had was vast and hazy, a mountainous region enveloped in low clouds. Setting up her classroom in the mornings, she thought, *I'm sure there are men out there that I could find attractive; I just haven't met them yet.*

Patricia and Libby were careful at school. They would never leave together, never arrive together. Having met Patricia at work, having no way to reliably separate her two sides, gave Libby headaches, which often left her nauseated in the ladies' room after breakfast. She laughed to think that, if she slept with men, she would've thought she was pregnant.

Patricia was out at work. Unlike Libby, she saw no reason to hide. Being an administrator, rather than a teacher working with the kids, gave her a certain freedom. Patricia's sexual preference, then, was public knowledge, like her love of cold apples or strong black iced tea. Some people knew, some didn't. She never made any kind of announcement, and neither did she hide it. If the subject of spouses came up in conversation, if she needed to use a pronoun, then she did. There was no pause or pressure and no arousing curiosity or suspicion. She just was.

This ease infuriated Libby; Libby saw herself as less of a lesbian than Patricia, and therefore better able to fit into mainstream culture. So why was it Libby who found herself skulking around with secrets, unable to relax? Patricia would laugh and tell her that no one who loved to fuck the way Libby did was part of mainstream culture, except maybe men. Libby wondered if that wasn't an excellent reason to start sleeping with them. They, that great army of libido, liked sex the way she did, liked women the way she did. Common interests. This would've made her mother happy.

The hat had a spray of fake lilacs on it; this was unlike her mother. It must have been a gift. Libby liked them, though, the fake flowers. She took off the hat and tucked a few tiger lilies beside the plastic lilacs in the hatband. The hat was becoming hers now, she thought, the dirt smudge now darker on the right, instead of the left side of the brim. Her mother had been left-handed.

Suddenly she wanted to cry. To take her baby brother in her arms and cry into his long, unwashed hair. To tell him that she had fed him, put him down for naps as a baby. He knew this, she had told him before. She was sure he had grown up knowing that she, more than the others, took care of him. And here he was, like a salamander on a rock, gray on gray. He needed to be brought back from wherever he had been, wherever he left himself when he wasn't at school. There would be no watchband secrets with this one.

She didn't need a baby. The boy, the house, she raised them. Even at ten, she raised them. She didn't want to play house with Patricia. She knew how those games ended.

Though her parents were eventually happy together, she had the inexplicable feeling that living with someone, being married to them, was essentially a terrible mistake. She remembered her early childhood. Before Danny was born her parents were, as she now understood, simply living out the drama of a teenage relationship with an audience of their own making. Those scenes should've been set behind bleachers and in detention halls, the tears, the bitter fights, the overacted violence.

She understood them as ridiculous, in part, because of Gwen. Gwen had always, when their parents wept amid the ashes of broken china, made fun of them and whisked her away to a game or a secret place or some other protected zone. Gwen's catalog of hidden spots was inexhaustible, in part because their parents let them go, wanting only each other, only to bask in another perfectly tragic moment between themselves.

Libby did not want to live out her own Noël Coward play. She wanted what they had later, but since it seemed to take a new baby to achieve that, it was beyond her, a distant and dreamlike place, a place where you could breathe underwater. But hadn't she tried that once, breathing underwater? It hadn't worked.

She didn't want babies. She had her students, her fifteen little children who changed each year. With them she had all the attachment, she imagined, of a parent. But at the end of a day she could zip them into jackets, tie them into shoes, send them home to their parents, and have a deep, heavy, sloshing glass of wine. This was plenty of parenthood for her. She'd much rather have a dog. And so that was her plan, to have the lesbian fantasy of a wife who lived in the house just next door with the dog they shared, a Newfoundland, preferably, named Roscoe.

Danny stood up and stretched.

"Want a beer? It's four thirty." Meaning that it was a perfectly acceptable time for her to start drinking. Though when they were there, on vacation, really it was acceptable to drink anytime, as long as the drink was appropriate: Bloody Marys with breakfast, beers with lunch, beers as pre-cocktails, cocktails with hors d'oeuvres, wine with dinner, and port or whiskey after dinner. Not that you availed yourself of all these options, but the ingredients were on hand just in case.

"No, I'm gonna clean up for cocktails and have a real drink. Thanks, though."

He walked out of the sun and into the shadow of the porch roof, and from the open screened door he turned. "Nice hat," he called back. She knew he meant it.

PART III

SEVENTEEN

ANOTHER SUMMER

Their mother knows. She already knows, or thinks she does. Or she doesn't want to. What she knows is this: there is someone. But having never seen this someone or even evidence of them, it is an internal certainty. It is a certainty best dismissed, tossed out alongside the remnants of a broken wineglass, along with the spent mothballs. There is no purpose to it, to the speculation. When sweeping the stairs under the moose head, she pauses and sits on the landing, the dustpan hanging from her hand; she thinks of the broken glass, of the family trips of which he opted out. She thinks of their girls, too young, and the boy, maybe not.

She wonders what she must look like, this other woman who loves her husband. It's not jealousy but a morbid curiosity. She walks down the long dim back hall, the side door a hopeful bright spot at its end. Past Tom's room, the hallway smells of soil, camphor, the slick sharpness of kerosene, the metallic tang of oil on tools. This woman is her reflection or opposite. This woman is her in another space. The place where she didn't marry the first man she loved, preserving herself like an Egyptian queen in gauzy dressings. Their wedding night came and went, she entombed in crisp white sheets in an epic bed at the Ritz-Carlton, while he stayed at the bar. Neither of them knew where to begin; it took time to find the starting line. Having protected her virginity like a gem hidden in the center of a temple, having been told again and again of its value, her only value, it seemed strange just to toss it away.

The side screen door, only used for firewood trips and her own flinging of dust from a pan, creaks on hinges prickled with rust. She steps out into a patch of sun that seems to shine perpetually on that slim step.

The two of them didn't stay that way. He woke his queen, poured oil upon her forehead, and fed her grape leaves and thick liquor flecked with gold. And in the dingy top floor of a triple-decker they found, she thought, the appetite of gods, a divine devouring. Even here at this house, most especially here, with their first asleep alone in the nursery, they made the second on the front porch at sunset, made the wicker divan weep softly. An errant heel kicked a tumbler from the rail; it smashed on a rock that was covered at one end by lichen. She thinks of that other glass, shards found long ago, tossed along the edge of the wood at the side of the house. He doesn't drink wine.

Three days later she has come back early from a trip to the mainland for supplies. She managed to catch a ride on the mail boat. Ned, their postman, thought her too pathetic standing in the parking lot at the ferry depot in her dirt-smeared gardening hat, a flat of tomato seedlings wilting next to a deflated paper bag from the pharmacy. With her seedlings tucked carefully in the hold, they flew past the ferry, lumbering out to open ocean like a tired dog to the food dish. From there Remy met her at the landing and drove her back in his truck.

She pulls the flat from the bed of Remy's truck. She worries that the blazing-hot black ribs of the truck bed have cooked her little seedlings, which are looking sorrier than ever. He doesn't get out, simply holds a hand out the driver-side window before reversing up to the pump house and turning around in a chorus of thumps and scratching branches. She wonders how many decades must pass before he calls her Scarlet.

Neither of them mentioned the car parked up the road. A little thing, Japanese, that shouldn't even be allowed on a road like theirs, all hardscrabble and gullies. It is another wineglass, she thinks. The same, she hopes. She leaves the seedlings under the oak that dapples the meadow with its shadow and tosses her hat beside them. She wishes she were not a windblown mess. The sweat of a day on the mainland makes her shirt cling to her, her hair sticky with salt from the spray of the crossing; she had to sit on her hat to keep it from blowing away. Normally in this state she would drop everything on the back porch and walk through the house, leaving a trail of clothes, and head down to the dock naked, a treat for the lobstermen. Or this is something she did once, and she likes to think that is who she is, who she is when no one is home.

She yanks at the screen door, pulling down more than out to pry it loose from the frame, and calls into the house. The cool, dark wood absorbs her words. Shoes off, the wood soothes her, seems to suck the heat from her soles. She calls up the back stairs, then through the dining room and up the main stairs. No answer.

On the front porch she can hear music coming from the sloop out on its mooring. It comes small and bright across the water and up the rocks. She can almost make out the tune. No one is on deck, but she can see the open hatch of the cabin. The porch eases underfoot, rough compared to the smoothness of the planks inside. She carries her shoes in one hand, hooked on the ends of her fingers. She picks her way carefully down the path to avoid the pricking evergreens that send feelers along the ground, out into the empty sunshine and warm rocks. Down the ramp.

She stands on the float, and all the heat has rushed from her. Maybe because of the stronger breeze that makes it a few degrees cooler there, or maybe because of the hollow music that comes from her husband's boat and seems to pollute the empty sky. Or maybe it is the ominousness of high tide that has just turned. The water feels raw, like it could catch her in its current and send her away, slide her away. A kidnapping current, the shore shrinking away faster and faster. Then it is she and the dark rocks and the black sea, or just the sea, cold and willowy at its base.

The submerged ropes mooring the float beg her to follow them as they slant down through hazy sunshine. Through murk, their silken hair, soft cobwebs of brown algae, wave in a seduction, a lying reassurance that under the water is safe and warm. The wide, drifting fronds of seaweed, like six feet of freshly processed film, brown, transparent, slick, curled at the edges, reach out to pull her in. She ignores the siren call of kelp and lets out her own call. But there is no reply, the music too loud at its source.

Little Devil sits at the end of its line off the stern of the sloop. So she must take the big dinghy, beached upside down on the float. She pulls on her shoes, wanting traction, resistance, wanting in some small way to pull herself together. She rights the dinghy, holds it at the bow, and rocks it over. The hull knocks more than necessary against the decking of the float. She wants him to hear, have him come to the deck, express that he has been napping, soothed by the waves, that he will row to her. "Stay there, I'll come to you," she wants to hear him say. She doesn't want to catch, or see, anything. Still she pushes the dinghy to the edge of the float and slides it into the water. Holding the bow with both hands, the stern goes in first, dipping so close to the surface a bit of sea slips in.

She draws the boat parallel to the float with the bowline. She steps in the center with one foot and pushes off. She sits down fast to get out the oars before the breeze sends her back into the dock. She plugs in the oarlocks and draws the oars together across her lap. Once the oars are in the locks, she leans forward, dip, slice, pull. Smooth swirls and a glide out to the sailboat.

It takes eight strong pulls for her on a windless day on a weak tide. But today she goes slowly, watches the circinate fronds of each ripple. She even tilts the oars in, tucking the paddles inside the rail, allowing herself to drift, to feel the wind push the boat where it wants to go. The surface of the water feels elastic; it makes room for her but won't allow her to pass. She tests it with the tips of her fingers, then her whole hand. The cold of it makes her bones ache. Flexing her hand and then making a fist brings back the blood. She picks up the oars again, immerses them in the water. They cut the surface, back, down, through, up. *To be an oar, to have life and use, to be joined with the water and with a hand. To be both. It seems so hard to be both. To be mother and wife. To be tool and toy, to be bountiful and beautiful, to be expansive and inclusive. To cover the world and then to taste only a fraction of it.* She is sweating again. She wets her hand and rubs water on the back of her neck. Reaching the sloop, she ties the dinghy down and pulls herself up—hand, knee, foot, foot.

From where she stands now in the cockpit, she can see four bare legs in the berth below, sliding like oars together and apart. And then they stop. They must see her legs, her torn Keds, wet from the row in an unbailed boat, her slim cotton trousers, black with a purple bleach stain near the cuff. She will have to confront them in her gardening outfit. The legs spring apart, four become two.

A man, not her husband, bursts up through the open cabin door. His is a face she doesn't know, a square chin she's never seen. But she recognizes youth when she sees it, stripped naked on the deck of a boat she swabbed, reflected in all the bright work she's polished. He doesn't look at her, just moves past her in long-legged leaps, all tan skin and blond ringlets, ringlets everywhere. Everywhere. He pauses to hold a line, steps over the rail, and then dives off.

He swims for the dock in strong strokes. The man—boy, really—swims for the Japanese car up the road. She watches him; he glides like a boat through the water, no splash. Then he hauls himself out up onto the float, not bothering with the swimming ladder—hand, hand, foot, foot. He drips up the ramp. He looks even younger from this perspective too. She turns back to the boat. With his arms stretched wide on the back of the bench, her husband sits in the cockpit facing the house, watching too. She sits down beside him, and they watch the young man disappear into their house to leave wet footprints across their dining room floor. They sit there together like they are watching a sunset.

"He's a good swimmer," she says, her hands folded in her lap. Had it been a woman, she could've slapped him; there are a whole set of standard responses for that situation. But she doesn't know what to do with this. *Anger will come later,* she thinks, *echo out over the water, out of the screen doors and single-paned windows. It will turn and rage, a winter storm. The kind that moves beaches and pulls down seawalls. But not yet.*

"He's on the national team," her husband replies.

He brings his arms over his chest, so that even in the most innocent way he doesn't have one around her. He leans forward, elbows on knees. The music has stopped, and they hear the channel marker ringing, tipping slow on the wake of a motorboat. She puts her feet up on the opposite bench and stares now at the bleach stain on her pant leg: *How do you fix that?*

"The house looks nice from here," she says, though she isn't looking at it. The house and the kids should go to her, she thinks; both survived because of her. Food is bought and cooked because of her. Bellies filled, forms filled, checks written.

She has kept them all alive, but not herself, she is barely breathing. Her artwork is nothing but a block of unmolded clay drying out in their basement. She is arid, cracked, parched. They are sucking every last bit of moisture she has left. She thought she was drowning, but she sees now it is worse, slower, a long and brutal desiccation.

The anger builds in her, but the understanding that she isn't what he wants is stronger and brings up the tears she is sick of showing him. She is remembering how to do this, what should come next. But none of it is what she wants, only what she says, because she needs a script now, instructions, a booklet explaining how to assemble a family without a husband. The kids are at the quarry and will be back soon. She wants this settled before then. She can't stand when the kids leave their clothes in their duffel bags all summer. She can't stand waiting when a friend is late for lunch. She can't stand watching a sick animal die and has, as a farm girl, simply shot the thing dead. A mercy killing, but more for herself than the groundhog in a trap or the lamb who is slow to walk. The idea of recovery seems too dim, too slight a chance, too crushing a potential disappointment. So she will do what needs to be done.

"Stay for dinner tonight. We'll talk to the kids afterward, then in the morning you should go." This seems simple. Clean. Efficient.

"You don't want to talk about this." It is a statement, resigned, something he says to the water, to the house, not to her.

"I don't know what this means," he begins, but can't continue. The young man has been on the boat before. Many times. The other women are an effort to keep the young man away, to prove to them both that this is not the way of things. He has never brought him in the house. They are simply moored together on the edge of his life, where he wants them to stay.

He looks at her, and she at the house. He wishes he could put an arm around her. He wishes he could take it all back and have her be the one in the cabin. His love for her is as crushing as her disdain for him. He saw her once swim naked off the dock, when she thought she was alone. She was fire then. Since their littlest was born she has reverted to some frozen time before they settled into each other. They sleep without touching, a thin sheet spread over them like an altar cloth. He follows her gaze to the house. *It looks like a hymnal left out in the rain,* he thinks, *flaked and swollen.*

It is almost five, and she wants to start making dinner. She stands to leave. He watches her pull her dinghy alongside the boat and step in. She looks up at him, her face just over the edge of the deck, her chin suddenly knotted like a walnut and the tears coming. She pushes off. He calls after her, but she rows hard away from the sloop. He pulls in the *Little Devil*, untucking the oars and sliding them into the locks, pushes off, and he rows after her. The wind has died; the water is glassy in the evening calm. She stops rowing and turns around. He stops and lets his dinghy drift toward her. Two boats drift in the water, one after the other, like mated birds, together but separate.

"I want to stay," he says quietly. Oars in, he is at the mercy of the wind, but there is none.

"You're fucking men. You don't get to stay." This is much louder and, on the smooth water, flies clearly to the porch, where Tom stands, having beaten his sisters home by a good ten minutes. He watches his parents, two fools in boats, in what seems to be a slow-motion dinghy race, ending apparently in the demise of his family. Tom stands behind a pillar where he can see without being observed, and listens.

"One man," his father calls over the water.

"Of course, the All-American." Her husband loves her even more as she shambles about in the dinghy, kneeling at the stern, gesticulating, causing the boat to slap and slosh in the water. Lucky her oars have rubber stops; they hang unattended in the water, limp hands floating in a tub.

"The National," he says, correcting her. "Sit still. You'll end up headfirst in the drink. We've had one scare this summer; we don't need another."

"Jesus, Bob, I'm not a ten-year-old; I can swim."

Libby's accident had changed things for them briefly. Brought husband and wife together in a way they hadn't been since she was born. Their fear and their relief had injected the first week of that summer with romance. A profound appreciation ran through them both. Libby had survived, and they had too. The night after her accident they stayed up together on their small screened-in porch off their bedroom, drinking lemonade and discussing their impending middle age. Her feet rested in his lap, and he held on to her big toe as he talked. She laughed as he explained the correlation between his growing bald spot and his increasing belly. They talked about their first apartment. The neighbor who drove a bus and woke them up every morning at 3:45, so that most mornings at 3:50 they ended up making love. He told her he wanted to chew on her toes.

They came together on the blanketed floor of that porch as the stern lights blinked and the halyards clinked. But that was more than a month ago, and now they drift as they have for the last ten years. They drift, but he is always behind, always chasing her. Here at least she faces him; he's not sure when the last time she turned her face to him was. There was the night on the porch. She let him pull her to him. But she never draws him close, never comes to him of her own accord. She demands and she delegates, she gives him lists not looks. He waits for her to come to bed, and then she accuses him of sleeping on top of the covers, of not even joining her in their bed. But he would rather float above their bed, a cloud at the edge of her perpetual storm, than to be banished to the empty, clear sky. He would rather burn in the hearth of her rage than drown in the emptiness of life without her.

"We aren't telling the kids anything," he says. "I'll go, but we are not making any final decisions now. I'll go sailing. I'll leave for a few weeks, if that is what you want. But I will not end our marriage in one afternoon."

"I don't think it's just been this afternoon, Bob. I'm sure the All-American has been here before."

Tom feels sick, like when, during a recent driving lesson, he ran over the neighbor's cat. *Why do cats sleep under cars? Don't they know?* He stops watching them, and he sits down in a chair, but their words go on, floating in on the wind like so much pollen choking the gutters and covering the rocks with a yellow film. Disgust. Betrayal. Truth. Love. Why. I don't know. Germinate. Like briars around an ancient castle, trapping some in, keeping the rest out.

That is what their words are doing, growing weeds in his mind, blotting out his perfect day at the quarry where he ditched his sisters and made out with Gina Jo. She will come over tonight, and he will take her shirt off. He will see things he has never seen before. And he will rid his mind of all their words; he will spray them down and dig them up. He will put Gina Jo's face over every one of those weeds; he will feel her breasts pressed against him, not their spiny, furred leaves. He will lick her; he will put his tongue in her ear. He will gobble her up like a sundae, like a cigarette, like a nice strong drink.

Their father called the young man late last night, and now the two men stand beside his little Japanese car, just past the pump house and the bend in the road. The All-American is not easily convinced that it is over. Their father can only see the peaks of the roof, the chimneys. They stand there at five in the morning, the All-American in shorts and sandals, as usual. He always dresses for Florida even though they live in some misted Celtic hinterland, as if Hadrian's Wall stretched right out under the Atlantic, crossed the Northwest Passage, rolled boulders down glaciers until they petered out, just forgotten farm walls, cow paths snaking the coasts of New England. They stand in the ruts of the drive, ferns weeping at the edge of the road. The All-American has come to convince him that it is just beginning, to laugh at the ridiculousness of being discovered, like guilty teenagers bare-assed behind the bleachers. His curls jounce as he shakes his head.

"At least she knows now," the All-American says. "At least you can stop pretending."

"What was I pretending?" their father asks.

He knows his lies have extended to everyone, to this young man, only eight years older than his son. What lies has he fed this boy to keep him coming back aboard his boat? What lies has he told to keep him away? *Have I been pretending to love this boy? Have I been pretending to love my wife? Have I been pretending that I am a sailor and the sea is the keeper of all my secrets, of all my truest desires, and that no person can satisfy me like the high sun and a strong wind?*

He wonders why the young man isn't cold, his arms bare, the mist heavy in the skirts of the trees. Peeking through the foliage, the yellowed seaweed in the cove is a creeping jaundice. The seals have left; they sleep low by the spindle.

"You think you don't love me?" the All-American asks.

"I know I do. But I can't stay."

The cove is sick, the house is sick, mold a cancer in its walls. She cares more for the mold than for him. She skirts around him, turns from him as she would from a draft, pulls her sweater tighter. She forgets to leave a light on for him, so he stumbles up the stairs in the dark. She complains of the cold, and he adds a log to the fire, then she complains of the sparks. But she makes coffee in the morning even though she only drinks tea. Her nails are short and rimmed with black dirt. She makes things grow. She coaxes faces, bodies from clay, fields and flowers from paint and canvas. She makes things beautiful. She smells like sugar. He wants to bask in her, devour her, crawl inside her skin and sleep. He would drink her, eat her, inject her. But she leaves him shuddering, sick, sitting on the edge of the tub in the middle of the night wondering when she last called him by name. He is losing sleep, losing weight. She is heroin, and the young man, methadone. Monitored and controlled, the All-American doesn't make anyone sick, but calms nerves, settles stomachs. *My love for him is not a cancer or a cure,* he thinks; *it is a delay, a putting off the inevitable withdrawal.*

He encircles the young man's wrist with his thumb and forefinger. Usually the young man is all angles, his wrist a square of tendons and sinews that widen and weave up his arms, moving into the wide planes of his back. Their father loved to think how easily this young thing could overpower him. But here in the mist the All-American is so slim, a wiry rabbit, and he, the father, the husband, a lumbering bear. Or maybe he is just a man after all, a man who has taken this little rabbit into his hands to feel its fluttering heart, its whispered breath, and now the bones are too small, too brittle in his hands. He can't be gentle enough with any of them. Not with his wife, or with this boy. His love, his desire, is sprung and toothed and quick to snap. He has destroyed and devoured it all. There is nothing left for him on land. Maybe he is sick, loving too much, too many. Loving both of them, so none of them. Maybe he is the jaundice infecting the cove, the wet breath breeding mold in this house. He needs to be encased in fiberglass and sent singing down the Styx.

"Why don't you let me come with you?" says the All-American. "This can be just another cruise. Please, Bob."

He says this coming close, standing just inches from their father, from her husband. He can feel the heat come through the boy's thin T-shirt. With the All-American he can be just a man. He sinks into the space between them, lets his arms go around the young man's shoulders, lets his hands go to the back of his neck, the back of his head, his face. And for a moment they are at each other against the car. He wants to consume him, devour the All-American and keep him forever. He clutches at the young man's face, and they are frantic, their mouths and hands. They are desperate. And his sweater is up and off, and the young man's shorts are down, and then her husband is on his knees, worshiping the All-American. *He is god of the water, and I am just a man on the sea.* And every satisfaction is a prayer, the young man's hand in his hair, a blessing, together, a gratitude. He has spent four years putting forth offerings, trying to keep this boy that he should lose. They have always had a tendency to pull and rip at each other, like lions, like children. *It is one of the All-American's best qualities,* he thinks. But all that play is gone, now. They finish and come apart, pulling their clothes back on. Their father stands up, lichen stuck to his sleeve. The young man tugs at a tuft of hair that curls above the neck of her husband's sweater.

"This is mine," the All-American says. He holds their father's hands in his as if reading his palms. "These are mine. You are mine."

He feels as if he is shrinking. Before this thin reed of a man he is receding, growing bent. It is barely light out, the sun shining only on the sky now, not yet touching the land, not yet shining over the rise or the blueberry bushes. Only the sea and the sky are lit, one reflecting the other.

He needs to leave before they wake up. He should've left last night. But he couldn't go without this, his forehead pressed into the dip of the young man's collarbone, their fingers laced together. Their father shakes with sobs. Can he ask the young man to come with him? No. But God, how can he leave him behind? He has never left him behind. Every trip, every cruise, they were together. Maybe it is the young man that makes the wind blow, and without him her husband will drift and flounder. But he wants her. He wants him because he can't have her. He wants her with him. He wants her to ask him to stay. He is happy to be loved, and destroyed to be loved, by the wrong person.

"I'm still hers," he says. "I want to be hers."

"Even if she doesn't want you? You're pathetic." The All-American goes to his trunk, the hatched back of his little red car, and takes out a small box. He dumps its contents onto the road, by their father's feet. Stones, gray and speckled, frosted nubs of sea glass, and one knotted bit of rope lie scattered in the grass of the track. He recognizes the lump of red glass, like a gnarled raw ruby found deep underground, given on their second trip in honor of their first time. There was a stone, black and polished, from their sail to Brimstone. They had talked about sailing away, down the coast, to the Vineyard, Provincetown, farther to Fire Island, where they could be just a bear and his cub. But they always stayed close to shore, close to their summer islands. They always came home again. The All-American stands with the empty box in his hands. Their last four summers now mixing into the gravel of the road.

"This is your chance to get out, and you are too weak, too fucking cowardly to do it. You love your safety, Bob, you love your children, you love your 1950s sitcom life," says the All-American. "That's not the same as loving your wife."

Her husband is receding, like a tide leaving, exposing the sad collection of rocks at his feet, leaving crabs to scuttle for shade, for forgotten pools that grow too hot in the sun. But this tide keeps going, keeps leaving, out and out. And now boats are beached, tilting on their sides, and lobster pots snake their lines through the caked sand out to cages. Everything in him is emptying out: the house, the children, their love, his wife, her love, their twenty-four years of marriage, his dignity, this young man, his love, and the sweet relief of being with someone who wants to be with him.

Her husband grabs the young man by the shoulders, hugs him too hard, and says, "I'm weak. I'm a coward. I've brought us here. I've ruined things for all of us. I'm so sorry."

He cries into that thin T-shirt. He cries into those ringlets. He says his name over and over. Jeremy. The young man smells of deodorant and chlorine. *I will never swim in a pool again,* her husband thinks.

"How can I let you go?" their father asks.

"You're the one going," says the All-American. The young man's nose is red, and red flecks have appeared around his eyes too. Their father picks up the sea glass and puts it in the young man's hand.

"You're right. I'm going." He says this knowing there is nowhere for him to stay. Their father takes a deep breath; this is the last time he will have to pull himself together for anyone. Soon he will be able to let it all unravel.

"Time and tide, and all that." He tries to look bright, to look ready, but he feels cracked, worn. Again, he is a liar.

The All-American gets into his car; he reaches out the open window and pulls at the hem of their father's sweater.

"You are making a mistake," he says. "I won't be alone for long."

He imagines the young man swimming with a school of porpoises; the alternative is too much for him to even consider. The car throws up dust as it backs up the driveway. He hopes it can't be seen from the house.

Their father is drowning in the dust, in the air, in the sunrise that is coming up too fast now. She will be up soon to make coffee. He will have to sneak around the side of the house to go down to the dock, to get back on the boat, to find the sea that is disappearing. He will sail away. He will let this tide go out, and her love go out, though maybe he never had it to begin with. This thought makes him wretch, doubles him over, spitting into the ferns. He wants to walk into the kitchen; he wants her to see him, to stop him, to tell him. But then he'd have to say why he is still here, why he was out in the drive, and then she wouldn't say anything he wants to hear. He knows that once he is out on the boat, out past the thoroughfare and into Penobscot Bay, then he will let the weight of what is gone return, and what is now too exposed and dried up will be destroyed in the churning flood. There is a tsunami coming. He will go aboard his boat and drown.

EIGHTEEN

Tom

July 9

Tom had started the morning out on the south porch with everyone, drinking coffee and eating honey toast. First, the women went off to start their day, and then Danny, leaving Tom to finish his lukewarm coffee, squinting at the cove and thinking of how much he wanted sunglasses but refused to wear them. Sunglasses, he felt, on anyone over thirty were the first signs of a midlife crisis. From the small precarious base of sunglasses, he knew, a house of cards could be built that included sports cars, affairs with younger women, and, worst of all, nostalgia for one's youth. Youth, he was sure, had been horrible for everyone and just seemed wonderful in hindsight. He figured many middle-aged people, in the face of sagging skin and stamina, longed for seventeen. He did not.

The smell of raspberry bushes growing around the south porch, with their serrated leaves and bristled stems, was strong at high tide when the smell of the ocean drowned itself. The lichen, too, was strong now. It grew not just on the rocks but on the tree trunks and tangled in the branches of a fallen pine, clogging the fine mesh of its limbs. With the tide high the seaweed, light brown, plumed on the surface of the water. It was windless, the fog having just burned off. So the seaweed rose and fell on the glassy surface like the gentle sleeping breath of the sea, still calm in the late-morning sun. But all that softness hid the rocks below. There was menace in those plumes, given what they were anchored to. They were scattered, an archipelago. As you glided over them in a small craft, the waving forests of corpuscled weed looked softer, strangely less wet when underwater, more graceful and serene. The sharp points of their rock base could be much deeper or just below their fronds. In the silly look of seaweed, all bumps and shaggy locks, Tom saw the shadow of death at sea, broken hulls and misjudged dives and dark storms and misread charts. The seaweed didn't soften the sharp edge of death among the rocks, but hid it.

He followed the sun to the front porch. From here, facing the water, the fog had gone completely and the Camden hills showed blue over the treetops of Crabtree Point.

The pines here have started to die, he thought, *reached the end of their life span.* It must have begun a year or two ago, but this summer suddenly the trees that framed their view from the porch had gone dry and rust colored, listing precariously to one side. Even the low shrubs along the path had begun to lose parts of themselves, large regions gray and dead, overtaken by lichen. Things had been changing. Even the mussels seemed to be disappearing. Once his mother could spend hours in the rocks of the boathouse beach pulling up their dinner, and now, not a mussel remained there. They still clung to the large boulders just down from the house, but less each year.

He could see the ferry in at the landing, a hulk next to all the sailboats and lobster boats moored in close to town: *Dorothy Gail, Ladies First, You Bet Cha, Reel Life, Doctors Orders, A Parent Lee Knot II, Jolly Roger, Miss B. Haven, Santa Marine,* he never understood why naming a boat was an opportunity for bad puns, slogans, testaments of love. Like permanent bumper stickers. Even his own father, a lawyer, had felt it necessary to name his first boat the *Misdemeanor*. Tom preferred simple names that connected with life on the water, *Osprey, Leeward, St. Ann*.

The *Native Son* just motored past and slowed up, resetting traps. Hook, pull, check, bait, back. The stern man couldn't have been more than about eight, just a day out with his dad, what a different life. Tom couldn't imagine spending time with Buster at his office, much less in the confines of a working lobster boat. He tried to get his son interested in boats, taught him to sail early, but seasickness won out over father-son bonding. And Kerry, he'd felt awkward with her ever since she turned eleven; knowing that she was no longer a gender-neutral child, that she was entering a world of femininity. It made him nervous. As if she already understood her sex in a way that he would never fathom. He did what he thought little girls might like to do with their fathers, took her to tea at the Four Seasons, bought her dresses of all types—sailor, flapper, sun, and party—he gave her an assortment of beads and yarn, thinking that while he did not know what to do with these things, she would.

Tom couldn't remember what his father did with his sisters. He'd been too busy rushing out of the house himself to notice. And even if he had he would've done the opposite, striving to be the opposite of his own father. He promised his children honesty and assumed the rest would come. But the rhythm of parenthood was in constant flux; just as he understood and adjusted, things would change. "Ride the wave," Melissa would say, sounding disturbingly like Gwen. No, he was relieved that the kids had chosen to stay home this week, to leave this place to the adults. He didn't want the pressure of trying to make them happy too; to understand their moods and needs too. Melissa was enough, too much. Hot from the sun, Tom decided to head down to the float to consider the water. He, in the last few summers, had become less willing to swim.

On the float he found Melissa, Libby, and Danny. Melissa and Libby had gone down with intentions of swimming. Danny had given up the porch with the intention of going for a row. Tom found that all their good intentions had been submerged under the high tide. Libby and Melissa lay on small bath towels facing each other on one corner of the float. Libby, in a black one-piece that she had been wearing for the last ten years, lay facedown, a straw hat over her head. Melissa lay face up, arms stretched out wide beside her. She wore a small bikini he had not seen before, purple. There on the hot, gray planks against her baby-pink towel, she seemed to be drawing the light to her. She looked thin and young, and Tom thought in that moment she was strangely unchanged physically by the two children and fifteen years. Danny lay on a large pile of life jackets in the bottom of the *Little Devil*, which floated away from the dock, its bowline tied to a ring on the float. He had one leg hung over the side, and with each lazy wave his limp heel was kissed by the water and then released. Gwen had apparently gone to take a nap. She was napping a great deal this trip. He assumed she was living too hard at home.

Tom stood on the end of the ramp and thought how young they all looked. How old he felt. How Melissa's breasts curved lasciviously out from her rib cage. He wanted to lick them, wanted the rest of the family to disappear. *Should've come here alone,* he thought, *just the two of us. That hot day, skinny-dipping, how long ago was that?* He wanted to fuck her there on the hot planks, get splinters in his knees, the heels of his hands. His stomach turned, ashamed to want her here with his family draped all around. Ashamed that he couldn't control those feelings. Scared at what could be behind them. He wanted to fuck her in broad daylight in a public place. He wanted to tie her up. He wanted to feel her thumbs press against his windpipe, to feel things go black. He wanted to turn her over and find a new place to fuck her. And these thoughts as he looked at her body, barely covered, made him burn with the heat that runs up the back of the neck before vomiting.

She had let him tie her up once, on the guest bed with the pine-apple posts. He wouldn't do it in their own bed. He had never come so hard. And for days afterward he didn't want to look at her. She had defiled them both by letting it happen. Really, it had been her idea, a game, an experiment, like she was just testing a new recipe or attending a costume party. She wanted to do it again, and he had explained that he hadn't liked it. She had laughed at first, had thought he was kidding.

He wasn't going to let himself like it. Because if he did, if he tied her up and fucked her ass and devoured her body, forced her to do all the things he wanted, she would see what he truly was. Or what he truly was, something even worse, something that he could not even imagine, would find its way to the surface. Because there could be some even more perverted longing inside him. He knew what happened when these boxes were opened. He knew if he stayed, eventually she would find out. She would force open the lid with all her good intentions, the writhing contents would pour forth, and she would leave disgusted.

He had to leave her before that happened. If only she'd let him alone, let it go. His predilection might not be his father's, but he was sure there could be much worse, that really it was all the same in the end. He would not find out, but he knew all the same. Melissa said she was always up for anything. He knew that was simply a saying, a phrase that, if tested, she would regret ever uttering. So he would love his wife as he should, face to face in their own bed, no rope, no throat, no covenant broken. Soon he wouldn't even be doing that. God, he wished she'd cover up.

He pulled off his T-shirt, with an uncertain impulse to give it to her, but instead let it drop to the decking. He felt the nausea rise, felt almost faint from it. He stepped down from the edge of the ramp, walked to her side where she lay at the edge of the float, and dove over her into the water. He went down deep to where the water felt heavy and sharp, so cold he felt his body seize for a moment, then he turned up and pulled strong for the surface. The feeling that his air might give out before he broke the surface made him swim fast, fighting the cold. Sputtering and thrashing he stroked for the float and hoisted himself up, not willing to swim the long way around to the ladder.

Danny gave him a cheer. "Takes balls to jump into that shit."

Libby peeked out from under her hat as if to verify that he'd actually done it and not just thrown a rock into the water. But Melissa sat all the way up, having to move quickly out of his dripping, panting way.

"You alright?" she asked.

"Just hot. Water's nice, you should go in." She looked skeptical and, pressing into her feet and one hand, like a crab, lifted herself from the float, pulled her towel out from underneath her, and handed it to him. He scrubbed his back and head vigorously and then sat down beside her with it draped over his shoulders. They looked out toward town. Libby flipped over. Danny adjusted a life jacket behind his head.

"That's new," Tom said, nodding at Melissa's suit.

"You like it?" she said, smiling, pulling at a strap.

"Aren't you a little old for a bikini?"

A thumb still strung under her shoulder strap, her smile gone, she stared at him. Then she stood, turned her back on the town and the water, lifted the towel from his shoulders, and walked up the ramp toward the house.

Danny shaded his eyes with his hand. "Dude, you will never get laid with comments like that."

"I don't think getting laid is your area of expertise, Dan," Tom replied.

Danny leaned out over the rim of his boat and with a sweeping arm showered the edge of the float with water, with Libby bearing the brunt of the splash. Libby sat up quick as if the water burned her, her hat falling into her lap.

"Holy!—Danny, what is your problem?" Libby smoothed the drops from her legs and arms.

"Sorry, Bibs. Was aiming for Tom."

Danny's such a child, Tom thought, *still reverting to violence.*

"Yeah, well, I'd be careful who you catch in the crossfire; that boat isn't the best cover." She pushed at the bowline with her foot, and the *Little Devil* immediately started rocking. But she was already losing interest, leaning back on her elbows, the soporific sun had too strong a hold on her.

Tom realized as the two of them settled back in that he shouldn't have said it. He didn't even know if Danny was sleeping with anyone; he just assumed not. He assumed that if Danny had actually done it that he would've told him. Not that Tom told Danny much of anything, but that was different. A man's marriage was private; a man's conquests were not.

White downy thunderheads rose soft on the horizon and gave the water a porcelain cast. The sea's native green lost beneath the reflection. Tom wanted to be this, to reflect the purity of the clouds, to let the green darkness within him stay sunken with stones and traps. He would let himself be wide, expansive, smooth water that had more to do with the sky than the sea, more to do with clouds than sailboats and rowboats and other things that grow barnacles on dark undersides of their hulls. Tom picked up his T-shirt where he had dropped it. It had grown hot in the sun. He put it back on, then pulled the Whaler in from the outhaul, hand over hand, untied the line from the soggy loop, stepped in, and pushed off. He'd go glide across that porcelain sky.

NINETEEN

ANOTHER SUMMER

Their mother takes the sheets off the bed. First the pillows shaken from their cases. She removes one blanket at a time, folds each carefully and lays them over the back of the rocking chair with the broken cane seat. She tugs the top sheet up and off, luffing like a sail. Clambering across the bed, she unhooks the banded corners of the fitted sheet, too well secured to come up with a simple yank. These sheets she rolls into a ball hand over hand, making a muff around her wrists. Then she lets it fall to the floor on top of the dead pillowcases. She lies down on her back on the bare mattress, striped ticking, like an engineer's hat. The hard buttons dig into her shoulder blades, sink into the flesh of her rear and the backs of her arms. She lies perpendicular to the bed, her feet hang off the edge. She opens her legs and arms, stretches and becomes an *X* in the middle of the bed. She closes them and becomes a line pointing toward town. She opens and closes, an *X* for here, a line for there.

Here, there.

Should she stay here and let the thing grow, like the ocean between this island and her husband's boat? Not a call from him, not a letter.

She wonders if the All-American is with him. She wonders if that would make a difference, if he came back. *Will he come back?*

There.

In the town there is the ferry. On the ferry is the long hour of islands on the horizon, of porpoises chasing the boat, of chance after chance to change her mind, to take the boat back, the one that crosses their path at the midway point. Off the ferry there is the taxi ride to the hospital, to the doctor who will tell her it is a miracle at her age, though she has never felt old before, just a year out of her thirties. *Is this when miracles start? Do I need them already?*

The doctor will ask her, "Is four really too many; with one about to go off to college, it's like a trade-in, a newer model." She hasn't changed a diaper in ten years. After their littlest's first day potty training she and her husband sat on the porch, watched the sun set down across the water, over the town, and toasted to no more diapers.

Here.

Maybe this will bring him back. Maybe it will keep him away.

There.

If I get rid of it, maybe he'll never forgive me. She brings her knees to her chest, wraps her arms around them. She wants to freeze time, make no decisions, hold everything as it is. Not just this thing inside her, but her oldest too, hold him home.

He stays out longer and longer. He comes home and ignores her. At night he sits at the kitchen table, eating bowl after bowl of cereal, keeps the car keys in his pocket, says he's going out again. She can't force him to stay, all of seventeen. But still too young.

She squeezes her legs tighter and rolls on her side. *It is inside me like this,* she thinks. She wonders if it can cry in there. *Can eyes that don't open squeeze out tears?* She will have to write him, explain. She never understood the ship-to-shore. *But where to send it?* She doesn't know which port, doesn't even know his course. *Has he told anyone? Is there someone to notice if his ship goes missing?*

They almost never made love on this bed, even when it was something they did, not on this bed. The ancient springs send a chorus of rusted squeaks through the house, just turning over seems to be an undoing, the bed giving a final death call. So they used to cover the floor with blankets, tell the curious children in the morning that they'd fallen asleep having a picnic.

They had many picnics in this room. They had picnics in every room. They had quick picnics and slow, savoring picnics, even one unfortunate picnic in college that had bugs. They were healthy eaters. Outdoorsmen. The last time on their little screened porch, on these blankets now hung so neatly on the back of the rocker. The blankets had been laid for him, too sticky in bed that hot night. Such a rarity here; hot nights are the domain of the city. Here nights wear pants and long sleeves. But that night, after their littlest was brought up from the floor of the cove where she had drifted for the briefest moment, just long enough to make them think she might not surface, they sat together on their porch. And then they lay together. It wasn't the purposeful smoothing of blankets onto the floor, a conscious decision, we do this now, this is the time. Instead it was a slow progression from chair to blanket, and then they drew together, dovetailing. First their feet, the soft curve of arches over each other, then calves, the tender back of a knee snug over a kneecap. Then hips, bellies, arms, chins, shoulders. And lips. The curve of his lower lip, like a drop of honey about to fall from his mouth. She bit it. And he her cheek, and they tore at each other. Clawed and tangled and tasted. A chair went over backward. He pulled her hair, and she took him into her with the hunger of a decade, even if it had only been six months. They chewed and licked and panted and cried. And then he had her face between his hands, and his lips on her face, cheeks, eyes, lips; he pressed his forehead against her neck, raised his head, looked her in the eyes.

"Where have you been?" he asked. She had no answer, no words, barely any breath, his weight so deliciously heavy on her. With bent legs and curled toes it ended, finishing with a great expansive clarity, the height and freshness of a sky after rain, wet air that is about to dry. *I am here.*

Suddenly she wishes not to wash the sheets, not to have taken them from the bed. She wishes she could sleep in them every night until he is home again. The last of his smell is in these sheets. How can she think of drifting off without that smell? Even through the camphor and sea air she can smell it. But it is too late. The sheets lie crumpled on the floor. They have been removed; again she has made a step out of habit or expectation that does not match what she truly wants. What she wants comes late, a realization too late, a missed turn on the highway. That was it, wasn't it, back there? *Don't go. I'm sorry.*

She gets up, not wanting to be here, or there. She gathers the linens in her arms and shoves an elbow in between the door and the jamb to unstick it, everything in this house sticks, squeaks. She can't get the mothball smell out of the mattresses, the pillows. She uses two cases to try to diffuse it. When they first bought the place she tried everything. Burning sage, incense, candles, a fire in every fireplace, cedar sachets, scented shelf paper. But smoke cleared; candles melted, leaving gleaming white drip castles on the lips of wine bottles and smooth ponds in the centers of tables; mice built nests in the cedar, their babies born in the warmth and tidiness of a pouch with an embroidered shell; shelf paper yellowed, curled, in the closets with windows, of which there are three, went white like a photogram. She wishes she had thought to put leaves on them, creating a permanent shadow. The smell remains. The mice remain.

During a heavy rain, the floor of the great room is pockmarked with buckets, washcloths wet at the bottom to muffle the drops, drippity dropping, the kids used to say. The whole roof needs replacing. She must have Remy find someone; if she tries they will give her the summer rate; Remy can get the local price. He is always the go-between, always this lobsterman vouching for them.

Remy will know where he has gone. A wave of relief sweeps over her. *Remy will watch his course, the weather, will have gassed up the boat, repaired the anchor, got the boys at the boat shop keeping an eye on things.* Remy will know her husband's next port.

She walks down the long balcony, looks out the bay window in the great room at the empty mooring. *Put into port, lie anchor soon, crave a haven with shops and other boats, need something, run low. A letter is coming.* Down a few steps, up a few steps to the hallway and the kids' rooms. She will write the letter while the clothes churn in the washer. She is about to nudge open Libby's bedroom door, strip her bed too, when she hears a noise. With the girls off at sailing and her oldest never home anymore, she is alone in the house. She hears it again, a rustling and squeaking, *this house,* she thinks. Hinges, floorboards, steps, bedsprings, sashes, faucets, chairs, all a symphony of squeaks, whines, groans. The faucets, those are the whines she hates the most. Late at night, early in the morning, she wants only the soft sound of running water. She drops the linens in the doorway and heads farther down the hall toward the sound. A window left open, a breeze kicking up, she guesses.

Gwen is in her room with a local. They tied up the boat down on the beach, only visible from the porch. She was supposed be teaching him sailing, a year younger than she is. Instead, she has brought him here in their small sailboat. Her mother must be having a nap, she says. She takes off her shirt. The local fumbles with the bra clasp; finally she turns around, so he can see what he is doing. It is unhooked, and she turns to face him. He leaves it there, hanging limply from her shoulders, and she takes it off. His shirt goes on the floor, his pants, her pants. She is faster than he is, and she lies naked in the bed. Gwen feels as if the world is now made entirely of afternoon sun and an ocean, not this cold thing, but one warm enough to stay immersed in. She is swimming. Kisses are strokes, short splashing, broad, full, deep, and propelling them ever forward.

The tempo varies, they slow, they stare; there in the afternoon light of her small tower of a room, a rookery, a beacon, the gray shingles of the walls, like mirrors, maybe it is she, and not the sun, that shines. Maybe her light is spreading out over the sea and bouncing back, maybe her fire will ignite the whole sky. The tempo speeds, mouths move to places they've never been. And she is ready, she has prepared. She produces a small, gleaming square from a shoebox beneath her bed; she hands it to him. But this breaks the rhythm, and he seems confused by it. Together they figure it out, rolling and unrolling. But then, they can't figure it out. What seemed so easy now is challenging, and there is a maze of movements and spaces that they can't navigate. He flags, fades, he doesn't want to stay, to keep trying. They have an hour, and it has only been twenty minutes.

He stands at the foot of the bed; he puts his briefs back on. He can't, they can't, she thinks; it isn't as easy as she has been expecting. And now he has his pants in his hand. She doesn't understand; *isn't this what boys want? This is what I want. Is this not what I should want?* she thinks. He has one leg in his pants, he knocks a book off the windowsill, he's about to say something. The door opens, her mother, in the spotlight of the sun stands and doesn't see, and then does.

"Dear God, close the door."

She does. Now there is nothing left to say. He knows how to sail, he says, he can get the boat back. She knew he had taken the lesson only to get close to her; now she's shown too much, and he has seen everything, and she has found out nothing about what is on the other side of afternoon sun and nakedness. And her mother, now she has seen, and knows what Gwen is trying to discover. For the first time in five weeks, she is glad her father has gone. She knows he is not just cruising, he is running, just like this local boy will be, blazing across the thoroughfare, leaning hard into the wind.

Her mother stands on the other side of the closed door with her hand still on the knob. Their Gwen is fifteen, and she has learned what beds are for; she is ruined now, gone too, like her brother. She has lost them both. Never again will she be the one they love most. At least she has her littlest for a few more years, before this shadow falls on her too.

She drops her hand abruptly from the knob, not wanting to run into the boy as he leaves. She hurries down the back stairs, forgets the sheets in a knot on the hallway floor. She goes to the kitchen first, but then decides he will come through here. Then she nips quick through the china closet and dining room, *must avoid him if he has the nerve to come down the main stairs.* She runs into the rug room and sits in the chair by the fire, the one spot that can't been seen from the dining room or the front door, in case he leaves by boat. *Had there been a boat at the dock?* She hears the back door slam; *he must have biked, or God, driven, what if he drives?*

Her husband would've taken the boy by the scruff of the neck, down to the Whaler; "Men can only really talk in boats," he used to say. Now she knows what that means. She feels sick. Sick at too many things, and she laughs at what her husband would say to this boy who has taken something from their daughter.

"Well, now you have to marry her." A straight face, just to see how long the poor kid could take it, to watch him grip the edges of the boat, looking for a way out, for some alternative. Then he'd make the boy scrub barnacles off the rocks in front of the house, and if the boy asked why, her husband would say, "Snails too," and in answer to the boy's questioning look her husband would respond, "Keep going and you'll be musseling these rocks." At lowest tide the lower edges of the rocks shine blue and black, sharp as ravens' wings. Often she has stood precariously on those rocks in rubber boots, shorts, and a bra, with a cultivator and leather gloves. She'd pull and toss, pull and toss. Off the rock and into the bucket. Her husband would've made a good dinner off that boy's big mouth, if he were here. If she hadn't run away from the boy. If she hadn't chased away the man.

Gwen, clothed, comes downstairs ready to face her mother, or at least knowing it can't be avoided. Gwen looks out the front door first to the wide-open porch, its sun and shadow. She isn't there, or in the kitchen. She has to, of all things, call her name, "Mom." Her mother sits in the rug room. Gwen sits down in a wicker chair, *so much wicker in one house,* she thinks, as it creaks under her. Her mother looks into the cold ashes of the fireplace. And Gwen looks at the oar hung above the mantel. It is small, three feet at most. She often wonders what it was for, *a canoe? Maybe a toy, do they make toy oars?* Her mother sighs. She can't just say, all her yelling with their father, and she can't just say. Always sighs. *This is why he leaves, always disappointment and no chance of redemption.* Gwen refuses to be the first to speak. She will not apologize, no matter how many sighs make her feel queasy and dirty and wrong.

"You'll need to see a doctor." This is what her mother says. This is where she begins. Practical. Gwen is not sure that this is better than yelling, than questions, than outrage. *Is this what she expects of me? Did she already know?*

"You'll need to have tests," she continues, "begin a prescription, and you should ask the boy, I'm afraid I don't know his name, for any history or pertinent information."

Is this desire? Is this what my mother thinks sex is? A questionnaire, a form to be filled out in a waiting room. What if it is? What if sex is boys backing out of rooms with their shirts in their hands? She needs to find the answer. She needs to find a source beyond her mother, whose hands tremble in her lap, who, in these last few weeks, attacks the ringing phone only to be disappointed. What will the local boy tell his friends? What can she tell hers? There is nothing, and so they must try again. There must be more to this thing. Her mother continues: Pill. Blood test. Pap smear. Contraception. Conception. Infection. Medication. Infatuation. Graduation. How soon can she see him again? Tomorrow? Can they try again tomorrow?

Their father returned two days ago, their mother's letter in his hand like a plane ticket, a boarding pass. And they were sent to the Shaws' for the weekend. Kicked out of their own home, they felt resentful and confused. Libby, only ten now, will not be the youngest much longer. They have gathered, and this is what will come. Their parents sit together at the same end of the dinner table, the end closer to the front door and the large window that looks onto the porch. The sun is setting, pouring its light over the steps and the porch, through the picture window with its arched pane, lighting up the backs of their parents' heads, making their ears glow red. Their children, ten, fifteen, and seventeen, squirm and squint, all orange and pink. The thick oak table shines black with a century of elbows. Libby can't sit still; she is too excited to have her father home again. She wants to jump up and run a lap around the table and stand between the two of them, so close, and hold them both. She sits up tall and reaches her arms out along the wooden tabletop, the table's edge pressing into her armpits. Her father reaches for her hand and squeezes it. She squeezes back. She moves her hand, wraps her fingers around his wrist. She sits up from her seat, leans over the table, and kisses the top of her father's hand. She will kiss it better. He pats the top of her head, pulls his shirt cuff down.

Gwen sits next to her and Tom across from them. The two of them sit back and low; Tom has one knee up on the table, pushing his chair back, tipping, balancing on two legs. Libby knows it is things like this that made her father leave, his tipping chair. She knows that Tom has been out of the house most days, and most nights that their father's going seems to be because of that, that and a neighbor's dead cat. Of this last part she is sure. She saw the ruptured thing before her father wrapped it in a towel, before he shooed her back to the house. She saw Tom stand by the side of the driveway and cry. She had never seen him cry before. And her father had a look she didn't understand, and then two months later he was gone.

Sit up straight, she thinks, she begs him. *Don't chase our father away again. Don't put the dessert spoons where the soupspoons go.* She has been spending early mornings, when everyone is still asleep, sorting through the silverware, putting each piece of cutlery in its proper felt-lined drawer. She knows that her mother likes this order, and that Tom doesn't seem to notice, and then her mother yells at her father, though it is Tom putting the flatware away. He is always doing things his own way, not the way of the house. Her parents cannot bear more mistakes, she thinks, or accidents or carelessness. She fans out her fingers wide, like she is holding the table up with the power of her little knuckles. *My hands work hard, my hands do good, my fingers have picked wax from this table, this whole spot is clear of it, though still a bit sticky,* she thinks. She will ask her mother how to get rid of the stickiness.

They begin.

"We wanted to talk to you all together, to get a few things out in the open."

Here Tom's chair hits the floor with a thud. *He will ruin this if he is not careful,* thinks Libby.

"While I was away," her father says, "your mother and I had a chance to think about things. And we've talked, and we want things to change."

Here the word "divorce" flashes through her mind like headlights over her bedroom ceiling in the winter, and then it is gone.

"No more fighting," they say. "No more crying. We've cried enough," they say. "We will talk with someone."

Here Tom leans his chair back again. *Doesn't he want them to stop fighting? Isn't he glad their father has come home?*

Then they change, then they look like they have a surprise, like there is cake in the kitchen, like they are going to take them on a trip. Her parents hold hands and look at each other.

A baby. There will be a new baby. It is growing, curling, a fiddlehead inside their mother's womb. Now the older two sit up and forward.

"You're too old!" Incredulous, outraged.

"We're not changing diapers."

"You could've asked."

"We weren't aware we needed permission," says their father.

"You don't own this family," says Tom.

"I'll feed it," says Libby. "I'll burp it and babysit and give it my favorite green baby quilt." Though she regrets this offer immediately, she knows the impulse is right. The other two are full of sarcasm that she is just beginning to understand.

"Just what this family needs," says Tom.

"Things will change," they promise.

"Yeah, right," says Gwen.

"We can't promise no more fights."

"No kidding. Shocker."

"But we can promise it will get better. We do not want to go back to where we've been."

To this Tom says nothing. He looks at his mother and shakes his head. Libby watches him, watches him refuse to look his father in the eye.

He will spend his time avoiding his father's eyes. His father will be confused and afraid to make things worse. Tom will see this in every pained attempt at conversation. But Tom will not back down; he will not be the one to make it easy. He will stoke his little fire of anger, keep it glowing soft under brush and through rain, through heavy hands on shoulders, and small victories. When the acceptance letters come, Tom will have a moment, forgetting the fire, and look at his father with a proud and happy face, and then remember, *stoke the fire, do not share joy with a liar.*

His mother is now like a child, like Libby, not strong enough to stand up for herself. She sits at the head of the table, a hand on the back of his father's neck; even her hands are dishonest. He can't respect her when she is happy to live a lie. Not just live it, but birth it, bring about a new life built entirely on sand. He thinks of this new baby, a monkey in a lab. He sees the monkey's long fingers cling with love to its mother, a metal armature wrapped in a blanket. Underneath nothing but emptiness and wire. He wonders how long he has to sit here, the car keys growing warm in his pocket.

Gwen stays at the table, Tom outside, the back door bouncing at his exit. They talk about names. Gwen pretends it will be fine. She understands now. She has been lost for the last six weeks, not knowing why he left, but thrilled to have him gone. She had assumed her father was sick of dodging plates, that he could no longer stand to watch the remnants of their wedding smashed to bits against the kick plates and wainscoting. But Gwen understands now; he was driven mad wanting to be close to their mother. She sees this in his face, as her mother's hand squeezes the back of his neck. He so much like a dog, afraid to be left behind. He has been searching for this.

Her mother would stand just out of reach and then accuse him of not trying. Gwen had heard that fight before, and then felt it herself in the last year. Her mother standing at the edge of rooms, in doorways and at the tops of steps. *Come down, come in,* Gwen would think. *I can't, I'm not wanted,* said her mother's figure on the other side of a door. There was no convincing her, and the distance remained.

It had been so easy before, to fall into her lap, to lay a head on her soft breast and breathe in the smell of sleep and home. And her mother would rub her back, tell her stories, listen and listen, to Gwen, yes, to her father, no. But then her lap became the cushion beside her, then the chair beside that, then the next room. Kisses left, and listening went dim and far away like a foghorn, a moment and already fading.

Gwen understands her father's leaving. Sees now that her mother will not tell him about the local boy. Her interest in Gwen has now officially faded away. It is this baby that has taken her attention from them, that has absorbed what little she had left, stored it away in her womb. This is the summer her mother, not her father, left her. She thinks about boarding school. She looks at her little sister, thinks better of it. Libby will need her back rubbed, she will need to have someone while their father has their mother and their mother has a baby.

They knew they could count on their littlest, and here she is living up so much to their expectations. "She will be the easy one," they said. Even as a baby, she the quiet one, so quiet forgotten one day at the school, asleep in her stroller. Arms full of coats and bags, ears full of tales of stone soup and multiplication, they were at the car before their mother realized, *my littlest.* And here their small girl is listing names, mostly the boys from her class.

"What about Daniel," says their middle child.

"Sounds like a prince." Their littlest. Gwen will come around, too, they see it; for Libby she will come around too. But Tom has carved himself a new life out there on the slim roads of the island. Out in the Whaler on the thoroughfare. They hope it's a boy, something to bring Tom back. But there may be nothing that can.

The sun is lower now, and the light has gone red. Their mother gives them fifteen minutes to run around, drink Shirley Temples on the steps and watch for seals before setting the table. The two girls go out, and the two adults are left alone. They will make dinner together. He will help more, she will let him. She will make room for him, she will call back all names she has called him, knowing that they were parts she cast him in, not ones he wanted. She will live up to every word in that letter. And asks that he show it to her so she can remember—*don't let me forget. Don't let us go back there. Reach for me; I will not retreat, not a slick fish against your searching hand. I am not sand or water; reach for me, I will stay, a shell, a stone. Put me in your pocket.*

PART IV

TWENTY

Danny

July 9

In an awkward arabesque—a hand on each side of the boat and one foot in it—Danny pushed off the float with the other foot. Then he quickly swiveled down onto the seat, took the package wrapped in a plastic bag out from under his shirt, and tucked it under his seat. He plugged in the oarlocks and oars and took his first strong pull. The movement of the stubborn, squat dinghy was a tug at first, resisting the water. But by the third pull the water unseamed, and they—boat and boy—slid through.

His back to the bow, Danny watched the float recede. The house became a house, not a mountain, not a ship, not even a grand pile like a giant stone Buddha forgotten in the jungle. It was vulnerable there on its point, so close to the rocks. How many more storms could it withstand? Danny felt the water just beneath his feet choose to allow his boat through. *Really,* he thought, *it is the ocean that owns the planet. Humans think they're in charge, in control, but really the ocean lets them play. "Poison me all you want. My vastness is beyond your stupid comprehension. I am a universe. I will keep your islands of garbage only to deposit them back on your little shores. The land is just a third of this surface. I am in all dimensions. And your little land is shrinking. I am coming."*

Danny could see the sea flexing up over beaches, over seawalls, over the undulating bricks of the Back Bay. It would put out the gas lamps, burble up through the city drains of Cambridge until Avon Hill was an island, Fresh Pond a bay, and here . . . All this gone like a town drowned by a reservoir, forced out of existence by others' needs. It is a ghost. Danny looked at the house and saw fish swimming through broken windows. He felt sick. He realized he had stopped rowing and was drifting in toward the boathouse beach. And the ocean said, *I will drown cities. I will send my hunters to your safest shores. I will take whatever I like because no amount of rock or sand can stop me. I am time. I am deadly.*

Here, at the boathouse beach? Too close to the house; they might hear. But he stayed there for a moment, twisting one oar and then the next to keep from drifting. He was so tired. That after-lunch haze mixing with an exhaustion he couldn't get away from. He was so tired he could sleep anywhere at any time. He'd nap, not just a midday resting of the eyes, but a deep, dreamed-filled sleep, full REM. His subconscious welcomed him home at any time, all he had to do was open the door. He could sleep forever right here in this boat.

There were no waves in this little cove. The water was just absorbed by the pebbles of the beach, not soft like the lapping of a lake. Here the slopes of granite turned back into the ground and left a small-pebbled shore that seemed to filter the water, not withstand it. The water came in quiet and ragged, *like breathing through your teeth.* Danny took a few breaths through his clenched teeth. He held the oars out of the water and looked. To him this little beach always seemed like the place where a great sea monster—a scaled, long-necked amphibious beast—would emerge to look for food for her young, or come ashore to lay her eggs in the gravel that, to her gigantic clawed feet, actually felt soft and yielding. It was a place where arctic mermaids with blue lips and key-lime skin would lie on the soft, slippery rocks pillowed by seaweed, arms spread like cormorants, creamy breasts turned to the sky. But he was tired of mythical breasts. He was tired of things mostly existing in his mind and on TV. Even when things were right in front of him, it was as if he watched it all on a screen. He tapped his heel against the package beneath his seat, checking to be sure it was still there.

He swept the oars in opposite directions to keep the boat steady. The water looked black. He held the ends of both oars with one hand and touched the water with the other. It was cold enough to make his hand ache. He left it in until his eyeballs started to hurt. As if the cold was rushing up through his blood to his brain. An ice cream headache. He used to like ice cream. But now all he could taste was the fat. Lipids. He couldn't eat with a word like "lipids" floating around in his mind. But this was new. He used to want ice cream all the time. Actually, he really only wanted one thing.

He remembered the three of them on that small beach: Danny, at fourteen, watching his parents mussel. Really his mother had mus-seled, and his father, as he put it himself, had supervised. His mother, wearing blue running shorts over a black bathing suit and green rubber boots, had stood in the mounds of seaweed-covered rocks. She parted the strands of seaweed to expose the rock, like hair on a giant head, pulling mussels from beneath, the same way she picked lice from his head when he was nine. His father was shirtless; his endless body hair glistened with sweat. Danny had always wondered how anyone could have so much hair not on their head. He had wondered when he might have chest hair and if his father looked this way at fourteen, a teenage yeti. His father's beard was a three days' growth, and he wore the same faded pair of madras swim trunks he'd worn every summer that Danny could remember. His father stood knee deep in the water, facing the sea, smoking his pipe, his back to Danny. They talked, his parents. They seemed always to be talking.

"Should we move the mooring into the cove, or is it better off the float?"

"Should we buy Gwen a new car or get Tom to pass his on to her? What about a trade-in?" Danny had thought about the stones under his feet.

His father turned from the water, wanting to show Danny how to build a cairn. The forest edge was rough and brambly, webbed by lichen in the low branches of the underbrush, looking decayed, brittle, flaky. Knitted with the desiccated trunks was soft, flat moss, a thin overlay with the tapered fingers of roots that surfaced, the ancient hands of the trees coming up, knuckles first, through the forest floor. The trees themselves seemed to pull at the earth, drawing the moss up their trunks where the trees pull up the hem of their skirts away from the damp. It was at the edge of this that they needed a cairn, his father had said, something to mark the trail.

"A trailhead must be marked, the place where the sea stops, where the highest tide cannot reach." His father said this in a low, booming voice that he projected to the back of some imaginary theater.

"Oh, God," said Danny, turning on a heel to go back to the water's edge. His father threw a small rock at his leg.

"We'll make a trail," he said. "This will be the start, a trail to the ridge and then out to the point."

Danny had liked this better. He needed more ways to travel, more places to go. And he liked watching his father collect the perfect stones.

"Like this," his father said, "round but a bit squashed. No, bigger."

They hunted together through the large stones at the high-tide mark, kicking aside tangled bunches of seaweed; the dry ones crunched, the wet ones squelched.

"How's this one?"

Danny and his father made a pile of stones to choose from, and his father began, explaining as he went. They each began a cairn about four feet apart. Danny could hear the pipe click in his father's teeth. The smoke swirled up into the pine boughs. The tobacco smelled of Sunday afternoons and naps on the couch, and what he imagined Morocco must smell like—ivory, vanilla, cloves, cardamom, ladies with veiled faces.

"Start with the largest," said his father, "then work your way up. The weight should keep them steady."

Danny's stones kept toppling to the ground in a tumble of clunks and taps and a quick jumping of toes. His father's tower grew higher, and Danny felt at once proud and defeated.

"Keep at it, my man. Hey," he whispered, "what should we do for your mother's birthday this year?"

"Either Constantinople or rafting down the Amazon," said Danny. They always ate lobster on her birthday; they celebrated it here every August. Just the three of them.

"I'll book the raft," said his father. "You bring the life jackets."

Danny had made a pile of rocks that looked nothing like the articulated corpuscles of his father's cairn.

"Your mother's really the master of this," he said. "You should get some direction from her."

"I'm a little busy," Scarlet said. They had forgotten how easily their voices traveled over water. There was strain in her voice as she yanked two handed on her cultivator.

"And I have one word for you," she continued. "Piranha."

"What would a vacation be without the local fauna," called his father.

"Bob Willoughby, biologist extraordinaire. I'm pretty sure your interest extends only to those species that can be boiled and eaten with butter," said Scarlet.

"I have unexplored depths, Mrs. Willoughby," said Bob. He stood, brushed his hands on his suit, and said, "Our work here is done. The trailhead of the mystical path is marked."

They will know where to begin, but not where to go. Danny left his father to admire his handiwork, and began to pitch stones into the cove, practicing his throw. He felt in this posture he looked more manly. He'd been practicing. His father made his way over to his mother and rested his hand on the small of her back as she bent over to pull up mussels.

"Time for a swim," said his father. He moved off the rocks. The slick seaweed and sharp barnacles never seemed to affect him. He walked like he was descending the stairs in the great room. Then into the water with his pipe still clenched firmly in his teeth, he began a smooth backstroke. The water is so cold, Danny couldn't understand how his father could bear it, how he could keep his legs moving under him, keep himself from settling on the floor of the cove forever. Swimming here feels like a fight. But not for Bob Willoughby.

Scarlet had brought her bucket and stood next to Danny and they watched his father swim out toward the mouth of the cove. A stone warm from the sun lay in his hand.

"When I met your dad he taught me how to really swim."

From out in the water came his father's voice, remarkably clear despite the distance. "Damn straight," he said. "And preferably without suits."

"Gross," said Danny. "Don't talk like that around me." But they always did.

His father emerged from the water, all that hair in jet rivulets down his chest and stomach, a great walrus of a father who lumbered from the sea. Danny had thought of his own pale thin chest under his T-shirt. *I need more sun,* he had thought, *and more testosterone.* He had imagined himself doing pushups and drinking egg yolks. None of which sounded appealing. His father set his pipe on a bed of seaweed and went back in to dunk himself under. Then he returned to shore, picked up his pipe, and said, "Ablutions and libations, in that order." And with that he grabbed the bucket full of mussels out of his wife's hand and headed toward the house. Danny was theirs, hers. She put her arms around him as they watched his father walk away through the woods, a towel draped over his shoulder, the bucket swinging heavy in his hand.

"How lucky I am to have a son like you," she said.

He wondered if she said this to Tom too.

"Oh, yeah?" He said. But he knew he was lucky too. He had suspected that to her he was different from the others. Sometimes that felt good. They looked out at the ocean together, at the town and at the whole universe that seemed to swim and sail past their little cove.

"I love you the way you love summer vacation," she had said.

"Thanks, I guess."

She had taken the stone from his hand and, whipping her arm, had hucked it far out to the center of the cove. She had a good arm. Had had.

The blister on his hand burned. He watched the boats chugging toward their moorings, all those little satellites, all those distant stars. He knew what she had meant. She was the sun and his father, the moon. And Danny had been caught between them, standing in their light, in the love they had for each other. At least they saw him. Even if it had just been a way to watch each other.

They were gone. Danny's chest hurt, his stomach clenched. His breath went short and shallow. He pulled the heavy plastic bag from under his seat and set it between his feet. They were gone, and his siblings were basically missing in action, sucked into the battles of their own lives. Here, they were always about to leave. There were good moments, the first day or two were usually good. Here their rooms were still theirs. But then they drifted. First to their own rooms and then to boats and then ferries and then back to their own houses. Back in Archer Avenue Scarlet had turned their rooms into studies, guest rooms. Tom's old room had become just a collection spot, an eddy in the stream of stuff that moved through the house. They had called it the Bird's Nest. And then the house wasn't even theirs anymore. Sold. Her little apartment was gone too. Now he had no room at all. One day this place would be taken and them with it. It was this thought that got Danny rowing the boat again. This and the package at his feet.

Danny sat in the *Little Devil*, hauling at the oars, letting the little bathtub-shaped boat follow the shoreline. He thought the squeak and clunk of the oars in their locks was saying, *Big black hole, big black hole.* The universe wasn't expanding, it was imploding; it was going to crush them all to death, one by one. It was already happening. Everything sounded far away. He could've taken the Whaler, but he had never felt comfortable in it. Driving boats belonged to his siblings. Just another way the world kept him young. He was incapable of learning all those knots. He rounded Zeke's Point. It was hard against the wind, still high, still early afternoon. So he stayed in close to the rocks. The plastic bag at his feet rustled in the wind. He found the cove he was looking for, long and thin with a small bridge at its far end. It was fringed at its apex with sea grass, the sharp kind that cuts your legs. There were wands of purple blooms deeper in the grass, where the land thickened and the sea was forced back. "I pine for lupine," his mother used to say. Danny scraped his blister along the edge of the boat, ashamed that he had ever felt embarrassed by her. Maybe they were irises. He couldn't tell. He was already forgetting.

He imagined her sitting in a creaking wicker chair among a diminutive forest of lupine. He wished there was a grave, a place to go, a place to plant lupine. Instead it was just the urn, his mother in a knickknack. The bridge, still in the distance, was flaking white, and here at the cove's mouth he was out of the wind. Still a good roll of wake from a passing boat could send the *Little Devil* dancing, send it over. He imagined this bathtub boat turtled, claw-and-ball feet turned toward the sky. This was the place. He would give himself a place.

It was just far enough. They rarely ever came up this way. Usually Tom preferred to head out the thoroughfare past town or deeper into the island, not toward open ocean.

He liked imagining his mother looking out toward him. And then he didn't. He hated imagining her face; he hated that he already struggled to see it in its entirety. He could remember her nose perfectly, the snaggle of an incisor, the mole on one ear making them looked pierced though they weren't. But he couldn't put those pieces together, except in dreams. There she was whole, and he hated that more. He hated waking up crying.

He had chosen this dinghy on purpose. He didn't want to taint the house with one more death. He drew the oars into the boat and took the oarlocks out. They hung like empty bells from their strings, clunking the hull. Danny picked up the plastic bag; from that came the package wrapped in newspaper and twine, like a packed-up piece of fish. He had thought about the discovery, the cleanup, about what would be the least traumatic for the others. He thought about the bathtub in his parents' bathroom. He figured if he did it when they were out on a walk, most of the blood would drain before they found him. But then the thought of another death in the house made him feel nauseous, and the *Little Devil*, another tublike thing, came to mind. And then he would be with them, sailing, swimming, rising, falling, rolling in waves and sun and sky. He would be a proton, no, a quark. So small, he would pass right out the other side of the black hole into a new compressed dimension. He would just be energy, raw and pure and immeasurable, hidden and everywhere.

Here in the cove, once done, the dinghy would inevitably dump him into the sea. Back to the sea and the lobsters and the ashes. His pockets were filled with rocks. Danny tightened his belt. Just one more bad thing in a boat. That was what his mother always said, "Bad news comes in boats." He knew his father had left the summer he was conceived. Sometimes he wondered if he wasn't some lobsterman's baby.

But he wasn't natural enough on the water to be a seaman. Plus, he looked like Tom, like Tom after a long illness that weakened his bones and thinned his hair. Maybe that was it, he was a shadow of Tom, never meant to be born, a spirit that should've flown over his parents, not stopped and taken root. He was never supposed to have been on a boat.

Danny was living on a boat the day he found out his father died. He had been on Outward Bound for weeks, living on a sailboat, just a few hours from their house. One night, when he had to hang his ass over the side in front of the sleeping heads of the other kids, he thought, *I am only three harbors away.* Danny felt a constant pull to steal the boat in the middle of the night and sail past seals and gulls right to his own dock. He knew the way. The next morning the "captain" took him to the bow, put a hand on his shoulder, and told him there would be a boat to motor him home. "Because of your father." Danny wondered if he had made it happen. *Careful what you wish for.*

The water moved with the wakes, the trees with the wind. Everything was reacting. The wind rubbed against the trees like a cat, nuzzling up branches and pressing leaves flat against each other. Danny watched the path of the wind wind through the branches. Perfect. And it would be gone soon, taken by fall, by cold and frost. Taken away by some fucking suit who saw investment potential and market growth. Real estate winter.

"Fuck him," Danny said. *Everything is going out, the tide can take us all to the East.* He just needed his place. His face went hot and felt full of pins and needles and his lips shook. Danny clapped his hands over his mouth. He could taste the salt on them. He pressed his mouth shut, his lips still. Holding his own face so tightly meant the air whistled fast in and out of his nose. He squeezed his eyes shut and opened them again. The periphery was beginning to grow darker, and Danny was sinking into his body. *If I pass out now it will all be ruined.* Slick with sweat, his hands slid into a cup over his mouth and nose. Slowing his breath helped bring the color back into the sky, the blue into the black. This was the place.

Danny started to untie the twine around the package in his lap. He picked at the knots with his fingernails. Danny wanted the quiet sea to enfold him too, swaddled in waves and seaweed. He didn't want to make a sound. He wanted it to be silent; the world would go to sleep with him. But sound travels over water. The knot came undone, and he turned the package over, letting the twine unwind. It was close to high tide, but he wasn't sure if it was going in or going out. Libby and Tom seemed to have an innate ability to know the tide's direction, like an Australian aborigine who can be taken blindfolded into the windowless basement of an office building and still tell you which direction is north. *I have no internal compass now.* Bob and Scarlet had been those forces, north and south, high and low; they were tides and oceans and stones and love. And he was just there, the water boy, the alternate. They were the answer to some bizarre family equation, and he was just the remainder. Even Tom and Gwen and Libby were integers, factors, participants.

And yet he felt like maybe he loved his parents more than his siblings did. They didn't seem to miss them. They seemed to just go on, and that made him hate them a little, and need them even more. *How do you go on?* He didn't want to think about Scarlet, or his dad, or his siblings. He wanted to stop thinking completely. He was drifting closer to the bridge, and he knew he had to do it before he got there. He needed a moment of privacy; he didn't want some summer kid in his father's speedboat to see him drop, see some red flash bright against the green trees. He wanted it nice and simple. Danny unfolded the paper from the tight bundle in his lap, each layer pulled back like gray petals around a great black seed.

He looked up at the sky; there were no clouds, and he wondered if God wanted a clear view. Then the dinghy, having turned slowly horizontal to the oncoming waves, rocked violently with the frothy wake of a speeding yacht, not a real one with a sail, but a double wide outfitted with a motor. Danny clutched at the sides of his dinghy; the package sprang from his lap and fell hard to the bottom of the boat; his hands sprang up, shielding his face.

"Having some trouble there?" Danny turned to see Remy in his boat pulling up the only lobster pot in the cove all of twenty feet away. "It helps if you use the oars."

Danny's hands were shaking. His spinal cord pulsed with heat. *How long has he been there?* Danny pushed the package back under his seat. *Did he see?*

"I was just enjoying the view. But thanks for the tip." Danny began fumbling with the oarlocks, half on purpose, wanting Remy to leave before he had to try to row.

"You wanna tow? I'm going your way."

"That's okay, I got the wind on my side." *Please leave. Please leave.*

"But you ain't got the tide."

"Really, I'm fine. Just hanging out." Locks of Danny's hair were pasted to his sweaty face. He tried not to make eye contact. He didn't want to look a guy like Remy in the eye right then. Remy probably had never cried.

"I suppose when you live in the city you get that peaked look. All that soot." Danny imagined that the last city Remy set foot in resembled Worcester during the industrial revolution, offal in the gutters, powdered manure in the air, palm oil in every man's hair. Maybe Remy was an immortal living in this place separate from time so no one suspected. Remy Everlasting. He didn't need to cry. He'd seen it all. Danny looked up at him, the heat in his spine receding and a powerful nausea taking its place.

"My mom really liked you," said Danny, his voice shaking.

Remy nodded. "She was a good one, that's for sure." Putting slowly, he pulled his boat alongside the dinghy.

"Here." Remy tossed a coil of towline, which unraveled in the air soft as a ribbon, but clattered into the bottom of the boat with a small splash. Danny tied the line to the cleat on the bow. His hands were still shaking as he looped the rope under itself and over again. The rocks in his pockets knocked together. He hoped Remy didn't notice.

"You set?" Remy looked over his shoulder from the wheel.

Danny nodded.

"You forgot your life jacket."

Danny shrugged.

"Me too." Remy gave him a wink and eased on the throttle. The dinghy's bow tilted up as they pulled faster out of the cove. The water in the hull sloshed toward the stern, but the package stayed at his feet. Danny breathed hard, felt his lunch come up fast, and he leaned over the side, letting his hot insides pour into the cold sea. He was glad Remy didn't turn around. He thought of Gwen throwing up in the ladies' room of the ferry depot on their way over. He thought of Libby in Scarlet's hat. He thought of Tom pushing him up the gangway in front of him, of throwing an arm across Gwen when they pulled over to the side of the road, of folding a sweater Melissa left in a ball. He rinsed his mouth with a handful of seawater. Now his escape pod had been jettisoned without him. Maybe there was no easy way out. He replaced the oarlocks and felt his stomach drop with each wave. *How do you keep going?*

Ten feet from their dock, Remy stalled in neutral, and Danny untied and threw back the line.

"Thanks for the tow."

"Yup." And off Remy went, without a look back, just a hand held high over his head.

Libby came down the gangway as Danny started to pull the boat out on the outhaul. *Why is everyone everywhere today?*

"Everything okay?" She nodded at Remy disappearing toward town.

"Oh, yeah. I ran into him and he offered me a tow." *Because I'm pathetic.*

"You feeling okay? You're sort of gray." She put her hand on his forehead. Danny rolled his eyes. He couldn't let her look too closely.

"I'm probably anemic. I'll go eat some raw beef right now!" He bounded up the gangway, a plastic bag heavy in his hand.

"Don't blame me if it turns out you have SARS or Lyme disease or mono," she shouted after him. Danny stopped on the porch and looked back. Libby was pulling the dinghy in, looking it over carefully.

TWENTY-ONE

ANOTHER SUMMER

Their mother is here alone, came up a few days ahead to open the house. Her husband will come tomorrow with Tom, Gwen, and Danny. But Libby comes home today; she is not so little now, twenty-five this year. She thought it would be just them for the night, her Libby, all to herself. But coming back toward the house in the small boat, there are three. Libby has brought a friend. Riley. Arriving on the late boat. The sun sinks enough to make them think of strong drinks in low glasses, cheese, legumes crystalled with salt.

She has been busy, the chairs are out, the cushions in place. The ice bucket is full, and she sends Libby to make drinks; their bags sit quiet in the dining room by the door, no rush, let us sit, quiet the errant hairs. Feel the sun, watch the lobstermen chug toward home and dinner.

"Like men in suits coming from the subway at 5:15," says the friend. Libby's mother imagines those men streaming toward lit doorways and set tables. Libby makes the drinks. Her mother sees the wedding ring on the friend's finger, asks about her husband, her own suit streaming home to an empty house.

"How is it that you're here and he's still home?"

She is charming, the friend, and makes a sweet response; she has slipped away, leaving him to fend for himself. This friend is easy in the wicker chair, not too comfortable, but not stiff. She is complimentary.

"This place"—she sighs, looking around her—"there are no words."

"Yes," Libby's mother says. She likes that this girl understands. "Words are too small for this place," her mother continues, "and they don't smell as good." This one will fit in fine, she thinks. She can always tell in the first few minutes. Can they be a guest, respectful, thoughtful, always volunteer to do the dishes, while they are as relaxed as they would be in their own home? This is what it means to fit in here, to carry your own weight and still appreciate this sharp point piercing the waterway, making only the houses on the other side of the thoroughfare visible.

"Too bad your husband couldn't join you."

"He wouldn't get this place; it would be all hassle, the car, the ferry, the boat." Libby's mother recognizes something. A distance she is familiar with.

"How long have you been married?"

"Two years."

Two years and no honeymoon shine left on her is a bad sign. Again the friend says that she has escaped from her life, slipped under its slim gate, and stolen off to watch lobstermen work.

The friend is conspiratorial, the friend wants to bond with her, wives that steal away. But Libby's mother only knows husbands that slink away, and even that was a long time ago. The girl is less charming every minute.

Libby comes with the drinks, with the ice tinkling soft in full glasses, and there she sees it. Her mother sees that thing that she once spent four years blind to, or closed her eyes upon. Libby hands her friend the glass, already frosted with the cool of the drink, the warmth of the sun. Her friend takes it with two hands, like they are passing a bird between them, holding it delicate and tight, wings in. The friend looks up into Libby's face, and there between them goes something, a reddening of the lips, a widening of the pupils, and for a moment the sun moves, shines from a space between the two of them, above the folded bird of a glass. This is the moment, if they were alone, when they would kiss.

Her mother sees this kiss floating between them with the sun and the glass, this undone kiss is the soft bird they pass between them. It is the thing that shines so glaring to her mother's eyes. It is a mirror reflecting the light back into her face. The glare makes her put down her own glass, stare intently at the cheese, cut a rough slice. She chews slowly and looks away from them over her shoulder, over the steps, the water, the other island, to the real sun, whose light, in comparison to theirs, is soft, full of honesty. It hides nothing. It will set, as promised. It will rise, as promised, over the eastern tip of their island. It will keep appointments, it will lay bare all, it leaves nothing in dark cabins or in the wet bottoms of unbailed boats or in black footprints on polished wood or unmentioned until it steps lightly from the ferry boat, lighter with the husband left at home.

The friend needs the bathroom, and Libby gives her directions, says her room is right next to the bathroom down the back hall. The friend takes her bag as well, will settle in and then be back to finish her drink. She goes smiling through the screened door, through the dining room and the china closet, toward the kitchen.

"She's great, isn't she? I knew you'd love her. What?"

Her mother looks as hard and gray as the pebbled beach by the boathouse, like she may be sick.

"Are you all right?"

"You should've asked, Lib."

"I just figured, what's one more person, one friend apiece, right?"

"She's not your friend."

With this Libby is brought up short. She doesn't understand. Hadn't she just seen, through the dining room window, her friend's charm radiating from her like heat, and her mother basking in it? But Libby has somehow let it be known, some little unconscious action has revealed something meant to be hidden.

"You should have told me." Her mother says it again, clearer this time. "She is not just your friend."

"No, not just a friend." Libby feels that she has been caught stealing from her mother's jewelry box, a string of illicit pearls curled in her hand. She cannot put them back.

"She can't stay. Tell her after dinner. We'll eat, and sit by the fire, and in the morning she will go. On the early boat. Simply tell her that there isn't enough room."

To Libby these words seem to echo through the empty house. Rooms will be filled tomorrow, when the others arrive, but still more will be empty, still half her bed will be empty. She had thought that her parents would love her friend so much, that after the first few days, she would tell them, and they would embrace the whole thing, hustle her friend up from the lonely back hall. "No couple should sleep in separate beds," they would say. She did not expect this. It is hard to keep back tears, to feel, in this moment, an adult.

"Are you sure?" she asks her mother, because she can't believe that she is sure.

"She needs to go home to her husband, and you need to stay here. I'm sure."

Libby sees. Her friend must go back to fucking men, and since there are no men for Libby to fuck at home, she must stay here, meet a nice lobsterman as her sister does every summer, every week; some weeks, every day. Better a slut than a dyke. She understands. Her mother's certainty has been tied tight around her for years, ribbons pulled painful in her hair, around her neck. Her certainty has sat beside them at dinners in this house, another summer boy. He goes to St. Paul's, Groton, Westminster, he plays lacrosse, crew, runs the paper, won a painting scholarship. This one will take what you have to give, what you have to lose.

The sun is low now, and her mother's hair is fire lit from the side, what is dark as earth and slick as rain, goes red with the light. And here her mother earns her name, in all her beauty and fire and cruelty. Scarlet upon the rocky shores; Scarlet burning bright as the sun dims. Scarlet is the destroyer of worlds with a hand bent delicate at the wrist, a tan line white where her watch has been. Those stolen pearls burn in Libby's hand, *they have hung beside the heart of a dragon,* she thinks, *and I have stolen them and they will burn my hand forever. There is no letting go, they cannot be put back.*

"We'll go to town," Libby says. "We'll sleep in the inn there. I will not have her stay the night."

I will not let her sleep in the house with a dragon, all curled and smoky upon her pile of gold. Greedy.

She wishes her dragon of a mother slept not on gold but on the dead pile of broken china, Royal Copenhagen, she had smashed at their father's feet. She had made some deal, once a beautiful princess asleep on the sharp stones of broken plates and the sad, closed faces of smashed teacups, she became a dragon to turn her bed to gold. To keep a man beside her. Libby can't believe she has never seen this before. For the last fifteen years of her life, she has not smelled this smoke. And now it forces her, her and her friend, out across the water, to the inn on the opposite shore. Libby heads into the house, to roll up her friend's sleeping bag, to put her books back into her duffel, to take her toothbrush from the edge of the sink. She will cough as they motor over the thoroughfare in the Whaler, a smoky scratch at the back of her throat.

TWENTY-TWO

Libby

July 10

After lunch the weather turned, and the fog rolled in thick; and now the sun was hidden, too tired to burn off the mist. "Soup" their father would've called it.

"The day had such a good start and now . . . ," said Melissa, coming into the rug room.

"Socked in," said Libby, motioning out the arched window.

Gwen and the boys were each napping. Fog inspired long naps. Libby sat on the chaise in the rug room, her legs crossed, a game of solitaire spread out before her, stacked and cascading, showing her efforts. She imagined playing at a casino, the dealer only letting her go through the deck three times. She was halfway through the second round; she must move slowly. Be deliberate.

Melissa flopped a pot holder on the coffee table and put a teapot on it. Steam slipped lazily from its spout. The table was half covered with a jigsaw puzzle Melissa had been working on since she arrived. Libby stayed focused on her cards. *It's here somewhere,* she thought, *the opening, the space, the place to lay the next card.*

"You want more?" Melissa pointed to Libby's empty mug.

"Sure, thanks."

Melissa poured and Libby set down the deck, decided to let the cards breathe for a moment, consider their next move. A plate of cookies sat next to the teapot, half of which Libby had already eaten. Melissa helped herself. They both stared out the window into the fog, the thoroughfare somewhere in it. Low foghorns bleated far away. *Even better than a train whistle,* thought Libby, *the sound of coming home.*

"Who's winning?" said Melissa. She tapped a cookie on the plate like she was ashing a cigarette.

Old habits, thought Libby. "I've decided that luck really isn't a lady," she said. "More like a fourteen-year-old boy. A distracted quick draw that is totally useless to me."

"I think that would make Frank Sinatra a pedophile," said Melissa.

"It's just a theory."

"I still can't get over that dinner on the Fourth." Melissa held her teacup close to her chest.

"Lobster can bring out the worst in people," said Libby, imagining Tom standing on a stack of cookbooks and espousing the slow-cook method. They both looked toward the view they couldn't see, ghost limbs of trees reaching black-sleeved out of the mist.

"You know that Tom doesn't mean to be insensitive or malicious."

Just controlling and condescending, thought Libby. "You're legally obligated to be on his side," she said as she shifted on the chaise, the wicker creaking.

"That's not entirely true. There are a lot of loopholes."

"You don't agree with him, do you?"

"It's not that simple anymore." Melissa sighed. She moved the cookie plate and tried to wedge a blue puzzle piece into an expanse of evening sky.

"It seemed like you were on our side. I thought you were as attached to this place as we are."

"I understand where you're both coming from, and if things were different, I would be behind you totally, but . . ."

"What's different?" *Why does that stupid offer seem to make everything different to Tom?* Libby wanted money to be what it was for her students, shiny coins best put to use when shoved up the nose or made of chocolate wrapped in foil.

"Bibs, I love you. I love this family. I love this place." Melissa turned the puzzle piece in her hand, spun the tiny bit of clear sky between her thumb and finger. "But giving up on it might be what has to be done."

"Why do I feel like a puppy you're about to abandon by the side of the road?"

"I just—I think Tom is trying to shield you all from what is going on with him, and in doing so he's coming off as totally insensitive. He doesn't want to give this place up, Bibs, but it's how he needs it to go." Melissa kept forcing the piece into different spots, wedging it and then having to torque it loose, a bad tooth. "Seven hundred thousand dollars would put both our kids through college with some left over. We need this money."

"Why on earth do you need it all of a sudden? Oh my God, you're not pregnant, are you?"

"God no—not possible."

"No?" Libby frowned. *That can't be good.*

"Tom and I are separating."

Melissa put her hand on Libby's, and Libby could feel the heat from her teacup still clinging to her fingers. Was this what her friends had all gone through as kids? Hearing these words from their parents, instead of siblings, hot hands on theirs, disorientation?

Funny that you can see something coming, thought Libby, *and it's still a shock when it arrives like a bus you've been waiting for, coming in too close to the curb, you have to step back suddenly, afraid it will clip you.*

"Are you sure?"

"He started the ball rolling, and the thing is, now I see I can't stop it. I tried for a long time. I still do sometimes, but now, I think too much time has gone by."

"Do you love him?" Libby wasn't even sure why she asked this. She had always assumed Melissa's love for Tom was unconditional, involuntary, like thirst or watching *It's a Wonderful Life* at Christmas. Something commanded by the autonomic nervous system, like blinking.

"The money, selling the house," Melissa said, shrugging her shoulders, "would cover the cost of the divorce. It would pay for us to become a two-household family. It would let us make a really smooth transition for the kids, for ourselves."

"Have you guys been to therapy? Is there someone else?" How could Tom want anyone but Melissa?

"There was someone, a while ago, but I ended it hoping that Tom would want to—that we could fix things, but now I can't pretend that Tom's ever going to give me what I need. I love him. But sometimes it's just not enough. I tried really hard." She began to cry now. "I didn't want this. Not any of it. I kept saying I'm not happy. I tried to get us into therapy. You can imagine how that went."

Of course there was someone else. Suddenly they, as a couple, made sense. Libby could see how Melissa had lasted so long held at arm's length. She had found company out there at the cold edge of Tom's fingertips. Libby stood up and took the two steps to Melissa's chair, hugged her hard. Melissa startled, then went limp in her arms.

"I cheated, I don't deserve a hug," said Melissa into Libby's shoulder.

"He knows, right? So I'll let Tom hate you for that one. When it comes to love, I'm not exactly rigid about things. I was with someone a long time ago," said Libby. "She was married. Sometimes things don't work. You want them to, and they just can't." She remembered two rings sitting on her bedside table. She remembered watching someone else's wife climb from her bed, put those rings back on. Libby had wanted to hide them, bury them in the dirt of her ficus tree, as if it were the rings that compelled her to leave each time, to stay gone longer, to never come back. *What if someone had told Riley it was okay to leave her husband?*

"Tom knows, but he doesn't seem to even really acknowledge it. It happened a year ago, and he acts like it never happened. Or that it has nothing to do with us. Or maybe that I don't. I've become a piece of furniture. He's obviously so angry, but sometimes it feels like he's been angry for years. And now I'm losing him, and you guys, and my entire life. We haven't even told the kids."

Libby moved back to the chaise so she could look her in the eyes. Melissa drew her knees up to her chest, rested her chin on them.

"He doesn't get to decide how this goes," said Libby. "You get to be in our lives, no matter what."

"I'm sorry. I shouldn't even be telling you. We decided not to tell anyone until the fall, but—I just don't want you to think that he's being adamant about the house for no reason. This is a piece of your family."

"You know it's okay to get divorced. It's okay to want to be happy," said Libby. Melissa sniffed and blew her nose on a cocktail napkin. She smiled.

"You could say the same thing about marriage."

"Well, I never really thought it would be an option for us, so—" Libby picked up a puzzle piece, black and speckled. It belonged to a building in the skyline.

"Sometimes it's better to let go than to hang on to the idea of something. My idea of my relationship will never be the reality. Maybe the idea of being single is what you need to let go of," said Melissa.

"I don't know." Libby slowly moved the piece over building after building in the half-assembled image. "I like being free."

"Lonely, empty freedom."

"How did this become about me? You're dumping my brother; this is about you."

"One, he's dumping me. Two, you are in a relationship that actually works, with someone you love. Just stop being such a chickenshit."

Sometimes courage isn't enough, thought Libby. *Sometimes you can take all the risks, and it still doesn't go the way you want.*

"Do you love the other guy?" she asked.

Here Melissa's chin knotted for a moment, she started to say something but stopped. Instead she nodded and shrugged. She began to sigh, but it caught in her chest.

"I love Tom more, but at a certain point it doesn't matter."

"That's so fucking depressing." Libby picked up the deck of cards and looked over her game, realizing she had played it as far as it could go. "Want to play Spit?"

"Is it too early to start drinking?"

"Never. You're on vacation, and your kids are at home. Go ask Gwen what she wants. She's reading in the great room. I bet you money she turns you down."

"Why? Is she on some cleanse?"

"I have a theory." Libby held up the deck fanned out and whispered from behind it. "She's been sleeping a lot, she hasn't been drinking, and she said something about honey being pasteurized." She holds the cards to her lips a moment. "I think she's pregnant."

"No. I was thinking her figure was looking a little more hourglass lately. I should've guessed. You think she'll keep it? I don't want to miss a Willoughby baby."

Melissa put her head in her hands and started crying all over again. Libby stood up and patted Melissa's shoulder, waiting for her breathing to slow, for the shudders to ebb out of her. She offered her a cookie. Poured more tea in her cup. Then went into the dining room to the sideboard, pulled out the whiskey, and returned to the rug room and the puzzle. She unscrewed the cap and poured a good swallow into Melissa's tea.

"A hot toddy cures all. Don't worry, Mel. We won't let you miss anything. You're stuck with us."

Melissa smiled weakly and took the mug from Libby's hands. Though Libby could see in her eyes Melissa didn't believe her. They both looked down at the puzzle, the San Francisco skyline at dusk, the only high-rises for a hundred miles.

TWENTY-THREE

ANOTHER OCTOBER

It is the packing up, the putting away that their mother has avoided, that has kept her here a month and a half past her usual departure. The smell of leaves is strong. The oaks in the meadow are yellow now, their leaves almost translucent, moist, reverting to the full, pulped look of spring, tender in their fading, in their falling. The grass has gone gold, and over it come the leaves that give it a skin, a surface that undulates like water. The water is golden now in the afternoons with the lower sun, and then it turns fast, going gray and finally black with the quickening darkness. Their mother has left it all, each pillow and mattress, each chair, all in their summer spots.

She is with him here; in the city he will be gone. He lingers here: his feet propped on the porch rail, his hands wrapped around the binoculars, his slapping feet with long toes that thump and shush along the great room floor as he chooses a spot for his afternoon nap. He was a cat always asleep in the sun.

He is in the water. Tom scattered him there. She told him to, to go alone in the sloop to the center of the thoroughfare and fling his father forth, to live in the atoms of the sea. To settle to the floor of the harbor and billow up when the lobsters pass, when the traps go up and come down. To twist against the rudders of the Johnnies during their races as they swing around the buoy, to shake with the ringing of the channel marker, to wash over the backs of seals and the pebbles of their own boathouse beach. He will have the best view of the jammers now, no need for the binoculars. And when the boats go too fast he can whip himself up into a storm or a fog, to slow the world to puttering motors and dropped sails, to the long bleats of foghorns, like birdcalls, *I am here, you are there.*

She made Tom do it. He didn't want to. She knew her boy hated his father. Her stomach turns when she thinks of that day, watching the All-American swim to shore, rowing back to the float, climbing out of that dinghy and up the path. Her throat closes when she remembers her husband—her ocean, her heart—say to her back, "I don't feel loved." She had heard him, but did nothing. She came up the steps, the wet footprints of the All-American still dark on the dry wood. And there was her Tom crumpled and small in the peacock chair. Her husband had stopped on the path, not yet in view of the porch, stunned by his own realization that maybe she didn't love him and so there was nothing to feel. She had put a finger to her lips, and took her son, silent, by the wrist, rough and fast around the corner to the south porch. They stood under a stone arch next to a broken lattice gate. She held him by both shoulders and looked up into his eyes. At seventeen he had grown three inches taller than she. He couldn't look at her; he flailed like a tree in a storm.

"Be still," she commanded. He went limp. "Look at me."

From his hanging head he looked through his eyebrows at his mother. She looked beautiful, her hair a thicket, her cheeks sunburned, her eyes bright.

"Your father."

He groaned. She would not let him go.

"He is the greatest man. Whatever he decides, whoever he turns out to be, his greatness is not diminished. Your good qualities are his; you hate him, you hate yourself. And whatever this is, I am just as responsible. I have made a hole in your father's life. He has responded badly, but who he is with is not the issue. Look at me. Not the issue."

And then she turned him loose like a dog desperate to be outside. He stepped off the porch into the meadow and huffed off toward the blueberries, his long legs preceding him.

And so Tom hated his father. Hated him for her. She knew her oldest had her best interests at heart. But as the baby grew inside her all she wanted was her husband; she no longer cared about the things he did and didn't do. She saw only how alone he must have been before their split, even in the house with her. How she had left him. She kept words and tenderness from him. She left him in empty rooms to read alone. She shunned his company, his heart. So he found someone who would stay. In the moment, the difference between the young man and his wife was cosmic. But no one better than the other. No, the truth was the young man was better then. Well, kinder. And she, she was lucky. She was not better for him, not for skin or flesh or satisfaction of genetic urges; he simply loved her more. He loved the All-American. She accepted that. But he told her once that the All-American was lightning, ephemeral and brilliantly blinding, and she was the sky, expansive and sheltering, without which there is nothing at all.

Tom couldn't understand this, the covenant that bound them. He saw only what pushed them apart, and then only the most literal aspects. Her husband had upturned a stone that lay upon his heart, and he would not be ashamed of what was beneath it. A son and a father share a bond that Tom saw broken, and he couldn't understand how a repair was possible, so he chose to believe it was a lie. Tom could not fathom that his father liked men. Let alone the fact that he could like his wife even more.

So she handed him the ashes and said, "Make your peace. There is no second chance." The rest of them watched from the top step of the porch. Tom put up the sails, but they hung slack on the windless sky. And so he motored out to the spot, the deep channel that ran the length of the thoroughfare. He gave them a wave, an arm stretched high and swung in arcs from one shoulder to the other. They waved back. *That's the spot; go ahead.*

They didn't speak. The sparrow called for *Sam Peabody Peabody Peabody*. They could see Tom on the deck of the boat, still as a perched bird. They must be speaking now. *To forgive, divine, little one.* And then an arc of gray mist swept up over him as both arms threw something into the sky. Gwen cheered, jumped to her feet, standing on the bottom step, and whooped and whistled with both fingers between her teeth. Libby and Danny sat on either side of their mother, hip to hip. They leaned in close, her bairns, now grown themselves. But still her children, still needing her. She squeezed their shoulders, and they leaned into her.

"A good send-off," she told them. "We done good."

Now, she is alone in the house, and the warmth of summer faded just a week after the children left. For hours every day she has been staring at the water. She heats up canned soup on the stove. Boils one lobster in the small stockpot for Sunday dinner. She melts butter. She paints the window frame on the south porch. She sits in the garden and pulls up marigolds. He hated them. She does all the little things he wanted to get to but never could.

Today she has to wear a hat and scarf while she drinks hot tea on the porch. Remy has told her that she must leave tomorrow. "The pipes," he warns. The float will be pulled out once she goes on the early ferry. She is not ready yet. She taps her wedding ring against the mug.

She thinks of selling. Once she leaves, coming back will feel like looking at a photograph, a hollow substitution for a memory that will blot out the real thing over time. She takes a few steps toward the door. Stands in the spot where he died. She wonders if his spirit could've been absorbed by the pine planks. Untreated, after all; that was his choice. Maybe he had planned it from the start. For them to turn gray, to show their age, to soak him in, in his final moments. She laughs and scrubs the decking with her rubber sole. It grates and splinters.

She moves to the steps and sits down where she watched her oldest pour her husband into the sea. She thinks of the All-American running up the path in front of her, taking these very steps two at a time. She wonders where he left his keys. She takes a slurping sip of her tea, wishes for ice cubes to cool it.

The tea's steam warms her cold nose. Soon she will have to start pulling cushions off chairs, and alone and tired she will have to drag the porch furniture into the house.

TWENTY-FOUR

Tom

July 11

They stood on the porch together, Tom and Libby, discussing the state of the wind. Tom just needed to get the mail in town, but Libby always had to discuss things, she couldn't just come along for the ride.

"Never seen this many days of calm," he said, sure that she would disagree with him. She couldn't let him be right about anything up here.

"There's often a lull in late July. Guess it's just a bit early," Libby said, "though there's a bit of something out there."

"After you get past the lee, but not much."

"The sailing class is out there on something," she said. The small flock of dinghies was jostling in a tight group, looking like the trim corners snipped from a sheet of white paper. They were at the far side of the thoroughfare, close to the shore of the opposite island, but the voices of the students came distinct across the water. Tom could hear the squeals of teenage girls, a boy shouting, "Nathaniel!" the clunk of two dinghies colliding, and the persistent honk of the instructor's air horn, and when he abandoned that, some sharp instructions about the mainsail.

"If they can avoid running each other down, they might get somewhere on that starboard tack," said Libby.

"The wind is a mess; from here it's coming in from the south, but if they're on a starboard tack, then out there it's coming from the west. It'll only get worse as it gets later."

"The real drop will happen around five thirty," Libby said. "Things always calm by cocktails, which gives us a good three hours. I think we should risk it."

Why? So the two of them could spend half an hour paddling across a glassy thoroughfare while Tom had to yet again defend his position on selling the house. Really he just didn't want her out on the water for so long.

"No, let's just go to town and grab the mail. If we try to sail, we'll just end up rowing back."

She rolled her eyes, but said she'd grab the mailbox key if he'd pick up the life jackets from the porch steps. He wondered why she was giving up so easily, why she just didn't go herself, the gaff rig dinghy was easy to handle on her own; really, she could've handled the sloop on her own, if they still had it. He worried she would ask about Melissa, though he couldn't imagine she'd picked up on it. Maybe there was something else on her mind.

He had the Whaler pulled into the float as she came down the ramp.

"I'll drive," he said. She shrugged.

Now he was sure that something was wrong. What if she was sick? He couldn't handle one more death. They had all looked to him as their mother lay in her hospital bed, the switch, not a plug at all, ready to be flipped. No lingering, she had said. Danny had been practically catatonic himself, Gwen had her hands full with him, and Libby had already begun coping with the funeral arrangements, the cleaning out of the Crocker Street apartment. She had a small notebook devoted to all things related to their mother's death, except this. Who should flip the switch?

He did. They had all paused, and he said, "I'll do it." He said it with confidence, a tactic he used often in conferences. So they believed that he could. He knew only that he must, that as the oldest, it was his job to spare the others from the act of killing their mother.

He wanted to cry, to hold Libby to him, no more switches. Not for anyone, not for his baby sister. He had already saved her once; what if he couldn't do it again? He wanted her to tell him there, standing on the float. He didn't want to be one step farther from a hospital, from trial therapies and second opinions. But instead he lowered the outboard into the water and started the boat. She sat on the seat just in front of the wheel, leaning back on the small wheel stand.

"Why don't we toot up Perry's Creek," she called over her shoulder, "see if the fornicatoriums are putting in for the night." Perry's Creek was a jaunt he loved, a long, deep, narrow cove, good for going fast or for drifting and catching sights of seals.

"Sure," he replied, totally unsure. He had always seen Libby as fragile. If one of them were to be hurt or sick, it would be her, of that he was positive. He was unsure of her own natural instinct to survive.

They cruised out into the thoroughfare and, in a great arc of wake, turned up Perry's Creek.

"Slow down, Tom. Look at all the work they're doing to the Burketts' house."

He eased the engine down to a slow putt, and shaded his eyes as he looked at the shore.

"A whole new slate roof. Christ, hate to imagine what that cost," said Tom.

"But it is gorgeous, and if you can get it on, then it'll last forever. Like copper gutters."

"Yeah, if you want to spend your money on gutters, sure."

"Let's go up to the creek head," Libby said.

"We don't want to miss the post office. I've had these letters in my pocket for two days." Tom hated to be late, or to miss things because he was rushed. He wanted to get things done.

"Come on, Gramps, we've got plenty of time."

But with that long-ago day on his mind, with the memory of Libby's limp ten-year-old body pressed against him in the water, he felt he needed to give her time to say whatever it was she was going to say. Maybe they'd have time to try all the things they couldn't for Scarlet.

The water was flat and held just the smallest undulations from their slow progress. Up into the creek the lobster pots all pointed their stems straight up. High tide, just about to turn, and then those stems would swing down and point out to sea. Got to watch those pots closely once the tide turns, especially farther up. Gwen had run this boat aground here before, forced to get out and walk across the flats to the road for a ride. Libby knew better, Libby knew to watch the pots. Fog clung in among the pines, a light blanket tucked within their folds, just forgotten scraps here and there. Few fornicatoriums could come up this far. But when storms came, they tried it, preferring to wreck their boats themselves rather than let the storm do it for them.

"So, Bibs, how are you?"

He was not able to make this sound natural, except maybe to strangers and business partners, people who would never be expected to answer it honestly. They had come to the quiet point of the creek, and she threw out the small anchor and cinched its rope to the cleat on the bow. Tom sat down behind the wheel. She was at the bow, facing him. Bad news in boats. He looked at her, waiting for the conversation to thread toward her health, to twist down some dark path lined with small, malignant stones.

"We need to talk about the house," she said finally. "It's pretty clear that you and I are the ones that will bear the financial brunt of keeping it."

Tom felt the buoyancy of the ocean, the way it repelled the boat. They were riding on the back of Neptune's hand. He felt the relief of a leeward port, of a homeward wind. She was well.

"Don't look so excited. I'm not about to give this place up." She stood up in the bow looking at him. "I think if they had to, G and Dan would step up."

"You're kidding? Those two can barely change a tire. Dan can't even manage to go to class. He tell you about that?"

"Well, he's committed to keeping the house, so—"

"Gwen didn't sound so committed the other night," said Tom.

"I don't think it would take much convincing."

"Well, you're going to have to make one hell of a case to convince me."

"I know. Because, it seems like your mind is made up."

"I have other places I need to put this money." Tom waved in the direction of their house as if it were made out of bricks of cash. For a moment he saw himself with a briefcase handcuffed to his wrist, full of bundled bills.

"Right. So it seems like there's only one option here," said Libby. Tom shrugged. He knew this was hard for her to face. She continued, "I want to buy you out."

And somehow it was like she was dying again; or maybe he was. He was some fading apparition in their lives, and she, tearing a check from her checkbook, would snuff him out. He could hear the perforation of the check unzipping; he was fading into the fog. He rested his head on the small steering wheel. He wondered what happened if you passed out on a boat.

"Tom? You alright?" She had moved to kneel on the bench seat in front of the center console. She rubbed his shoulder.

"So, what would that even look like?" he said to the wheel. "Would you guys still come up for the Fourth? Would I not be welcome?" *No place for me here, no Melissa for me at home.* He looked up at her. "How could you even afford it?"

"I've been saving for a down payment. I have my 401(k). And I'm sure I could get a loan. If Gwen and Danny help, I know I could swing it. Eventually. We'd need some sort of installment plan." And he wasn't sure how to ask his question again. Was the idea of losing him so easy to accept? She wasn't hearing him.

Libby had her fingers wrapped around the edge of the wheelhouse, and she was looking up at him, like a rabbit peeking out of a burrow, like his little sister.

"Do you remember when you jumped in the water at Bar Island?"

Her hair was lighter then, with a slight wave at the ends, which she had since outgrown. It had always seemed to bounce in the wind instead of snap. They had taken a day trip to Bar Island for a picnic and swimming. She was just ten, narrow and pale, still early summer. Tom had watched Libby from a rock where he sat leaning back on one hand, holding half a tuna sandwich in the other. He watched her talk to their father on the pebbled beach; watched her point at the big, whale-shaped rock jutting into the little cove; saw her plead and their father shake his head. Then she'd stomped right past Tom, nearly trampling his fingers under her demanding little feet. She kicked at a tide pool.

He could see the idea come to her, saw her looking from her father to the rock. The decision forming in her mind, "Why not just jump? The water isn't that cold." She tapped the surface of the pool with the ball of a foot, as if to prove it to herself. Tom laughed at her, though, *let her catch it from their dad. Let her sulk in the back of the boat all the way home under the cloud of some infantile punishment, no candy for a week, no friends over this weekend.* Let her see their parents' dark side can come down on her too. He challenged her, dared her, silently. And she obeyed.

"I was just telling Melissa that story—Dad, the big hero, diving in and fishing me out. The rest of the details are kind of hazy."

She had stood at the back of the rock, up on its tail for a moment and then had taken a running leap off its head and into the center of the little cove. It had to have been twelve feet deep. The rock blocked his view, and he stood to get a better look. Tom waited for her to surface, waited for her to come up shrieking from the cold. But he heard nothing. She did not rise, but he could see her through the flat surface adrift at the bottom of the cove. It was her hair and hands that he could see. Her hair dark as seaweed danced up from her head. Her hands were white and limp at the wrists, dead fish.

"When you came out of the water you were unconscious. You weren't breathing."

He remembered dropping the sandwich into the tide pool as he stepped fast from rock to rock. He ran the length of the whale rock too in two strides. And then he dove.

Before his feet left the rock he was aware that his father was wading in fast from the beach, the water parting around his waist like a launching ship. Tom didn't feel the cold until his arm was around her, until he had to pull them both to the surface. The urge to gasp was hard to control; he pulled her heavy against the cold, against the dark of the cove floor. She did not move, not deep in the water and not at the surface. *Swim,* he told himself. *You swim, she lives, you breathe, she lives.*

Her hair hung over her face, a terrifying veil. He held her to his chest with one arm and used the other to pull toward shore. When he could touch the bottom his father grabbed her knees, and they held her high above them, out of the water, carrying her up, less drag. On the beach they laid her down, his father stepping to her side.

"I can do it," Tom had said. "I know how." He didn't think of the failure at life guarding, he thought only, *water out, air in, water out, air in.*

She had already gone blue at the lips. *So fast.* He rubbed the hair away from her mouth and nose, rough and quick. He tasted salt on her lips. The water was hot as she coughed it up, pouring over his hands as he leaned her to one side. She started crying at once, maybe before she was completely conscious.

Their father squatted in front of her, and she rolled toward him, and he gathered her up in a towel. Tom had looked for his mother then; she was on the deck of the *Misdemeanor*, anchored just outside the cove, must have rowed past him as he swam. She had the ship-to-shore in hand, trying to get the Coast Guard, the sound of clicking and static came across the water. He waved at her. She had waved back, nodding her head. Gwen had watched the whole thing from a driftwood log on the beach, silent, tears running down her face. Libby had spent the rest of the afternoon sitting in the beached dinghy wrapped in a towel staring out at the whale rock.

"We almost lost you that day," said Tom.

"I didn't realize it was so bad." She wrapped her arms around her shoulders. "Did Dad have to do CPR?"

"No. I did. I brought you out. I did CPR." His eyes burned and his stomach went tight. "I was closer, I got to you first."

She reached out and held his hand for a moment.

"I don't want you up here without me," he said. *I need to be able to get to you.*

She smiled. "We'll figure it out. There are no rules. We'll work it out together. We'll still be together."

She squeezed his hand, then tucked her hair behind her ears, looking at him like it was her birthday, all warmth and humility. Then she moved back to sit in the bow. She pulled on the anchor line to check it, shifted the life jackets beneath the bench.

"You know, Patricia," she began—he nodded, still catching his breath, happy to talk about something else. "She and I aren't just friends."

Libby clasped and unclasped her hands, alternating the weave of her fingers.

"We're thinking about next steps," she continued. At first he registered only his relief that they were done talking about the house. He didn't want to talk about where that money would go. He didn't want to talk about how terrifying it had been to see her half dead on the beach. She must have read this on his face.

"And we are really happy together. We've been friends a long time, and then it just grew into something more, you know?"

"Are you saying you're gay?" he asked, wanting her to say yes, wanting her to be honest with herself, finally.

"I'm saying I'm with Patricia."

At this he saw their father, not because of the last three years that she had been lying to him, but because she had been lying to herself.

"You don't have to look so disgusted, Tom. You know, I realize that you believe the coming flame will wipe out people like me, but maybe you could drop the neo-con crap for five seconds and just remember I'm your sister."

They were silent for a moment.

"You think I care that you're gay?" He said this quietly.

Tom couldn't look at her as he spoke. He surveyed the slate tiles on the Burketts' roof, looked for their striation, the tooth at the end of each shingle. "I care that you can't talk to me about it. I care that you've been in a relationship for three years and you've been pretending it's something else. Call a spade a spade. I care that you've been lying to yourself and me."

His mouth was dry, and a hot sweat at the back of his neck made him feel sick. He felt seventeen again. He felt the urge to run, to start the engine and fly from this quiet spot. To find the car keys and take to the small hills of the island too fast, making his stomach lurch up into his ribs. *I don't care that you're gay,* he wasn't talking to her anymore. *I care that you cheated on my mother, that you've been lying to all of us for decades. I care that you are worthless and that I am ashamed. I care that you are dead and never came clean. I care that without even realizing you taught this sweet girl to perpetuate your lies.*

Tom looked at her here now. She was flushed and her hands dangled from her wrists, resting on her knees. He and Libby were the hope for the future of the Willoughby clan. Gwen was a lost cause, and Danny not far behind her. But only if Libby accepted things, only if she could stop living the lie that their father had so mastered.

"If you are just experimenting, fine. But a three-year experiment? That is not an experiment; it's a way of life. At first I waited for you to say something. I just kept thinking maybe you weren't that serious about her, but eventually it seemed you just preferred the lie. Is that it? Are you not serious about her?"

Libby's fingers worked over each other, picking at nails and cuticles, careful and slow. She looked a bit confused, the way she always looked when doing homework as a child, or trying to work out a burr from the dog's coat with a doll comb.

"You don't want me to be straight?"

Why did they all think he was oblivious? Why did they spend their lives underestimating him?

"Of course I—Hawk—" He pointed, his finger following the bird's path as it soared over them. "Of course not. Just because I voted for Bush twice doesn't mean I'm a brain-dead bigot. Melissa and I have talked about how long it would take you to embrace it. To be open with me. Why has it taken this long?" Libby crossed her arms, watching the hawk. It circled back over the island and then out past the mouth of the creek, looking for fish. She seemed to be considering something, the same expression on her face as that day staring at the whale rock. He wondered what part of her was dying now, or was being resuscitated.

"We are serious," she said. Here he saw something he recognized. A sheen of embarrassment in her eyes. At least she was telling him. At least there was no dark path, no looming loss. She would not be buried with her lie.

"So you'd call her your girlfriend?" he asked.

"What, would you prefer I say wife?" She leaned back against her hands and looked him in the eyes.

"If that's what you mean, if that's the truth, yes. I mean, you could do a lot worse than Patricia."

"Well, she wants to move in together."

"Then 'wife' would be the more appropriate term, don't you think?" His sister with a wife, and he about to lose one.

Libby sat up straight, took a deep breath.

"Yes, actually. Patricia is my wife." Suddenly, all relief and assurance, she was the image of Scarlet. And he wanted to cry. Because she was gone. His mother. And because Libby would be a wife too, and he knew too well what happened to wives. But maybe a wife with a wife of her own was different.

The lobster pots began to dip now. The post office would be closing soon. He stood and clasped the wheel.

"So will you be the wife who cleans or the wife who cooks?" He smiled and started the engine. "Hoist that anchor. The mail waits for no man."

Libby rolled her eyes, but she laughed and pulled up the anchor. Tom doubted Libby could actually afford to buy him out. Would she still joke with him if he took this house from her?

TWENTY-FIVE

DANNY

July 11

On the covered portion of the porch Danny sat on the wide white rail, leaning against the gray shingles of a pillar, his legs stretched out and crossed at the ankles, a beer leaving a damp ring on the thigh of his jeans. Gwen and Libby sat in wicker chairs facing him, and the setting sun behind him.

"There's a lot of smoke, but they don't look worried," he narrated.

It was Tom and Melissa's night to cook. Danny watched them down on the concrete pier in the soft glow of sunset and the brightening light of the lone dock bulb, both of them staring down into the coals of the barbeque that was chained to the rusty pipe railing. Danny imagined that they struck the same postures when conceiving each of their children. He saw them standing together in white lab coats, looking skeptically into a petri dish, Tom gently agitating the contents, Melissa with her arms crossed.

He wondered what they said behind closed doors. Their house was a collection of closed doors. After Scarlet died, Danny stayed with Tom, stayed with each of his siblings, passed between them, like a mild virus or an infirm house cat that couldn't be left alone. Until winter break was over and he went back to school.

Tom's house had been almost too alive in some ways, the rhythm of school and breakfasts and homework, Kerry and Buster eating meals with their jackets on before going off to "practice." Danny could never remember what sports or plays either of them did. Eventually he had to stop asking. But when he had the place to himself, the house was a maze of closed doors. In that quiet, he half expected to wake up one morning and find every piece of furniture covered with a white sheet, all the drapes drawn. A closed house.

There were only five bedrooms, but Danny kept going into the wrong room. With all the rooms painted subtly different shades of blue, he had to look for his copy of *Surely You're Joking, Mr. Feynman!* face-down on the nightstand to be absolutely sure it was his room. He had wondered if he died would Tom leave the book there, open to the last page Danny had read, would this become the Dead Brother Room? No. His old room in his mother's apartment would've been his shrine, but it had been packed up while his mother lay in the hospital. Packed up by dudes with duct tape and dirty quilted blankets. Packed up when they realized she wouldn't be going home. His room was gone. No shrine. No offerings of folded laundry at the foot of the bed, no fresh glass of water on the windowsill.

First he had stayed with Libby. "Stay with Tom a few nights," she had said, "and then go to Gwen's; this way Tom won't feel bad." At Libby's he slept on her pullout. At least there he never lost track of his room.

"Good thing they left us with all this cheese," said Gwen. The round wicker table between them held a glass tray in the shape of a giant lettuce leaf spread with an array of oozing and sweating cheeses. To Danny they looked fleshy, like pieces of meat. A small basket beside the plate contained various crackers and breads. Danny built a triple-decker hors d'oeuvre, alternating different cheeses and their starch vehicles. Then, once settled back is his spot, he dismantled and reassembled them into separate selections.

He didn't want to think about his lost room, or the fact that he had only read another five pages of *Mr. Feynman* in the last six months. He hadn't been able to read anything: textbooks, novels, even cereal boxes. He could pretend. Sit there with a book in his hand. Or worse, actually try to read, but the effect was the same. After a few sentences his mind would drift away. Most of his spring semester he spent walking the campus, following dirt footpaths forged over grassy quads and through copses. Forgetting where and when his classes were, showing up for dinner an hour after the cafeteria had closed. If he managed to make it to a class, to find the right room at the right time, there was invariably a quiz or paper due—a living stress dream. At least his teeth weren't falling out and he wasn't being forced to take a shit in front of a waiting and impatient crowd.

The birds were more muted now. The wind had died down. All seemed to quiet with the softened light. Even the distant motors moved slower, purred lower. The smell of honeysuckle was thick in the air, its tendrils wrapped the railing of the steps, snaked up the shingles and spread forth to obscure one of the rug room windows. *These pretty vines want to choke the house,* Danny thought, *to pull it back into the sweet mangling arms of nature.* There would be another hour until the light fully disappeared, a long, slow cocktail hour. Usually a languid time, tonight it felt pulled, swollen, stuffy. The slow got slower. Danny felt time thickening, hardening. He grew hotter, a prickling at the hairline, making him roll his shoulders. He rubbed his beer bottle on the back of his neck. He wished that he could take off his shirt, he'd just put it on for dinner, and already it felt heavy, stale, grimy. He envied Tom and Melissa down on the pier, where it was always cooler, a soft wind periodically luffing the flag even on such a still evening.

He watched Gwen take a long sip of her drink. Usually she'd be cradling something low and amber, but tonight, these days, she was experimenting with seltzers and juices, with ginger ale or 7 Up splashed with mixers or bitters or sprigs of mint. Danny wasn't sure if Gwen was doing that to hide the nonalcoholic content of her drinks from the others, or just to entertain herself. At least she wasn't drinking, that was a good sign, right? Or was she sneaking vodka into her spritzers, hiding it in an effort not to upset him? The next time she put her drink on the table he would go over, ostensibly for a cheese and cracker, and give it a quick sip to be sure. He sniffed in the direction of her glass. He was a bloodhound. He would find out. He needed to know.

There were too many things he ought to know. Danny was tired of questions. Tired of exam questions, of shrinks' questions, of friends' questions. He just wanted the peace of this house, this place of quiet. He hated that Tom was trying to ruin it, trying to cast doubt on every shingle. This place of sameness, of certainty, of every summer for twenty-one years, built on a granite slab, withstanding a dozen hurricanes in its 125 years. Tom made it all quiver with his talk of taxes and interest and equity. Tom made the place sound as if it were built on sand, as if an earthquake was coming, and all those grains would liquefy and wave like the ocean dragging them all down. What if it all went without him? *I need to go down with the ship.*

Now the tears started to come. He looked out to the water, over the sputtering barbeque and the bickering cooks, over the float, past the spindle and its cormorants, out toward town, keeping his face turned as far from his sisters as he could manage. He pinched his nose, tilted back his head, but it was no use. He could tell he wouldn't be able to stop the works. Gwen and Libby were discussing the cheese.

"I think it's more that all Gorgonzolas are blue but not all blues are Gorgonzola," said Gwen. She handed pieces of each cheese to Libby for a taste test.

Danny shuddered, one violent breath racing through him faster than he could control. Both his sisters leaned toward him.

"Dan, you okay?" Gwen said, a hand already on his shoulder, prepared to perform a quick Heimlich if he wasn't able to produce words. But if he spoke he would cry, so he just nodded.

Here he was again, the child unable to keep back the motherfucking tears. Gwen pushed his feet off the rail, turning him to face them, and perched right where his feet had been. Libby stood up in front of him and squinted against the sun's last glow to look into his face. Now the tears came fast. He was glad Tom was busy. Glad he'd kept his hair long.

"Is this about school?" Libby asked. Danny looked at her, his lips shaking now. *What does she know about school?*

"What about school?" said Gwen.

Danny couldn't even begin that conversation. School felt like some irksome problem, an inconvenient symptom of a much larger disease. As if his mother's cancer had spread to him. But of course his deformed and rapidly dividing cells had been there for a lifetime. He had them as a child, watching his siblings race away in boats and cars, going farther and farther, boarding school, college, grad school. It wasn't until the last few years that they seemed to stay, that they seemed to want him around. Here in this house they were together in a different way. They were a family who all ate at the same table, who all slept in the same house, something he had never known as a kid. In Danny's earliest memories Tom and Gwen were already away at college. Libby at boarding school. Holidays were short and busy. It was only here since Danny could be considered an adult, too, that they had been able to do the things that siblings were supposed to do—fight over the bathroom, argue about what music to listen to, talk in whispers behind their parents' backs.

"We can't let Tom sell this house."

That was all Danny could say. That was the best he could explain it to them. He couldn't say, "Without this house we will go back to what we were. Separate. Without this house we will just be adults in different stages of life. Without our parents." What had seemed slow was now exponentially accelerating, the sun sinking fast, the light changing from yellow to a failing pink. Danny felt now that even his smallest movements were happening in fast forward, and it made his stomach turn. He pinched his hands between his knees to keep them still, to try to keep them alive, to slow down the blood that raced from his fingers to his heart. He wondered if he would be the second Willoughby to die of a heart attack on this porch.

"Dan, Tom can't do anything on his own. This is our decision. No one's going to let this house go if it isn't what we want. We'll just buy him out." This was Libby, so practical, a seawall holding firm against the pressure of Tom and all his surging ideas. But even with her solid tanned hands on his knees he could not stop. The tears caught only to flow again, stuttering through him.

"Alright, Danny, tell us what's happening," Gwen said.

He felt like his chest was imploding, his hands were prickling with pins and needles. His arms were stretching, feeling as if they were ten feet long and limp, draped slack down the steps of the porch. Danny flexed his fingers and made fists. Gwen took his left hand in hers and began massaging it, rubbing the palm and then squeezing each joint of each finger between her thumb and forefinger. She paused at his blister and then worked around it. He wanted to run, to dive, to plunge his sleeping limbs into the ocean, to wake up. Wake up.

"What happens if we sell the house, Dan?" Gwen asked.

"Then there is no place for us." Without this place he'd still have Gwen, maybe. Libby would slip away into her own world. Tom was already trapped in his own world, maybe he always had been. But really, Gwen was too unpredictable. If only she held onto this baby, something to keep her grounded, something to keep her near him. The baby would need a man in its life. Danny had learned from a good source; he could do it, if they would all just stop leaving things behind, stop pressing forward, no matter what washed away in their wakes—houses, babies, parents, ashes, brothers.

The wind shifted, bringing the smell of smoking briquettes up to the porch. Snippets of conversation, too—

"Everyone uses lighter fluid."

"Everyone who wants their dinner to taste like lighter fluid."

Lobster boats and small cruising yachts were coming into the harbor. Many were already at anchor, their captains wrapping mainsails in their cocoons around the booms. The lobstermen tied up at their moorings and rowed their tenders in smooth, wide strokes across the yellow harbor toward the dock. Dan knew they should be setting the table.

"Dan, let's put all these decisions on hold." Libby said. "The house. We are years away from needing to decide that. Okay?"

"Well . . ." Gwen trailed off. Libby shot her a look. "Who is gonna buy a place that's caving in anyway?"

"And school too. College isn't going anywhere. And we have until the eleventh of August to get our deposit back for the fall semester. So let's wait until then to decide, and if August comes and you still aren't sure, we can just decide that you take a semester off. Just like that. Give yourself a little more time to make up your mind."

He didn't even care how she knew. It was so much like their mother, who never needed telling, who absorbed all the pertinent information telepathically, broke it down and rebuilt it into solutions and options.

"There is time for whatever you need," said Libby firmly.

"Do you want to drop out?" Gwen said this with so much surprise she didn't sound like herself.

"Time would be good." He said this to Libby, not wanting to look at Gwen. "I wasn't doing so great there." He said this to his knees, to the ends of his hair. "I slept all the time. Sometimes I would wake up and not know if it was day or night, or I would think I was back at Archer

Avenue. Sometimes I would wake up crying. My roommate asked for a transfer."

"It's okay to miss her," said Gwen.

And at that moment Danny felt some perfect polished floor within him—some big empty ballroom with a chandelier reflected in the gleaming wood—he felt it all collapse. It collapsed in splinters and billowing drapes. It collapsed in shards of crystal and fragments of crown molding. It collapsed under a great rush, a flood, under a river, an ocean. A luxury liner at the bottom of the sea. It had been so exhausting keeping it at bay, walled up, preserving that perfect room with however many dikes and dams and locks and quays. With his sisters in front of him, tucking his hair behind one ear, with their voices traveling over the top of his head, with some smell in the air he had been avoiding for months, he didn't have the strength to hold it back any longer. And he saw his mother's hands and her rings and her fingers curling around a stone and the sharp point of her wrist bone like a perfect buried jewel. And he cried without trying to stop it, without controlling his breath or hiding his flattened chin and curled lips. Then it slowed and, for the first time, stopped without his forcing it. He turned his head to one side and wiped his nose on his shoulder.

Gwen was still holding Danny's hand, but she had stood up and was looking out at the water. She was far away. She was not used to being out of the loop; usually she knew everyone's secrets. Had he disappointed her, too? Danny squeezed her hand. She came back from where she had been, her eyes glossy. She squeezed his hand back.

"We should've brought her up here," Gwen said. "I hate that urn. I hate trading her back and forth like she's a goddamn set of silver. What was Tom thinking, what was she thinking?"

"I never want it," said Libby. "Tom just shows up with it, and— what am I supposed to say? I feel like it makes my house smell of smoke. But Tom's just doing what she wanted; it's not his fault." Libby, the soother of rough edges. *She must do this all day,* Danny thought, *smoothing ruffled heads when moms and dads leave.* She has left them. He heaved a stuttering sigh.

"I'm sure she loved the idea of being able to keep an eye on us," continued Libby, "but now we get to decide who sleeps where. Now we're the grown-ups."

"She probably just wanted to give us more time," Gwen said, quieter now, able to look at Danny again, fully back from wherever she had gone. "To wait 'til we were ready to scatter her. I think we all need more time."

But Danny knew why Scarlet had wanted the urn, the cozy place on the mantel, rather than swirling under all that ocean. *You can move an urn; you can't move the sea. You can't take it with you when you go.*

"I need to give you guys something," Danny said. "I'll be right back." He went up to his room, went into his closet, and found what he was looking for. He came back out to the porch holding a package wrapped in newspaper and twine. A tight triangle like a folded flag. He sat down in a wicker chair, the package in his lap. His sisters stood in front of him, their shadows cast across his hands. The string untied, he unfolded the paper, letting the package unravel slowly in his lap. And in the center of the open newspaper, next to the headline "Glacier Shrinks" and "Death Toll Passes 500—City is Surrounded," was Gwen's gun. More accurately, Scarlet's gun.

Danny had kept it in the bottom of his sleeping bag, but afraid of possibly blowing off his own foot, moved it to the back of his closet, behind a box of mothballs and a pile of tattered pillowcases. After killing the deer, Gwen had put it in his hand, the barrel still so hot it had burned his palm, left a blister. She'd handed it to him as if it were an apple core she wanted him to drop in the trash.

It had given him a profound sense of relief, sitting in the back of his closet waiting for him. Some days he'd just pat the closet door, knowing through it was an escape, a key, a ticket out.

"Jesus Christ," whispered Libby. Danny looked up at them. Gwen was biting on her lips.

"I don't want this anymore," Danny said.

Libby bent over and pulled Danny's head to her, practically climbed into his lap. "I'm so sorry," she whispered.

He nodded at her. His tears were back, though softer this time; he could breathe through them now.

Gwen took the gun from his lap and stomped down the porch steps. Libby and Danny went to the rail and watched her stride down the path, dumping the bullets from the cylinder into her hand. She went past Melissa and Tom without pausing, and down the ramp, stopping only at the very edge of the float. She stood, looking out as if she was about to dive in, to swim to town, to boil the sea with her rage. And then she hurled the gun out in an arc like a boomerang, and sprinkled the bullets into the waves at her feet as if feeding the fish with lead. Danny thought of the gun at the bottom of the harbor, of giving the lobsters a fighting chance, of arming the Crustacean Revolution. He would tell Gwen that when she came back to the porch; she'd like that.

TWENTY-SIX

GWEN

July 12

G wen was drawing on the south porch, overlooking the small cove that led to the Shaws'. The cove had a spit of low sea grass at its center and a stand of pine jutted a rocky foot toward the open channel. It was certainly picturesque. Too much so, really. The type of landscape popularized by so much diner or motel art. But not the typical washed-out pastels of southern beaches, beaches as far north as, say, Cape Cod; not here. These were primal colors, colors that ran in the blood of lobstermen. Color she had been avoiding. Washed-out watercolor was the most she could manage. She didn't want to be so committed to the paper.

Make it. Don't define it, or interpret it, or line it up against older work to assess how you're progressing. No. Just make it. Gwen took a slim tin of Cray-Pas out of a canvas bag that bloomed with charcoal smudges. She rolled one between her fingers, drew bright lines on the edge of her paper.

She used pencil first, but almost right away the color too, and then carved the pencil back in on it, seeing the indent of the line. She worked slowly, and sank deeper into the image, into the looking, the seeing. Soon she saw only what was there, not what she knew or remembered. Her knuckles occasionally locked under the intensity of her grip. Tom came around the corner, stood under the stone arch and then sat down on the railing, watching her work.

"I like what you're doing," said Tom.

"Thanks," she said, as surprised by the comment as she was by his presence in this quiet moment. Tom shifted on the porch railing, facing the house, his back to the water. She could feel his unease, like a wobbly chair, there was no balance, no solidity. She wanted to slide a cardboard coaster under one of his feet.

"How are things going?" He motioned to the drawing. "With everything?" Tom owned one of her drawings, a portrait of Libby reading the paper at her kitchen table. He'd bought it through the gallery; Gwen hadn't even known he was the buyer until she saw it hanging in his study.

"Things are good. I had some decent traffic at my last open studio, some interest. Celeste keeps telling me I need to work larger, and in paint. She's tired of my black-and-white shows. She says, work big, make us both money."

She knew his asking about her work was his go-to procrastination technique. He had done something similar when the three of them told Danny their mother was dying.

She kept drawing, waiting; he'd get there eventually. Like waiting for a snail. As kids she and Libby would pull snails from the rocks at low tide, hold a small, knotted shell on their palms, staying still until the slick trapdoor opened and the snail slid out. Gwen had always felt sorry for them, having to carry their houses on their backs. How tired they must be.

"Keeping it is just not realistic, Gwen," he finally said.

She put a hand to her belly, surprised, offended, but then she followed his gaze as he looked at the roof, the stone arch, the sagging gate leading out into the meadow.

She rolled her eyes at the cove. *He can't let this be.* She turned to him, rubbed hair out of her eyes with a bent wrist, fingers already sticky and green.

"Tom, I don't think anyone, besides you, is ready to make this decision. You gotta back off."

"It may not be a question of readiness. It may be a question of necessity," said Tom. "Think how much that roof will cost to replace. A whole new shingle roof, maybe seventy thousand dollars."

"I wasn't the one up there hammering away at it with a broom," she said. She felt sort of sick at the thought of anything costing that much.

"That doesn't even include the interior work. I don't have that kind of money to spend; I need an influx of income right now."

"You got a bookie to pay off?" She liked this joke, the one about him living a secret, illicit life.

"Divorce lawyers, I guess, are kind of like bookies," Tom said. "Just a shade above breaking fingers."

She had been fearing this, she and Libby had been theorizing. She could recognize the signs, when love stops, or when it stops being enough.

"Well, fuck." She stood there a moment, both surprised and not. "Being a divorced man just isn't as sexy as being a divorced woman, you know? I wonder why that is?"

"Thanks, G. Very nice."

She sat down on the rail beside him, rubbed her fingers as clean as she could get them on her shorts, and put her arm around him. He was taller than she was, and it was uncomfortable to sit that way, but she didn't move. He slumped down a bit, maybe to make it easier for her, maybe because he could either sit up straight or not cry, but she could tell he couldn't manage both.

"Sometimes getting divorced is what you've gotta do. You know I love Melissa," said Gwen.

At this he sniffed, almost harrumphed—ever his father's son. She was amazed he hadn't already made a break for the Whaler.

"But I love you more."

He nodded, leaned into her a bit. Then waved his hand at the house. A question.

"This place," she said, "is ours. It brings us all together, Tom. That's not something I'm looking to get rid of, okay?"

"But we'll always be together. You three are my best friends."

Gwen blanched at this. Blanched at the sad idea that this was his notion of friendship, of closeness. *What must life be like for poor Melissa in the vacuum of his heart?*

"Funny that we both end up divorced, when Scarlet and Dad somehow magically made it through," said Gwen. "I'm convinced they must've been sacrificing goats or babies."

"Yeah, well, it's easy to stay married if you don't care how you make the other person feel. Lies are a hell of a lot easier than the truth."

She assumed he was talking about himself. So much bitterness; she had no idea it had gotten so bad.

But then he went on. "What was so twisted is they knew the truth and still believed the lie. How does that even work?"

"Which lies?"

"Their split."

"Their relationship was shit before that," said Gwen. "God knows, but I don't think there was much lying going on. Sometimes I think if Scarlet had just not told him about being pregnant and jumped right into therapy he would've never had his lost weekend. You know, like John and Yoko."

Tom looked confused.

"They split for a year, and when they were back together they referred to their break as John's 'lost weekend.'"

This was how Gwen had always explained it to herself. The baby, their unplanned little Danny, heralded the split, which was like a log jammed against a rock in a river. The waters rose, hiding their love under feet of water, making it appear gone. But then the log broke; their father missed her, wanted to be the husband he hadn't been, the father too. And so he came back. The waters lowered, and there, revealed in the shallow depths: their love.

"Anyway, Dan was a surprise; you don't think they planned that, do you? And Dad didn't want to go through the whole rigmarole again, he wanted it"—she used a low voice here—"taken care of." Then back to her normal voice. "Scarlet told him to get on his stupid boat and fuck off."

"Why do you think he came back?" Tom asked.

"He's a sucker for her. Once he really thought about her having another Willoughby without him, my bet is, he lost it. Or maybe he just got a taste of life without her. Why do you think he came back?"

"I think he didn't want to give her the house," Tom said.

"Wow, man." She took her arm back. "You're going through a divorce. I think that may be coloring your views a mite cynical."

He sat up straight now and looked at her.

"You don't know," he said.

Gwen was pretty sure she knew most things.

He continued. "It wasn't the fucking baby, Gwen." His swearing made her nervous, made her feel like maybe he might break a window. She had only heard him swear twice before, once when he was rear-ended in a mall parking lot, and once, under his breath, after the doctor told them Scarlet's prognosis.

"All those trips he took, all that cruising without us? He wasn't alone."

"Really? I always figured if one of them cheated it would be Scarlet."

"Yeah, well, there was another man . . . so you were half right."

Gwen gave him an incredulous look. She didn't appreciate his pulling her leg like that, even if he was depressed and on the verge of divorce.

"I saw them, G. Scarlet caught them together on the sloop, and the guy just dove overboard naked. He was young, like twenty—looked like Luke Duke. I had a front-row seat." He motioned to the front porch. "He walked right past me, left footprints on the porch, he didn't even see me sitting there. Then Mom and Dad each rowed in from the boat. It was in fucking slow motion."

Tom's voice got louder now, the words coming faster. "Scarlet came up the path ahead of Dad and yanked me over here"—he pointed to the stone arch and rubbed his wrist as if she had just let go—"like she was trying to hide me from him, already protecting him."

Gwen watched Tom's trapezius twitch. He held the edge of the railing and drummed it with his fingers. She was sweating, the south porch always a bit hotter, always in the sun and out of the wind. She wished a cloud would pass over the sun.

"What did she say?" Gwen asked.

Tom made a guttural scoff, a noise she heard regularly when they were teenagers. He was stretching taller, straining toward the sky, toward the water, like he wanted to run but was tied to the railing.

"She said, 'Your father is like the ocean in a storm. It changes with the weather, but is always the same underneath. He's the same man, same as yesterday, the same tomorrow.' Only he wasn't really a man at all, was he?"

"He was gone so much anyway, and then that trip. But I never thought . . . Was that why he left? Because he'd been caught? Have you told—"

"Who can I tell?" he said quietly. Not a question at all.

He looked her in the eyes, and she knew there was no one. *Maybe Melissa, but not anymore.*

"So this house? I don't want this place. I don't want to run into that guy at Schooners. Fucking Jeremy. I can't." Here he deflated, his shoulders dropped. He hunched over slightly, as if examining his knees. She understood. The house didn't hold the mending of his parents, that taming of the river—it had happened after he left for college. He only ever knew them as some couple that crushed down secrets and desires for the good of the children. He knew them as liars.

"That guy? Shit. I still think Mom and Dad loved each other," said Gwen.

Could that love have been fake? I don't buy it. She squeezed her hands between her knees. *All that fire and heartache was love. Wasn't it?*

"They were kids when they were married; no one taught them how to have a healthy relationship. There was no Oprah," said Gwen. She stood up and faced the cove, her hands on her hips leaving green fingerprints on the hem of her shirt.

"One dude, Tom, no matter how hot, does not a gay man make. They probably felt like they had to separate, to go to hell to see that they didn't actually want to move there. They had to find other options, you know? Anything, because being apart must've just felt wrong. And then the baby brought them back to each other. Danny saved them. That's still the bottom line, right?"

She folded her arms and paced between Tom and her drawing. Tom shook his head. He seemed to be growing smaller, his arms close to his body now, knees squeezing together.

She was reeling, defending a stance that didn't quite make sense anymore. *But they seemed happy, eventually. Was Scarlet just a beard? What a sad, pathetic thing for her to be. Were they happy just because he was off fucking college boys while she . . . What was she doing? What was her happiness? Danny? Keeping the family in some false state of togetherness?* She's always thought her mother was stronger than that, better than that. She didn't want to believe it.

And yet, she could see it. She saw the two dinghies float one after the other, she saw it all in her sad and defeated brother. It was certainly true for him. She saw that.

She saw it all now. How he'd been carrying this house on his back for two decades; how it had made him tired and old even in his youth. The effort of it had taken him away from them.

She stood in front of him now. She wished she could take it all from him, to be the one sitting on the porch that day, to have beat him back from the quarry. She took a deep breath, tried to breathe in his pain and breathe out relief for him. Standing in front of him, she hugged him to her, and felt ashamed that she had somehow allowed him to be alone in this for so long. Tom leaned into her and hugged her, both arms around her waist.

When he let go, Gwen sat down next to him again, looked at her hands. "I wish you'd told me sooner."

Tom nodded.

"I'm so sorry," whispered Gwen.

Tom put his arm around her and kissed the top of her head.

She wished she had remembered to take off her rings; they were already coated with green wax. She tried to rub her knuckles clean on her shorts, but she knew the color would leach into the lines on her hands, aging her. They sat silently, Tom looked out at the cove as she assessed her drawing. Funny how it had stayed there, the same, even as the rest of her world changed. Even so, the lines kept going, kept calling her to continue where she'd left off.

She thought of the baby inside her. Not a baby, just a collection of genetics incubating. And yet it was her genetic collection, something she had made, her tiny but epic installation. Because now it was all different. Babies didn't fix families or break them. They were just another piece of a long and intricate history, another tick on the timeline. Danny hadn't saved her parents, or ruined them. Her mother could have had him alone, could have let her husband disappear across the sea with some frothy-headed coed. *Would it have made a difference? Could they have been happier alone? Would it have made a difference to Tom?* She picked up Tom's hand and held it. Figured he could use a little color on his skin.

"We're going to be forty soon," said Gwen. "Funny, huh? That's how old she was when she had Danny."

"You've got four more years, Pipsqueak. But, I'll keep it warm for you." He squeezed her hand.

She saw him then, her big brother, curled beside her in her little bed in the nursery; saw him pulling her sister limp out of the sea; saw him flip a small switch on a machine in a hospital room. And she thought, *This is what he has always done, and I didn't see it. He's always gone first, scouted ahead, cleared a path for the rest of us. All the errant branches whipped into his face first as he broke through them, keeping the rest of us safe, leading forth, and leaving clues for the journey home. Just like now.* She was on the path to forty, and Tom would lead the way.

Gwen had always imagined that next decade as a heavy arched door with scrolled wrought-iron hinges that sat at the top of circuitous staircase. A dark mystery, that had to be answered, opened, revealed. The baby would not put it off, nor did she want it to. When she passed through that door she didn't want to leave anything on the other side. Not brothers, not babies. There would be an exhaustive inventory, and each thing folded and wrapped in tissue and stacked in a steamer trunk for the journey, jars of shells, a velvet box holding a sand dollar, a black stone polished by the sea wrapped in silk. All vessels would be filled. She would start now with this baby, a perfect pebble turning softly in her belly.

Gwen and Tom both turned toward the meadow as they heard the pop and crunch of a car coming down the road. A shining, wide, black car not at all appropriate for their gullied dirt road pulled up beside the jeep. *All the windows up, air-conditioning on,* thought Gwen, *must be lost.* Tom stood up. A balding man stepped out of the car and gave them a wave. He headed across the meadow toward them.

"Tom?" he called.

Tom met him with an outstretched hand.

"Rafe Phillips. Is now a good time?"

Tom looked back at Gwen. She nodded.

TWENTY-SEVEN

OCTOBER

The four of them stand in the cockpit of the *Misdemeanor* as they motor from one town to another. They pass their house, which is not theirs any longer. Libby cuts the throttle, and they stall there in front of their sprawling memory.

The four of them have come up for the closing; since all of them are owners, they all must be present to sign away this place. They have given most of the land to the Maine Preservation Society, and the house, they have sold to a family who promises not to tear the whole thing down, though they know that is a lie.

The oak is yellow and peeks from behind the house. The glossy white windows of the great room look down upon them. It is cold and they all wear their foul-weather gear, bright-yellow slickers, except Gwen, in a red poncho to accommodate the swell of her belly.

Libby keeps one hand on the tiller and the other she slips into Tom's hand. He gives it a squeeze and then puts his arm around her. Danny moves from the stern to stand between Tom and Gwen. They all stand on the starboard side looking at the house. Libby and Tom, then Danny, his hand resting on his brother's shoulder, and Gwen next to him, her arms crossed over her protruding belly, her hair long and dark hanging down her back. She is no longer a beacon, but a buoy in her poncho, red right returning.

The sky is gray and low and promises a choppy ferry ride to the mainland, but there in the safe haven of the harbor it is calm and windless, and the house isn't empty, but expectant. The flat water, dark green now, lies empty, the float pulled out the month before. Going from town dock to town dock, there is no need for a tender. There is no way for them to come ashore, even if they wanted to.

A house like this is not supposed to exist now. It comes from another era. It is a ghost, like the schooners that sail through the thoroughfare every summer. It is an aberration, a figment. It is their great shingled memory.

ACKNOWLEDGMENTS

I owe an immeasurable debt to Rob McQuilken for being my ideal reader, my staunchest advocate, and my infinitely patient agent. Thank you to the publishing gods for Carmen Johnson; your devotion to old-school editing, and your creative support, encouragement, and collaboration have allowed me to untangle this stringy, knotted story. To the thoughtful and committed team at Little A, who shepherded the book through the maze of production. To the Vermont Studio Center for granting me the time and space to leap off the cliff of novel writing.

Thank you to all my readers: Wylie O'Sullivan, without you I would not have finished this book, or found Rob, or generally gotten where I needed to go. To Mike Sacks and Kate Papacosma for help and advice. To David Fogg for decades of friendship and inspiration. To the Papercuts: Erik Rhey, Mac Barrett, Jenny Barton, Joe Irvin. To Nora O'Connor and Emily Taylor, your support kept me coming back to this process even after months of ignoring, denying, and avoiding it. To Cecily Parks, my favorite poet, my trusted reader, my friend. To Lissa Fox, whose opinion I trust most in the world. To Shana Gozansky, my child's godmother (and probably my soul's as well), the perpetual velvet to my unwieldy hammer.

To the many ladies in my life who have forged a path as working artists (and artists who have other projects like jobs and children), I am so proud to be part of your clan. To All Body—the Smiths, Scaife-Smiths, Reeder-Smiths, Ames-Nelsons—my Fourth of July family, who taught me how to truly vacation. To my father, Marshall, for your belief in me, for your generosity, and for your love. To Cally and Brad, you are my siblings, but when we were kids you were also parents. Now, you are my best friends.

To Peter Twickler, because of you I get to be me. You are my ocean. To Ellery Twickler, you and this book began at the same time, but you are funnier, smarter, and far more magical than anything I could ever write. To E. B. Moore, my mom, my greatest fan, my solace, my hero. I only hope I can be a fraction of the woman, mother, and writer that you are. And finally, to Noni and my generous, welcoming relatives who own this house. The beauty in this book belongs to you. Thank you for sharing this perfect and wondrous place with me. I hope I did it justice.

ABOUT THE AUTHOR

Sarah Moriarty received her MFA from The New School and has worked as a writer and editor for *A Child Grows in Brooklyn*, *What to Expect*, and *LOST Magazine*, among other digital publications. She taught writing and literature at the College of Staten Island and Saint Ann's School, where she strived to prove to her students, and herself, that writing is worth the work. Sarah lives with her husband, daughter, and assorted fauna in Brooklyn, New York. *North Haven* is her first novel.